FULL OF

Paul A.

This is a work of fiction. Similarities to real people, places, or events are entirely coincidental.

FULL OF EYES: A REBEL BISHOP MYSTERY

First edition. June 13, 2024.

Copyright © 2024 Paul A. Barra.

ISBN: 979-8224847419

Written by Paul A. Barra.

DEDICATION

This novel about Southern priests is dedicated to the memory of a
Southern priest, diocesan historian and friend:
the Rev. Scott J. A. Buchanan
1968-2001

> "...(the beasts) were full of eyes within;
> and they rest not day and night."
> *Revelation 4: 8*

FULL OF EYES: A REBEL BISHOP MYSTERY

"You argue by results, as this world does,
To settle if an act be good or bad.
You defer to the fact. For every life and every act
Consequence of good and evil can be shown."
Part II, Murder in the Cathedral, T. S. Eliot, 1935

CHAPTER 1

A*pril 1861*:

I walked down Broad and let myself through the lychgate onto the cathedral grounds. Something rustled the underbrush nearby, but I kept my lantern dimmed. The early morning darkness was pleasant, and I knew the gravel path that meandered across the great sward surrounding the church. My mind drifted as I meandered myself, vaguely grateful for this time alone, not yet considering the day ahead. Peace was a scarce commodity at other times of the day, with South Carolina just seceding from what had been a nearly one-hundred-year union of colonies and with my religion being assailed on many sides. These moments alone in the quiet air, heedless of direction and moving easily to warm my muscles for the tasks ahead, were graces to be valued.

Still, I was happy enough to unlock the oaken side door to the great church and step inside. It was a damp spring in the coastal city of Charleston, and the interior of the tall wooden building was dry. Standing for a moment, smelling polish and wax and something else not immediately identifiable, I readied myself for what was to come.

I was thinking of the day's chores and duties, not ever contemplating the horror that assaulted my eyes when I opened the

FULL OF EYES: A REBEL BISHOP MYSTERY 5

shade of my lantern. I straightened in the sudden glare, drew in a sharp breath.

Poor Jamieson's remains lay crumpled in front of the altar rail.

The first thought that galloped unbidden through my mind was that my mother was probably right after all. She had warned me about heading south into slave country.

Mother was worried about Lowcountry diseases and temptations of the flesh that were concomitant with sultry climes in her mind. Her concern for me was genuine, even if she had never considered that the duties of her thirty-year-old son would eventually involve a murder.

That's because I'm a priest. That was my second thought when I saw the figure, his face frozen in the grimace of his final surprise. I rushed up to the man, saw immediately that he was dead. His head was crushed and he lay on the slabs of heart pine in drying brown liquid, as if a jug of molasses had broken, and his eyes had about them a soulless look. The corpse no longer had the texture of a living body, the solidity one sees even in a sleeping person, but I was still able to identify the red hair and dark eyes of Jamieson Carter. I didn't have my oils with me, but I administered the last rites verbally. The sacramental duties, the care for his spirit, kept me from dwelling on the outrage of his death for a few moments, but then I was forced to face the reality of my discovery. This person had been murdered in our holy building. He had been hit over the head with tremendous force.

The stench of blood was strong near the corpse, probably because the church had been closed up overnight. The stately building smelled like an abattoir during hog butchering time. April of 1861 had begun nearly two weeks earlier with warm days that had lingered. Bolted doors hadn't kept the flies away. They were crawling over Carter's body, eating and doing God only knows what else in the gore that had been a man's head. One fly walked across an eyeball that stared at the altar. I followed the sightless gaze for an instant, as if the stare of the dead could help answer some of the questions that were somersaulting through my mind in the empty quiet of the church. I could see the sanctuary lamp still burning and the glistening tabernacle closed and locked. Nothing seemed disturbed—except for the body on the floor. Something small scrabbled in a dark corner, motes of dust drifted down from the impossibly high ceiling of the place. The smell of old incense that had permeated the wooden interior seemed strong just then, though not strong enough to cover the smell of blood.

Breathing deeply through my mouth, I wobbled out to fresh air and then over to the house on Broad Street that served as a rectory. I had seen a few dead bodies in my work before I entered the seminary, but I had not known any of them in life. And none had been murdered in church. The bishop had enough trouble facing his diocese already. He wasn't bound to welcome the news I carried.

I went to the massive front door of the bishop's house, rather than using the back entrance that let in to the business offices of the diocese and my own downstairs quarters. I was moving quickly when I reached out to push the door handle open. It was locked, and I nearly crashed my hand through the stained glass window that marked the house as a cleric's residence. I paused for a deep breath before I hammered the brass knocker.

Mrs. Ryan answered. Her thin, pale face was puckered in annoyance, her arms white with flour. She was wiping her hands on a dishtowel and had used it to jerk open the door, which she herself had locked even though she knew I had the early liturgy. She looked at me with tight lips, the way she often did since I'd arrived in her diocese some two years before. I thought she would have welcomed another Irishman in the house she ran, yet I could see her mind wrestling with respect for my Roman collar and vexation at my relative youth.

FULL OF EYES: A REBEL BISHOP MYSTERY 7

Compared to her ancient bones, I was indeed youthful, although the tremor in my knees at that very moment might as well have been an old man's ague. But my resolve was as strong as the Celtic blood that coursed through my limbs and brain. I fancied that I could hear it throbbing in my temple.

"His excellency is resting after his breakfast, Father Dockery. I—"

"I'm sorry, Mrs. Ryan. This just can't wait."

I pushed by her as I spoke and went down the wide hall at a good clip, the hem of my cassock whispering across the glossy floor. The housekeeper seemed stunned into silence. By the time she recovered and moved after me, I was already at the half-open study door. I knocked on the jamb and went through.

The Most Reverend Patrick Neison Lynch, forty-four years of age, looked up from his desk. He had been consecrated Bishop of Charleston three years earlier in the very same cathedral where the dead body now lay. He looked his age, and more, if truth be told. I hated to add to his woes.

"What ails you, Tom? You look like you've seen the face of evil itself."

"And I fear as much, Excellency. Jamieson Carter has been murdered in our church."

The bishop sat erect in his padded chair, his blue eyes reflecting the alarm he must have felt in his soul, ringed as they were with pain lines and moistened at the corners. He half rose slowly, his face masked in shock. Then he sat back down, heavily with a sigh that seemed ineffably sad. "Our sacristan? Are you sure he's—No, I'm sorry. I know you well enough to know that you would not come here with such disastrous news unless you were certain. Please tell me what transpired."

"I went into the cathedral to prepare for the seven. Mr. Carter was lying at the foot of the altar. I'm afraid, sir, that his head's been

8 PAUL A. BARRA

bashed in. I administered the last rites and relocked the church. I came right here. I believe he was killed but a few hours ago based—" I hesitated before adding the gruesome detail "—on his body's warmth. Forgive me, Excellency."

He nodded absently and with a thin smile.

"Yes," he said, "your pre-theology training. You are such a gentle man, Tom, I forget you were once a policeman. Did you then...er...detect any cause for the murder? Was the church burgled, the door forced?"

Impressed again with the prelate's ability to get right to the heart of a problem, I replied, "No sir, it was locked, and nothing seemed to be missing."

He shook his head slowly, adjusted his glasses, and resumed his administrative calling.

"It's nigh on seven. Catch Uncle Williams and have him position himself at the cathedral door and direct worshippers to the lower church. Say your mass there as usual, Tom. I'll take the oils over to poor Jamieson." He raised his voice slightly. "Mrs. Ryan, please send Flora to summon the police. Have them come without fanfare to the side door of the cathedral."

Mrs. Ryan stood in the doorway behind me, mouth open, arms hanging loosely, and eyes as big as palmetto bugs. She snapped to on the bishop's orders and retreated toward the kitchen. Bishop Lynch sighed again. I nodded as I caught his meaning. We wouldn't have to worry about Charleston newspapers telling readers of the murder. It would be all over the chancery before the workday even began.

CHAPTER 2

I went back to the cathedral and prayed my way through the Thursday liturgy in the chapel below the main church. It was cool and quiet, with its thick stone walls, so we were all just as happy with mass there. Even at seven a.m., it was a muggy day beginning. There were three-dozen of the faithful in attendance, half of them nuns from the convent across the street. Those women were dressed in black, their faces shone from the work they did before mass and were outlined by the white cotton wimple that was a mark of their order. Some older lay women in shawls and bonnets were regulars, a young Negro woman with her fair-haired ward in a white muslin dress were occasional worshippers during the week. She sat next to Uncle Williams, the other Negro in the congregation and the parish dogsbody. A few Irish workingmen in coveralls knelt here and there, preparing themselves for another hard day on the docks and in the rail yards.

I didn't think any of the worshippers knew yet what had happened in the nave above them, but no one commented when I skipped the Confiteor and whispered much of the Latin. I could have been reading Portuguese poetry for all they knew, but I was, in fact, praying very hard indeed. I could sense the people behind me, praying on their own for a way through the dark times ahead. Their concerns had nothing yet to do with a murder in their cathedral. For despite the morning sun shimmering through the narrow crypt windows of the lower church, the outlook of these good people was probably gloomy because of the tenor of the times facing them.

The Diocese of Charleston was in great peril early in 1861. War seemed imminent, Catholicism was still under attack from nativists, money was tight, cotton prices were at a low ebb, and the great issues that threatened our fledgling nation threatened also to rend the Christian community of the South in two. It seemed as though we were being forced to choose between our land and our faith. But we were not alone at least. Many well-respected southerners, like Jefferson Davis and Robert E. Lee, had balked at secession until we finally faced the brink of conflict. Now people were beginning to talk of the possibility of actual war between the northern and southern states.

Our bishop had turned from a man of peace, a man who had pleaded for patience and understanding, to a vociferous advocate for secession. He thought he had no choice, now that things had gone too far, now that the rhetoric of northern abolitionists had left little room for compromise and now that Union soldiers were bivouacked in Charleston Harbor. His sincerity combined with his magnificent preaching manner had made him an unlikely hero to southerners. Unlikely, since he was after all a Roman Catholic cleric, a papist, in the local vernacular. I didn't think that his religious superiors in Rome and his confreres in the rest of the country were as energized by his secessionist stance as were his secular fellows in the southeast. It was one more source of potential acrimony and dissension.

As I turned to face the small congregation to dismiss them, I could hear footfalls on the wood floor above. Before I blessed the people, I addressed them.

"We were not allowed in the main church today because of a great tragedy that took place in the cathedral proper."

FULL OF EYES: A REBEL BISHOP MYSTERY   11

Their faces were blank, as palpable as late blooming cotton bolls in a withered field. Their eyes were round and dark. The churchgoers had the haunted look of beasts in a pen, wondering what other misfortune could fall about their weakened shoulders. When they found out about Carter's murder, they murmured, and they drooped some more. They filed out slowly.

The police were waiting for them.

And they were waiting impatiently for me in the person of Gordon Becknell, chief of police for the City of Charleston. He was wide, red-faced and bald, a Charlestonian from the wrong side of the tracks. That still gave him what he considered to be an indisputable cultural advantage over me, a northerner and a papist.

He looked up at me with what could only be characterized as a sneer. "Please come into the church proper, Reverend, and tell me what you saw, and when. I know these here folks call you Father, but I am a God-fearing man and can't do that. The Bible don't allow that."

"I'm sure you don't mind your slaves calling you master, though, do you, Chief Becknell?"

He snapped a mean look at me and opened his mouth to reply, but I went through the doors of the Cathedral of Sts. John and Finbar before he could formulate a response. I often wished I could have the opportunity to explain how he had misinterpreted that passage from Matthew, but knew in my more realistic moments that he was not likely ever to listen seriously to scriptural exegesis from a Roman rite cleric.

Once inside the church, I hesitated, thinking of the gore that awaited me by the altar rail. I considered the irony of that—for I loved the place as God's house and as a symbol of the Church herself and what she stood for. I rebuked myself for my lack of self-control and moved with more confidence.

The tall interior of Sts. John and Finbar was brighter than when I'd made my awful discovery earlier, now that the sun was lighting up the stained glass windows. The glossy dark wood of the sanctuary glistened in the light, set off by the marble altar and painted statues. It was a majestic place, for the Americas, suitably elegant for funerals but never designed for murder.

The body had been removed, it's final resting place marked in chalk, but I had scarcely a moment to contemplate the death of Jamieson Carter. The police chief was peevish and made no attempt to modulate his voice for the sake of religious propriety. The other men on the scene avoided my glance and drifted away from the imposing presence of Becknell, who fairly growled at me. "What time did you discover the body then?"

"It must have been about half past the hour, Chief Becknell. I usually get here at about that time to prepare for mass at seven. I came through the side door, since I leave that unlocked behind me for parishioners who come to worship in the morning. I saw poor Mr. Carter immediately."

"You moved the body around, did you? Didn't you never think to leave him for the police to examine, man?"

"I did nothing of the kind. I'm a former policeman, if you'll recall, Chief. I—"

"A few years with the Blue Boys up in New York don't make no nevermind down this-a-way, Reverend. We run things different."

"Yes, of course. Anyway, I didn't touch anything. I administered the final sacrament to the man with a blessing."

Becknell shuddered at the mention of a sacrament, but he said nothing and wrote in a small notebook with a pencil stub.

"How'd the victim gain entry, do you think, if you found the door locked when you arrived this morning?"

FULL OF EYES: A REBEL BISHOP MYSTERY 13

"Mr. Carter is—was—a volunteer sacristan. He had a key. If the key is missing from his person, then the murderer could have locked the door when he left."

When I saw the twitch of his eye, I realized that Becknell had not considered that possibility yet, although I found out later from a source at the Charleston Police Department that the victim's key had indeed gone missing. In fact, his whole key chain was not to be found.

The chief had, apparently, decided on a motive already.

"Why was the victim here so early, then?"

"It was his duty to prepare the sanctuary for our morning service each day."

"So, people knew he'd be here, eh? Sounds just like I thought. Robbery. Anything of your golden idols gone missing, you can tell?"

I took the opportunity of the chief's nasty intimation to look about the church, trying to concentrate on easily moveable objects. I hadn't seen anything missing earlier, but I looked again in the natural light of early day. The plaster statues seemed to be in place, but they were too large to be stolen, or used as weapons. The candlesticks were in their glittering line on the altar as usual. Surely a thief would have seized them as valuables.

At first, I didn't notice what was missing. It was carved out of dark wood, a tropical of some sort, and blended in with the wood and stone interior of the tall church. I'd always wondered what point was served to have two statues that no one could notice from beyond the communion rail, but surmised that they were a gift from some prosperous patron. Now it looked as if one of them might have bashed in the skull of another prosperous patron.

"The Blessed Mother is gone."

"Who?"

I amended my language. "The carved statue of Mary is missing."

"Where was it?"

"There."

I pointed to an empty place in a niche cut into the wall that gave into the side altar of the Blessed Mother. The carving, maybe two feet tall and as thick around at the base as a man's forearm, was nowhere to be seen.

I pointed out that another statue of approximately the same dimensions, this one a mate and of Joseph, was in a niche by the other side altar.

"Musta been a killer with a sense of humor."

From his snarly tone, I knew Becknell was demeaning the Church again.

"I don't take your meaning, sir."

"Beat a papist on the head with a craven image." He barked out a laugh.

"Craven? I resent—"

"Never did understand how y'all could worship a woman like that. Ain't Jesus himself good enough for you?"

"We do not worship—"

"Ain't got time to argue theology right now, Reverend. We got things to do. Don't leave town, seeings how we might need to ask you some more questions."

He turned his broad back to me and walked slowly away in a swagger.

I clenched my palms and figuratively bit my tongue. Then the thought occurred to me that perhaps the ignoramus actually meant to call the Blessed Mother a graven image, but I was certain he meant to cast aspersions on Our Lady whatever he meant to say. Becknell's minions followed him out the door, leaving the nave silent in the wake of their boot steps. I relaxed and blew out my cheeks. Seconds later I nearly jumped in place when a strong hand clasped me by the shoulder close to my neck.

"Easy now, Tom. I didn't mean to startle you."

FULL OF EYES: A REBEL BISHOP MYSTERY   15

"No. No, of course not, Excellency. I'm sorry. It's just that heathen Becknell vexes me somewhat."

Bishop Lynch chuckled softly, patting my shoulder as he did.

"You're a grand one for understatement, Father Dockery. Now please tell me what the heathen got out of you."

"Well, sir, I discovered just now that the dark carving of the Blessed Mother is missing from the side altar. And—"

"The black one, the gift from Señor Bachman? That's an odd choice for a burglar."

"But not so for a murderer in search of a club," I said grimly. "As sacrilegious as the thought appears, it is a suitable size and heft for braining a man."

"My God in heaven. We'd better look the whole church over."

We did just that, finding nothing else missing or out of place. On our tour of the sacristy, we met a police sergeant named Moseley standing in place, looking at his notebook and shaking his head very slightly. I knew him to be a genuine sort, a country boy trying to do well in a job that usually required a lot more authoritarian attitude than he possessed, or at least was willing to display. James Moseley was smart, if not educated, and got a lot done by becoming friendly to witnesses and perpetrators alike, although I never doubted that he could be a stern officer of the law when necessary. When I had gotten to know men on the force, because of my interest in police work left over from my prior lay employment, he had fast become someone I could count on to cooperate with my curiosity. Although we were about the same age, we were not close socially, but I knew him well enough to call him a friend—and to recognize his perplexity. He was scratching at his sandy hair with the fingers of the hand holding a pencil.

"Something doesn't make sense, James?"

"Oh, hey, Father Tom. Morning Excellency."

He bobbed his head at the bishop and would have surely doffed his cap if he'd been wearing it in church. Moseley was a casual Southern Baptist by persuasion, but his respect for authority figures was deeply inbred.

"This old nigger I just interviewed is what's got me confused, Father. He seems like an honest and truthful fellow, but he told me an inconsistency that makes me wonder."

"What was that, now?"

"Well, sir, he told me he was instructed by yourself to direct worshippers to the downstairs church."

I nodded. "Ah, that would be Uncle Williams, and what he told you is true enough."

"Yessir, I figured that okay. But then he says that he went to church with them after he told them where to go, if you can imagine that."

"That's probably true enough also."

"Uh, nossir. I mean in the very same church as the white people was going to, not upstairs in the balcony or nothing."

"Yes, that's what I meant, James."

There was an embarrassed silence. We stood facing each other, Moseley with a stricken, slack-jawed look about him, me straining to hold what I hoped was a friendly smile.

After a pause, the cop pulled his facial muscles back into line. "Well, then, I guess at least he wasn't lying. I hear there's some Baptist congregations that ain't separate neither."

Then he nodded, with his eyes looking out the sides at us, and left the room in a hurry.

The bishop chuckled softly.

"I'm afraid you scandalized your young friend, Tom. Racial fraternization in church is not something he's used to. The Catholic church will be the subject of more gossip than the killing this day."

FULL OF EYES: A REBEL BISHOP MYSTERY   17

The bishop allowed a slender smile to play on his lips as he talked. It didn't last long. He shook his head slowly and wondered aloud what else would be added to his woes that day.

We decided to retire to the rectory to talk over our options about the murder and plan a course of action. The police would presumably tell Jamieson's wife and children about the killing, but we had a funeral to prepare and probably some sort of cleansing rite for the church itself.

While I was saying mass, Bishop Lynch had anointed poor Mr. Jamieson Carter's broken head with chrism oils to complete the official order of Extreme Unction that I had sketched out when I found the body. Now his concern was with the rest of us who remained living. The bishop liked to know where he was headed when he started out in a rush. And he had a lot to do that day.

On the way down the cathedral steps, we met Flora, coming toward us at her own pace. We seemed to be in a stop-and-visit style everywhere we turned, but as anxious as we were to plan our strategy, we paused instantly to let her make her way up to us.

Flora moved with a grace that never failed to impress me. She was not young and not complete. She had some congenital malformation of one foot, but no one thought of her as a cripple because she had made herself learn to overcome the deficiency. She was heavy, in the way of older African women who managed to escape poverty, and always smelled of herbs and spices from the rectory kitchen. Her face was smooth and regular, not what you might call handsome, certainly not pretty, but it glowed and was, therefore, attractive. She smiled a lot, flashing brilliant teeth made more so by the glossy hue of her ebony skin. The whites of her eyes were bright, and her amber irises glistened, reflecting the mind behind them which I found both keen and alert. Whenever I saw the light behind those eyes of hers, I asked myself was it true, as most Americans believed, that the Negro was a mental inferior to the white man? Or were we all just deluding ourselves? She was easily my equal, if not my superior, when it came to quick intelligence.

I had to force myself not to avert my eyes in embarrassment every time I saw Flora, nonetheless. Try as I might, I could not reconcile the thought of a slave living in the house where the priest in charge of both Carolinas lived. It was unconscionable.

I had adopted most of the ways of the South when I came to live here—it seemed the logical thing to do, to assimilate as much as possible, since I had chosen to be a part of the culture. And I had enjoyed most of that experience. The Southern way of life fit the climate in its pace, and the gentility I met on most occasions was a pleasant change from the harsh mercantile ways of New York, ways that were becoming more and more pronounced as the city commerce grew.

But the slavery issue was one that continued to stick in my craw, like a hardened growth. Along with many New Yorkers of my age, I was a Southern sympathizer, but I drew the line at slavery. It was one area where I disagreed with my bishop.

There was no time to consider that disagreement now, for Flora had news that could not wait. She dipped her head at Bishop Lynch. She was not smiling this hour.

"They's a white lady waiting in the big house for you, master bishop. She appears highly agitated."

"Thank you, Flora."

We set off at a rapid pace for the episcopal residence, the former Thomas Pinckney House that functioned as our rectory and occasionally as the chancery of the diocese. Flora waited until we started walking and then fell in a step or two behind us. We went up Broad Street and climbed the bowed staircase that led to the floors the bishop actually occupied. I knew the building well—not that there was much to know. The rooms were so large that the first floor numbered but four, and the ceilings were eighteen feet

FULL OF EYES: A REBEL BISHOP MYSTERY   19

from the oaken floors, so the whole house probably had no more than a dozen rooms on three floors. Below the stairs were my room and the chancery offices. The whole mansion needed paint here and there but was saved from appearing dingy by enormous windows that rose almost the entire height of the rooms. The house was airy and enjoyed a sort of sweeping majesty, perhaps in my mind because the bishop of Charleston lived there.

On this occasion, though, I did not pause as usual to enjoy the scale of the architecture. I was wondering what new problem awaited us.

She was sitting in what can only be described as regal posture on one of the silk straight chairs in the front room. Mrs. Jamieson Carter, Cynthia by Christian name, flattened her lips so that they assumed a more or less straight line when she saw the bishop enter. She accented this snob smile, as I thought of it, by extending her hand to him, wrist bent, arm in a languid arc. Bishop Lynch took the preferred hand and bowed over it slightly.

"Please accept my condolences on the passing of your husband, Cynthia. This must be a terrible blow—er—shock, to you and your family."

"Thank you, Excellency. It is worse than you can imagine."

Her thin face showed no emotion when she spoke these words. She ignored the bishop's inadvertent pun and the blush it caused him. She ignored her surroundings. She ignored me. Her face was long and regular, nose narrow and prominent. She was a slender woman of a certain age, tall and almost gaunt in appearance. My still undisciplined imagination flared into my brain a vision of Cynthia Carter naked. I shivered mentally and quickly brought my mind under control. Some things don't bear imagining.

"How can I help?" the bishop asked. "Is there anything I can do for you in your time of grief? Just say the word."

"I have had time, thank you, to reconcile myself to the loss of my husband. When he never returned last night, I knew something had happened to him. The city police confirmed my worst suspicions, in their own brutish fashion, an hour ago."

The lady paused to bring her lace handkerchief to her face. Bishop Lynch waited patiently until Mrs. Carter continued her conversation.

"Perhaps it is shock or some other reaction, but I feel decidedly clearheaded at this very moment and wish to seek your advice on a...uh...rather delicate matter."

Mrs. Carter looked pointedly at me when she said this last line, the first time she had acknowledged my presence in the room.

"Father Dockery is my closest advisor, Cynthia. If this has anything to do with the scandalous demise of Jamieson, I would prefer if he heard it from you also."

She said nothing, sitting bolt upright as she had from the first, and fanned herself, although the front room was still cool from the overnight sea breezes. The house was quiet. I could hear the clock chunking our the seconds as its pendulum swung. Then the lady turned full-faced to Bishop Lynch and said slowly and clearly, "My husband was having an affair with Gretchen Becknell and probably saw her last night before he was murdered."

CHAPTER 3

The bishop and I stared at her for a second, astonishment doubtless registering on our faces, and then glanced quickly at each other. His eyes were round and rimmed again, reflecting the pain in his heart. He rubbed his forehead with his fingertips and shook his head slowly as he removed his wire eyeglasses. Adultery was common enough not to be a shock anymore, not to us priests, but it still saddened my heart and, apparently, Bishop Lynch's as well.

Before he could reply, the Carter woman went on, "The capacity of that information to cause scandal is much on my mind, Bishop Lynch. Both to the Church and to my family reputation. I purely hated to mention it to you, except that I have become convinced that this, this foible of Jamieson's has something to do with his death. Do you take my meaning, Excellency?"

"I believe so, Cynthia. It pains me that you should have been put in this embarrassing position, but rest assured that the parish itself will look into the…er…relationship between your late husband and the Becknell woman. We shall not involve the police unless absolutely necessary."

Cynthia Carter nodded. "You, sir, understand me perfectly."

Just then there came a timid tap at the arched opening to the room, and Flora leaned in. "Miss Anne Carter is here, master bishop."

"Please send her in, Flora."

A trim young woman of medium height with billows of auburn hair came in quickly. She was wearing a long gray frock that she held off the floor with one hand as she bowed her head to me and curtsied to the bishop. She fell to her knees next to her mother, clasping at the older woman's hand.

"Can it be true, Momma? Daddy is dead? In the church?"

Mrs. Jamieson Carter patted the girl's head and hushed her gently.

"Be strong, child. Your father would want that. We have to think of the other children now, and the business."

Annie Carter nodded but could not contain her grief. She let it pour out of her as tears and sobbing. As her mother sought to comfort her, Bishop Lynch turned to me and spoke in a whisper, "I truly hate to ask this of you, Father—"

"I'll go see Mrs. Becknell immediately, Excellency."

"Yes, please do. And report back to me when you return."

Gretchen Becknell knelt in the garden, slathered with grease and looking like a shining vision from Greek poetry. From atop the diocese's red horse, I could see across the fence that surrounded her cottage on Partridge Lane. She was young and blond, dressed in a loose white cotton dress. When she heard Jasper clatter up to the front gate, she lifted her head so that I could then see her full face as well. She had big, light eyes and generous lips. She might well have been the exact physical opposite of Cynthia Carter and was such a handsome creature that I could not picture her wed to our bull of a police chief. I also wrestled my imagination into a quick submission. This was a woman I didn't dare imagine naked, neither now nor in

FULL OF EYES: A REBEL BISHOP MYSTERY 23

my dreams. I was, after all, a man vowed to celibacy, both actually and in my thoughts.

"Hullo."

"Good morning. Mrs. Becknell, is it?"

"It is indeed. Please, get off that pretty horse and come in."

I did just that, handing the gelding's reins to a Negro woman who slipped out of the garden gate. I joined the blonde woman in the dappled shade of a water oak whose leaves were already budded out. The yard smelled of turned earth and scythed grass. There were squares of color in the corners, flower boxes of what looked to be petunias.

Curiosity at the nature of a mid-morning call from a man in a Roman collar must have been bursting within the woman of the house, but if so, it was not noticeable. We sat on two small wooden benches with a round table between us. She had removed her gloves and now slapped them against her bare arms. She had a smudge of dirt on her forehead, almost, I thought irreverently, like Lenten ashes.

"We started at first light trying to transplant those seedlings, and the gnats were fierce then. I must look a sight with this grease all over me now. But it did keep most of the bugs away."

"It seems an intelligent precaution."

She smiled at that.

"Not a word people usually associate with me."

"I beg your pardon?"

"Intelligent. Why, few folks would think that of me, I'm afraid."

This lady of the South may have been anticipating some repartee at her modest claim, but my Irish wit seemed to have left me in her presence. I barely managed to say, "Oh."

After a few seconds of heavy silence, she spoke again in her bright voice. "Well, how do I address you, sir? Are you a priest?"

"Yes, madam. I am Father Dockery of the Diocese of Charleston. I'm sorry to tell you that I've come bearing bad news."

She did not reply to that but sat still, the remnants of her smile slipping off her glistening face as she took in the significance of my somber expression.

"A friend of yours was killed on church property last night. Jamieson Carter."

I watched her carefully as I said that, looking for telltale signs of disbelief or distress. I needn't have bothered.

Gretchen Becknell made no attempt to hide her devastation. The color drained from her face, and her jaw fell loose. She looked at me with wide eyes for a second or two, and then her face screwed into a mass of wrinkles and a piteous moan escaped through her clenched teeth. She threw her hands to her face and shook her head slowly. She did not cry.

I sat there uncomfortably, daring not to touch her in consolation.

"I'm very sorry."

She nodded, her hands still covering her face. I was indeed sorry now, sorry that I had broken the news to her so abruptly.

I was trying to provoke a reaction, maybe even a confession, but had not anticipated such obvious grief.

When she finally let her hands drop to her lap, her eyes were red rimmed and her face pasty white. She pulled a soiled hankie from her dress pocket. Holding it to her face, she spoke in a muffled, throaty whisper, "Jamieson was a good man."

"You were close, then."

Her demeanor hardened perceptibly at that. She crumpled the hankie and jammed it back into her pocket. I fancied that I could hear her mind whirl into action. She could grieve the loss of her lover at her leisure, she was thinking, first to deal with this threat to her family.

FULL OF EYES: A REBEL BISHOP MYSTERY   25

There was no doubt in my mind that Gretchen, the wife of the police chief for heaven's sake, had been an intimate of the murdered man. And she knew that I knew. I couldn't bear the idea of dragging out her misery.

"Mrs. Carter has made some...er...accusations, I'm afraid, madam. Normally, they would be no concern of mine, since you are not a parishioner of the cathedral, but in light of the crime committed, I—"

"Has she told the police?"

"No. Mrs. Carter is concerned about her late husband's reputation—"

"She should have been concerned about his happiness."

"—so she confided in Bishop Lynch and me—first. She wants to be counseled in what next step to take."

"I'm sorry. I'm being mean-spirited. It's just that he deserved to be happy. I'll have to admit to you, Father, in confidence, that Jamieson and I—we are, that is, we were—"

Gretchen Becknell broke down then, gave in to the storm that had been roiling around inside her. Fat tears rushed down the gullies alongside her nose, and her lips quivered so badly that she could no longer speak. I looked away, out into the garden, and tried to collect the thoughts that were running and bumping into each other in my head. Mrs. Becknell's maid servant had taken Jasper around the back, presumably to water him, and the two of us were quite alone in the garden.

I think that fornication is an abomination, to quote some of my more expressive fundamentalist acquaintances, *and a threat to the family structure that braces the foundation of our still tenuous existence here in America. Jesus, who I consider friend as well as savior, is distressed when his people can't resist the simple temptations of the flesh, when they can't sacrifice base pleasures after he sacrificed his very life to save their souls. Not that the sacrifice is easy, nor that I care to judge people.*

I did not believe, as I sat across from this crying woman, her shoulders shaking now and snuffling sounds sneaking from between her fingers, that Gretchen Becknell was one of those destined for promiscuity in life because she had so weak a character that she could not resist men. As appalling as it sounded for a man of the cloth to be thinking this, I thought then that she was in love with the wrong man. But if she had been paying for her indiscretions with shame and guilt before, she was paying now with a deep running anguish. It would get much worse, even if the affair were not a matter of relevancy to the investigators of the crime, because she would never be able to mourn properly. This was her one chance to cry the grief from her system. So I let her cry hard, without trying to intrude.

After a few more minutes of sobbing pathos, she suddenly got up and ran to her house. I waited alone in the garden, my thoughts in a whirl, but not for long. In five minutes, she reappeared with her face composed. Her eyes and nose were red, and her fair skin blotched but she had her emotions under a tight rein. As long as she didn't think too passionately about Carter's death, I thought she could probably carry on.

"Can you tell me what happened, Father?"

"You mean how he died?"

"Yes. Please do not think to spare my sensibilities."

"Well, madam, Jamieson was a sacristan at our church, as you probably know. He apparently went to the cathedral and let himself in during the very early morning, sometime between midnight and three or four, I would think—based on the time of death. I'm assuming he met his killer there, because the church would otherwise have been locked and there was no sign of forced entry. A blow to the head killed Mr. Carter. A statue of the Blessed Mother is missing and is the presumed murder weapon."

FULL OF EYES: A REBEL BISHOP MYSTERY

I realized that I was talking in a sort of official monotone, but could not bring myself to tell this poor woman the details any other way.

She surprised me by responding with a gentle smile, looking over the garden as she did so. "He would have appreciated that."

"I beg your pardon?"

I was sure the shock I felt at such a statement must have sounded in my voice, yet the blonde woman seemed to be unaffected by it.

"Jamieson." She switched her gaze back from the middle distance where it had hung for a moment. "He had a great sense of humor and an abiding love for the Catholic Church. Even though the demands of his faith were a burden to him—us—he could never quite let it go. He would have found it agreeable to die in his cathedral."

That confession of the heart threatened to break her down again, but she hardened her will and fought off the tears. I dread saying this, but I was beginning to see how Carter could have become enamored with this woman. It was surely a sinful relationship, no denying that. Even Jesus loved sinners, though, and told us all to try to understand them, if not their sin. I prayed quickly and silently, and not for the first time, that Jamieson Carter had repented of his sins before he was killed. Then I got back to business.

"The timing may be wretched, madam, but I'm afraid that some questions about your relationship must be answered immediately. My bishop and I promised the widow to inquire privately and tell the police only what is pertinent to their investigations. I trust you understand."

She nodded, watching me, and I went on. "Where were you last night?"

"At home. My husband can verify that."

"Thank you. Did you and Mr. Carter quarrel yesterday?"

"No. In fact, I did not see him yesterday at all. Our relationship was so discreet that we often went weeks without even seeing each other and usually...er...met but weekly. On Saturday mornings, to be precise. Since today is Thursday, you can see that I haven't even talked to Jamieson for nearly five days."

"Did you quarrel Saturday?"

"No."

"Do you have any reason to think that your husband may have discovered your...uh...affair?"

She twitched a small grin at my discomfort, but it trailed away so quickly that I may have imagined it. "No, Father. I don't believe that it would occur to Gordon Becknell that his wife would even dare look at another man. I would consider it highly unlikely for him to have discovered anything about Jamieson and me."

"Was he at home all night last night, madam?"

"Yes. At least, as far as I know. I retire before he does, and since we have separate bedrooms, I cannot absolutely guarantee that Gordon did not go out once I was asleep."

"I see."

I couldn't think of anything else to ask for the moment. There was no denying the woman's grief, but, still, I had the feeling that I was missing something, that her confession was somehow incomplete. But I could think of nothing else to ask. I hoped too that I hadn't revealed overly much to her about the details of the murder. She would have to be considered a suspect, after all, and she now knew almost everything the police did about the crime.

We sat there in the garden in silence, listening to the peeper frogs calling to each other in the boggy lands nearby. The woman started to cave in at the shoulders a bit, but she straightened smartly when I got to my feet.

"Thank you for your cooperation, Mrs. Becknell. I appreciate your candor. I don't really know what will happen next or how long the police will pursue this matter, given how much is threatening the peace just now in our town. I will keep you out of our end of it if

FULL OF EYES: A REBEL BISHOP MYSTERY 29

I can, although you must understand that I could never impede a police inquiry."

"Of course not. I'm grateful for your understanding. But what about your bishop?"

"What about him?"

"Might he be less understanding? You said that Mrs. Carter spoke to you and him, probably assuming I had something to do with Jamieson's murder—"

"Bishop Lynch is a charitable Christian man, Mrs. Becknell. I don't believe that I will have any difficulty convincing him that you were innocent...uh...of the murder, and that making your indiscretions public at this time would serve little purpose."

And that was indeed the case when I returned to the episcopal residence and explained at length what I had found out on Partridge Lane.

CHAPTER 4

Bishop Lynch listened without comment as I detailed the extent of my interview with Gretchen Becknell. When I'd finished, he tapped the nib of his pen on the side of the inkwell that sat on his desk.

"I worry, Tom, that this...um...affair between the Becknell woman and Jamieson Carter could be a factor of some import in the cathedral murder. If, let us surmise, the police chief somehow found out about it, would that not make him our prime suspect?"

"I agree, sir. A cuckold's vengeance could indeed explain the vicious nature of the attack."

"Yes, and we have ruled out robbery."

I had a certain intuition about the suspects I had spoken to thus far, but I also knew that my detecting hunches were not always reliable. I hadn't been a detective for long enough to have developed the instincts of the more experienced men. Still, I told the prelate what I thought.

"I didn't get the feeling that I was in the presence of a murderer when I spoke with either of the Becknells."

He flipped his pen to the blotter and slapped his hands lightly on the desk.

FULL OF EYES: A REBEL BISHOP MYSTERY 31

"I'm sure you are correct, Tom. At least, I am willing to grant that possibility until we learn more. With that in mind, could you sort of take the tenor of the thinking in the city? You may hear something that could help us decide."

I nodded assent. "Certainly. I'll ride in after dinner."

"And I will call on the Widow Carter and offer assurances that there appears to be no connection between her husband's murder and his alleged dalliance with Gretchen Becknell, wife of Police Chief Gordon Becknell. And that we will continue, in our capacity as church leaders, to pursue our own investigation of the murder of a valued parishioner."

I was happy to hear the bishop assume the responsibility of reassuring Cynthia Carter. He was welcome to that. Most assuredly he would not tell her what both of us knew full well, that if Becknell had learned of *l'affair* between Carter and his wife, he would be our number one suspect. We could not afford to leave the investigation of the murder of a prominent Catholic to a potential suspect in the crime. We needed to look into this ourselves. I was happy to bend myself to that task, rather than have to face Cynthia Carter again after the demeaning attitude she displayed toward me earlier in the day in our parlor.

"I'll tell the dear lady that we will do whatever we can to avoid a scandal that could besmirch the reputation of the esteemed and late Jamieson Carter," Lynch said. "I just hope, Father Dockery, that we are not keeping essential information from the investigating officers."

"I don't believe so at this point, Excellency. That could change at any time, of course, and then we will have to come clean, as they say. I don't mind telling you, sir, that I dread the thought of that. There's no telling how Becknell would react to the kind of news we hold in confidence now."

"Amen."

◇ ◇

32 PAUL A. BARRA

I was currying Jasper two hours later, my belly about done digesting an excellent bowl of chicken and dumplings. Her distemper notwithstanding, Mrs. Ryan could cook like an artist. We ate in the Southern style at the diocese, a big breakfast, prepared by Flora, and then dinner an hour or so after noon, and a cold supper in the evening. It suited the rice and cotton farmers in the area and, so said the bishop, it would suit us as well. In the intense heat of the summer months, it was nearly impossible to do any strenuous work at midday, so working men and women had gotten in the habit of resting after lunch. We did the same.

Now I was preparing the sorrel horse for some afternoon exercise and enjoying the affection and smell of his company. It had been a coolish spring, but the heat to come was hinted at with temperatures of the past two weeks, cool nights yet but days that wilted flowers by evening. Jasper dozed with one hoof lifted and a few flies buzzing around him. He blew suddenly, and his ears snapped to attention.

Another of the priests assigned to diocesan pastoral work and stationed in the city of Charleston entered the stables with the slam of a door. The horse snickered in alarm, and I felt the same sensation myself once I saw who was approaching.

I should mention that the Diocese of Charleston was founded in 1820 and still comprised the states of North and South Carolina in 1861. Georgia had been partitioned out of the diocese in 1850, to become the Diocese of Savannah. Our founding bishop was John England, and as marvelous and renowned as his incumbency was, the South was still a wasteland for Catholicism. In our diocese, there were no more than a scattering of us across the wide expanses that went from sea islands off the coast to mountains at the Tennessee border.

Charleston itself was slightly more amenable to the Church of Rome, being a fairly civilized city in the European fashion, but even here Catholics numbered perhaps ten percent, and many of those

FULL OF EYES: A REBEL BISHOP MYSTERY 33

were Irish immigrants mixing with the French and a few Germans. Five priests, including the bishop and me, served all the faithful of the city and surrounding countryside.

St. Mary of the Annunciation on Hasell Street was established as a Catholic church long before there even was a diocese here, when we were yet a part of Baltimore. Its pastor at mid-century was the Reverend Monsignor Raymond F. Reed, famous locally as a fervid pro-slavery advocate. Assisting him and also functioning as a roving cleric was a Society of Jesus émigré from Louisiana, Reverend Antoine Gagnon.

It was that Jesuit who thumped into the stables on Queen Street behind the grand cathedral, creating those frissons of anxiety in both myself and the young horse I was combing out. It's not that Antoine was so palpably unlikable or hard to look at. He was a slender man, clean-shaven with dark hair that fell across his forehead when he gesticulated, which was often. My problem with him was more his unfettered ambition—so unlike a member of the Society of Jesus, at least those few of my acquaintance—and his arrogance. Jesuits were famed for their education, which rates them above most diocesan priests, so I assumed that resisting a certain hubris must be a burden for some of them. Antoine Gagnon did think of himself as smarter and better educated than me, no doubt. It didn't help that he was also quick witted and often right in his opinions. Despite the fact that he looked a little effete, certainly compared to my robust Irish frame, and never failed to advertise the fact that he was a Roman rite clergyman himself, Father Gagnon also had a wide range of contacts in Charleston society, high and low.

"A murderous, sacrilegious fiend on the loose, and Detective Thomas Dockery is grooming his horse?"

He spoke too loudly. Jasper skittered to the side away from him and showed white in his eyes. Some people were not attuned to horses and refused to learn how to behave around them. I'm afraid Antoine Gagnon was one of them.

"Good afternoon to you, Tony."

"Please. Call me Antoine. We must keep up appearances in this barbarous territory."

"Afraid the horse will be scandalized, now?"

"Oh, we are sharp today, aren't we? But I know that, when you lapse into your brogue, you are concerned about things. Can you not determine who has done in our friend and benefactor, the esteemed Jamieson Carter?"

As usual, he had hit on the real cause of my anxiety, all right. I wanted badly to lash back but knew that it would not only be uncharitable to do so, it would certainly lead to further chagrin at his quick wit. I was no match for Antoine Gagnon. Thank God, I realized that. Nevertheless, I bit my lip and wanted to growl. I held my tongue instead and brushed a little harder. My refusal to answer his jibe had no apparent effect on the other priest. He closed his eyes, the long black lashes feathering along his prominent cheekbones as he tilted his head back and let his fine hair sway with the movement.

"Do you know what the Protestant denominations are saying, Thomas?"

Despite myself, I turned to look at him inquiringly. Father Gagnon curried the favor of the top Protestants in town and had a communications railroad that was unrivaled in the Catholic Church anywhere in the diocese. His coziness with the Anglicans, Presbyterians and Anabaptists was unseemly in my mind's eye. After all, they looked down at us, called us papists, mackerel snappers, and whores of Rome. Many made no secret of their support of the Know Nothings in that party's attempt to prevent foreign-born Americans, who were mostly Catholic, from voting. Reconciliation was not something that many on either side thought at all about, yet Tony Gagnon seemed to have actually cultivated friendships in that

FULL OF EYES: A REBEL BISHOP MYSTERY   35

quarter. When I said that he had contacts in Charleston society, I meant also within many of the steepled churches in the Holy City, as Charleston was often called.

It was indeed unseemly, yet...

"What do they think, Antoine?"

To his credit, he didn't smile at his little victory over my curiosity.

"They think it was Carter's lack of flexibility concerning the Confederacy that did him in. He was vocal, don't you know, in his defense of South Carolina's secession. And, apparently, his life had been threatened."

"By who?"

"Whom. Don't know for certain. I heard the preacher Quillery's name mentioned as one who was sort of violently opposed to leaving the Union, especially since we were the only state to do so for such a time. He opines that the move will be a disaster for the South."

Andrew Quillery was a wild-eyed fundamentalist not long removed from his western Carolina roots who ministered at a downtown church. He had no formal theological training, but that did not seem to have affected his popularity. He had a large and active congregation, and they supported the preacher in high style. He was purported to be very much the anti-Catholic, but somehow managed to be civil in all his dealings with members of our faith. He even considered the bishop a nodding acquaintance.

"The Reverend Quillery is not the only man in Charleston who opposes the Confederacy. Just because Jamieson Carter was a big supporter of the CSA doesn't mean everyone with federalist leanings is a suspect in his murder," I said.

Gagnon brayed out a laugh, causing Jasper to raise his head again.

"Why do you insist on attributing simplistic logic to me, Thomas? You state the obvious as if no one else in the world could have thought of it. I—"

"It creates discussion and allows people to express ideas that may not have formed yet in the silence of their minds."

"Ah. Perhaps. Anyway, I assure you that I have thought this through thoroughly—and in the silence of my mind. I mentioned Quillery because of his CSA opposition, but also because he was seen last night, early this morning rather, skulking down Broad Street and carrying something under his arm."

"You know this from a credible witness? First hand?"

Antoine nodded with a smirk.

"Aye and aye. I advised him to tell the police what he told me, but it is somewhat unlikely that will happen."

"Why?"

"Because the witness is, in the local vulgate, a nigger boy."

I hated when he spoke like that, and realized that was precisely why he did it, but I held my temper this time and asked who it was.

"Bones Fletcher."

My heart lifted a little at that news. Bones was the nephew of Flora, Bishop Lynch's house slave. I had never made the acquaintance of Bones but was certain that, as reluctant as he may be to talk to white authority, he would trust Flora, and she would almost certainly cooperate to help us get to the bottom of this heinous crime. That thought made me pause in mental mid-stride. "How," I wondered aloud, "did Father Antoine Gagnon get the information he had about Quillery from a boy who was frightened of authority? No authority figure could be more imposing than a tall priest dressed in black, a man whose employer forbad many of the devilish pleasures that people of color seemed to partake of so casually."

I realized the irony of my assumption even as I spoke. White people in their adultery might have caused a murder, and here I was making mental accusations against Negroes. I had scarce time to berate myself, though, since Antoine replied with some asperity.

FULL OF EYES: A REBEL BISHOP MYSTERY 37

"Of course, the boy didn't tell me, dear Thomas. I overheard his conversation with another lad."

"And where were you to have overheard two nervous slaves talking about a serious secret?"

"I was sitting in a room, a parishioner's room. He had the window open, and I could hear the slave talk. Why do you ask such a question? Do you disbelieve a brother priest?"

He huffed and puffed when he said the last and turned on his heel to stride out of the stable, banging the door again on his way. Jasper snorted, but I had other things on my mind. I was certain that Father Gagnon had lied about overhearing the conversation between Bones and another boy. I couldn't begin to fathom his rationale at this early juncture, but it was probably worth my while to check out his story.

The big gelding pawed at the dirt as I saddled him. The banging door and the visitor's loud manner could no longer be the causes of his nervousness. The red beast acted as if he anticipated more trouble down the road.

Jasper pranced and fought the bit on the ride to the business district. I had my hands full calming him and my mind full thinking of all that had come across my desk, so to speak, in the last few hours. Off in the distance, I could hear the rumble and ruptures of a thunderstorm over the water. It seemed to me as though even the weather was reacting to some universal source of incitement.

As it turned out, the day's drama was hardly done. There would be more discoveries before the day was out. One, in particular, would make my current confusion as irrelevant as a weed in a forest.

But at the time, I had no way of knowing what else might occur. I was heading to the city center to see some friends I had nurtured, friends who hung around city hall as a pastime while their hirelings and slaves ran their shops or farms. The farm owners were regulars, despite the travails of travel, because their land was not distant from town. Charleston was a major Southern city, but the rural reaches of South Carolina rolled onto her very doorstep.

On the brick walk outside Harry Seidman's haberdashery, three men lounged, two sitting on a bench, the other with his right boot on an upturned crate. One of the sitters was Gordon Becknell, chief of police. He got up and walked off as I dismounted at a hitching post twenty feet away. Skittish as Jasper was that day, I didn't want the horse tied too close to people.

Becknell's sudden departure left Charlie Barre, who lit a cigar and watched me approach, and Peter Fletcher.

Both men nodded to me, Fletcher even tipped his black planter's hat and took his foot from the crate.

I smiled back at them.

"Afternoon, gentlemen."

Fletcher grunted in friendly enough fashion and put his left boot on the crate. Barre said, "Same to you, Reverend." Neither man was Catholic, but their friendliness toward me was an indication of the esteem in which Bishop Lynch was held, at least in Charleston.

I nodded in the direction Becknell had gone and asked, "Was the police chief questioning you about the murder? Everyone's talking about it, I imagine."

"Sure enough, it's all the gossip hereabouts," Barre said. "Gordon wasn't questioning us, I wouldn't say. Just kinda poking around, y'know?"

"I imagine he was asking and, as you say, poking around and was not likely to give up much about his investigation."

"You got that right."

"Any opinions about who did the dastardly deed, then?"

"Expect everyone's got some opinion," Barre said. "Only one I heard I can put any confidence in is the talk about all the money the young'uns are fixing to inherit. They's three of them and a big business that can only get bigger if—shoot, I might as well say

FULL OF EYES: A REBEL BISHOP MYSTERY 39

when—war breaks out. Hell's bells, excuse me, Father, but the dadgum post office is delivering abolitionist tracts, in spite of the fact that this here sovereign state outlawed the practice. Y'all ever hear of such a thing? My sister lives in town, and she paid the postman two cents yesterday, and he gave her a flyer telling how bad slavery was. She ended up with that kind of manure right in her own house. Excuse me again, but I'm right provoked about it all."

I nodded acceptance of his apology, along with what I hoped was a sympathetic smile. I didn't know what I felt about abolition as a political issue, but I knew that the right of a state to govern itself was being imperiled in the state of South Carolina because of it. There were also consequences to sudden freedom for hundreds of thousands of slaves. I often wondered if the ardent abolitionists had thought those things through.

I did not agree with Barre that a war between north and south was unavoidable. Only madmen would provoke an armed conflict between parts of a free country. Terms would be agreed upon before serious friction arose, serious enough to kill each other in copious numbers, I meant, but what was certain was the inevitability of confrontations and flaming rhetoric and frightening incidents before some sort of resolution came about. I wanted badly to solve the terrible murder of Jamieson Carter before the whole world in Charleston changed. We could not rely on the police to be much help.

Then I caught myself. Solving crimes was for police officers, and I was a priest. But the idea didn't ease my concerns about what had transpired in the cathedral. I was not able to muster up much confidence in Police Chief Gordon Becknell's competence for solving this particular murder. Maybe I knew too much for my own peace of mind. He and his wife were both major suspects.

Against my better judgement, I found myself considering the possibility of inherited wealth as a motive for murder.

"Jamieson Carter was a ship's chandler, wasn't he, Charlie?"

"Yessir. Carter's Chandlery, sells rope and pitch and all those things you need to go to sea. Big business. Don't know how it'll fare without him."

As Barre, a rice farmer from west of the Ashley River, shook his head, Fletcher spoke up for the first time. He was a lawyer who specialized in civil disputes before the magistrate's bar, not one of the regular hangers-on but probably a good source of information.

The information he surprised me with was hot off the wire, as telegraphy jargon had it.

"The late, lamented Mr. Carter died intestate, as I presume you already know, Mr. Dockery."

"I had no idea, but I'm sorry to hear that."

I wasn't going to get drawn into small lies with a lawyer. I learned as a testifying police officer years ago in New York that they like to get you admitting you're on the inside track, and then suddenly turn on you like a mad hound. The fact that I wasn't up to playing his games seemed to trouble Peter Lee Fletcher, Esquire, not a bit, or perhaps I was just being skeptical about the legal profession.

"Yessir, I feel certain his wife was also sorry to learn of it. In this sovereign state of South Carolina, she'll be awarded but a third of his estate because Jamieson neglected to write a will. The children will get the other two-thirds."

"And you suppose it was a big estate, do you?"

"What Charlie says is true enough, Carter Chandlery's one of the premier mercantile establishments on the river. I'm not privy to his debt structure or his spending habits, but I'd be mighty surprised if Jamieson died anything but rich."

That meant, if true, that the three Carter children, one of whom was probably old enough to commit murder for greed, stood to become wealthy suddenly as a result of their father's death. Might

FULL OF EYES: A REBEL BISHOP MYSTERY   41

as well throw another suspect into the plot, I said to myself. Maybe more than one.

"I know three of the Carter children, Peter. Are there any more?"

"Just the three. The eldest is Annie. Went up to Virginia for finishing school and now works at her daddy's store. Must be twenty or so. Has a reputation for being a bit on the wild side, if you take my meaning, Reverend. She's old enough to marry, not old enough to vote if we ever grow up enough to permit female suffrage, that is. The youngest are boys I expect you know better than most. They're altar boys at your church, if I'm not mistaken."

"Martin and James Carter, yes indeed. They must be all of twelve or thirteen."

I decided that the boys could hardly be considered candidates for murder, but Annie now—she was a different story. I thought back to her obvious distress with her mother in the bishop's parlor earlier. Could the wild-haired young woman be a murderess? I needed to look into their inheritance a little more closely. Looks could be deceiving, although it pained my heart to think of patricide.

Barre was about to add to the speculation when he stopped cold, his heavy brows shooting up. Thunder down by the battery, not a half-mile from where we had gathered, cracked loudly and ominously. We looked to the sky, and I at least was perplexed to see no more than wisps of cloud floating here and there in an otherwise pale blue background, although there was dark cloud activity over the water. The storm seemed to be localized and heading east. We'd had enough rain for April already, and it was only the eleventh.

I was saved the embarrassment of a fatuous comment when a small crowd of colored men came sliding around the corner and onto Meeting Street, heading east. The three of us stared in a frozen tableau at the unlikely sight of Negroes running wildly in the heat of an April afternoon. They weren't hooting and hollering like they did when old devil rum got a hold in their brains. They were humping it as though someone or something was chasing them. Following them but not able to keep up were some older Negroes, one of whom I recognized as our faithful parish aide.

"Uncle Williams!"

He turned to look at me. His eyes were glinting, and his lips were drawn back, showing the tips of his mangled teeth. He was a freed slave who hung around the cathedral doing odd jobs much of the time.

He came up to me now, moving as quickly as I'd ever seen him do, his thin body canted over to starboard a little and his carved face seeming to strain the tendons in his neck. He was a smallish man, dark, with kindly eyes and demeanor. He lived a poor existence but kept his person clean normally. He was quick to do what he saw as his duty. I saw him at the back of the church at nearly every mass I said.

He was out of breath, glossy with perspiration. "Father."

Something was happening, and he didn't want any more change in his life. He drew a graying hankie from his back pocket and wiped his mouth.

"What's all the commotion, Uncle Williams?"

"Don't know for sure, Father Dockery, but talk be there gawn be trouble out on de water."

"That where everyone's headed?"

"Yassuh."

The three of us white men looked at each other and set off for the battery without another word.

CHAPTER 5

We walked with a sense of urgency but without unseemly haste. We came across other Charlestonians coming out from behind their garden walls and moving down the narrow streets in a similar manner. Some, however, betrayed their uneasiness by not having paused long enough to dress for a sojourn in public. Some of the men were in shirtsleeves, and a few women had forgotten their parasols.

Negroes, especially the children, made no pretense of savoir-faire and raced down the streets, leaping horse droppings and darting around the walkers. But even they were quiet. It was as if everyone wanted to find out what was happening but wasn't certain that the outcome would be as exciting as it would be frightening. I myself felt a deepening heaviness in my chest, less a fearfulness than a sense of foreboding as I saw the crowds starting to gather. That feeling was intensified by the sight of armed soldiers near the cannon that protected Charleston from the sea. The city sat on a long land, a peninsular finger that dips into a well-formed harbor. It was bordered on the east by the Cooper River and on the west by the Ashley.

Charlestonians said that the Cooper and the Ashley ran down to form the Atlantic Ocean. That made them sound inordinately proud of their birthplace, and I supposed they were, but I had always found the local folk to be so charming about their braggadocio that it was easy to forgive them. Even now, they were polite and smiling, although the air was fairly crackling with tension.

There were perhaps 200 people assembled in little knots near the seawall that kept Charleston Harbor off the dry land most of the time. One knot seemed larger than the rest, and I wandered over to it, listening acutely at conversational snatches that floated out from the islets of Charlestonians. The folks were in a stew about something.

In the center of the largest knot was a woman I recognized, although had never actually met. She was Mary Boykin Chesnut, wife of a colonel in the Confederate Army who was a staffer with Brigadier General Pierre Gustave Toutant Beauregard. I knew Beauregard by reputation, as did everyone in the Lowcountry, I dare say, and thought him a bit of a dandy for my taste. Still, he had a fine reputation as a soldier, had been trained at West Point, and commanded the 6,000 or so troops of the newly formed Confederate Army in Charleston, and he was a Catholic, after all. The fascinating story that had circulated through the episcopal residence and out again this week was that the brigadier had learned gunnery tactics under Major Robert Anderson, the Federal who was now the commanding officer of Ft. Sumter. It would be one of those ironies of war if it turned out that the student and his teacher fought each other in an artillery duel. For that seemed to be what everyone was anticipating, although I heard people saying that no shots had yet been fired in anger.

After a few minutes of unabashed eavesdropping from the outer perimeter of Mrs. Chesnut's circle, I deduced that the lady and her colonel husband had entertained Beauregard and other ranking officers and their ladies at an elaborate dinner party just now concluded. As she tittered on about the festivities, I thought I

FULL OF EYES: A REBEL BISHOP MYSTERY 45

detected a note of false gaiety in her manner. She spoke too quickly, and her twitching smiles did not seem to elicit a response from her eyes. Then someone asked a question, and I knew that my assessment had been correct.

"Was there talk of imminent fighting, Miz Mary?"

"I'm afraid—" She paused to wipe at her eyes with a lace hanky. "I'm afraid we are going to fool on into the black cloud ahead of us, after all."

That rather formal utterance unleashed a small storm of queries directed at her—we didn't know at the time that she was trying out phrases for her diary. She answered that her husband had already been out to Fort Sumter with a demand that the Unionists surrender the place. Anderson and his staff had rejected the ultimatum, but Beauregard was reluctant to attack the fort without further notice. It was all very civilized and polite, but neither side was prepared to cede, it seemed. The entire coastal Union garrison was encamped in Fort Sumter, prepared for resisting any assault, and the Confederates surrounded them with dozens of big guns. The die had been cast, in Mary Chesnut's eye. War was inevitable.

Of all the civilians and soldiers who had gathered at the Battery, she seemed to be in the best position to know something factual. There were no officers there that I could recognize. I strolled around a little longer anyway, trying to learn as much as possible before reporting back to Bishop Lynch. Anticipation ran high, although nothing was actually happening. Apparently, soldiers had been put on alert, and that was enough to stir the public angst. People wanted to be on hand when things did begin to occur. If war was really just over the horizon, then my charge from the bishop to find evidence about the murder in the cathedral was under severe time constraints. Once actual hostilities broke out there would be more deaths to worry about than one murdered sacristan.

46   PAUL A. BARRA

Finally, after trying to find out anything concrete for about an hour, I concluded that Charlestonians were keyed up but that nothing was happening at the moment. I strolled away from the seawall, wondering how the prospect of war was going to affect the investigation into Jamieson's death.

When I meandered back to them an hour or so later, Barre and Fletcher were deep into a heated discussion with four other men, so I left them to it and walked over to Jasper. He was gone.

His halter, still tied to the railing, lay in the dirt. The head strap had parted. As I held it in my hand, I visualized the nervous animal rearing back in fright at something else that day, much as he had in the presence of Antoine Gagnon. When the strap broke, he ran off. It didn't surprise me. If men could act crazily enough to push each other toward a war within their own country, there must be a wildness in the air.

I set off on foot to look for the horse. A big, red and saddled gelding with no halter or bridle shouldn't be too difficult to find in a city. He was a well-bred animal, and his fractious nature was more a component of his immaturity than of bad blood. I thought he would make a valuable mount as he grew older, although I liked him well enough as he was. I expected to find him close to where he had been tied, filling his belly with someone's early greens.

A long while later, my shirt was sticking to my back, and I was panting like a blue tick hound on a deer scent. I was hot and getting exasperated and had wandered into a poorer section north of the city center. I had been all over town and into its outskirts, trudging everywhere and asking as many people as I saw. No horse. It was time to head home and summon some help in the search. As so often happens—God knows instinctively how long to allow the fates to torment us—I spotted the object of my search just as I was about to give it up. He was grazing placidly in a patch of unkempt grass fronting a semicircle of shacks. The houses had windows without

FULL OF EYES: A REBEL BISHOP MYSTERY

glass and sheets of dingy cotton cloth for doors. Their unpainted siding had weathered to a light gray where it hadn't mildewed and the roofs were rusting tin. One was patched with a sign advertising a store tea. But the clumps of early grass were light green and healthy-looking.

The gelding was tethered to a tree by a thick rope that looked to have come from a ship after the deck boss figured it was too frayed for tying off to a pier. It was still good enough for a horse, even if it ringed his neck like a Tahitian flower lei in one of those South Seas daguerreotypes that were becoming so popular, with bits of unraveled strings outlined against his dark chestnut hide. Jasper looked up and nickered as I approached. I had been thinking about God and instincts for the moment, no doubt fatigued from traipsing around half the town and most of the adjacent county, it seemed, looking for the beast. Then I'd focused on Jasper once I caught sight of him. I hadn't been paying attention to the houses and was surprised to notice a Negro lounging at the doorway of the first house. He was shirtless, his pants baggy at his knees and tattered at one ankle. He was big around the chest, and his belly bulged like a mating frog's throat. He scratched idly at his paunch and looked at me without saying anything as I eased up to Jasper and ran my hands along his neck and sides.

"Hello," I ventured.

Nothing. His eyes fell to half slits, and he continued to stare in silence. Before I could say another word, a second man slipped out behind him. He was younger and lighter than the first, a pecan next to a black walnut. His skin looked burnished where the older man had a sort of dusty coating to his chocolate shade. Neither was especially ugly or fearsome—except for the look on Walnut—but something about their attitude stirred my policeman's instincts. Still, I reminded myself, I was a man of God not an enforcer of the law, so I continued in an amiable tone.

"This animal is Jasper, gents. He belongs to me, and I certainly appreciate you catching him up for me."

Neither Negro answered. The younger one drew a long, thin-bladed knife from a sheath at his hip, a type commonly known as an Arkansas toothpick. He began cleaning his fingernails with an air of nonchalance. The older one just stared. My throat was beginning to feel parched under what I perceived as veiled threats from the two of them. But I was determined to recover my horse, so I slipped the rope over his head. I had repaired the bridle as I walked around searching, but now that required that I tie off the replacement string behind the gelding's ears. It took forever, and my hands felt stiff and unwieldy as I worked. I kept one eye on the weapon in Pecan's hands. Neither man offered to help. My black cassock was sticking to my lower back. The horse decided to stay calm, and I thanked him for that in low tones as I worked around his head.

Finally, the knot was secure enough. At least, I hoped so. I surely didn't want to lose control of the horse as I made my getaway. I cleared my throat just as the paler man murmured something.

"I beg your pardon?"

"You owes us for de horse."

He had finished with his nails and was slouching insolently against the doorjamb bouncing the knife in the palm of one hand, smirking without showing any teeth. The knife didn't look too big, but the two men continued to look decidedly unfriendly. The sky was losing light. There was no one else around that I could see. The nearest house of any substance was behind me a good quarter mile, too far to offer any hope of assistance.

The knife made the difference. I could easily bang the two men together, since neither was particularly robust. I could probably cow them with my authoritative voice. Priests aren't supposed to act like that, however, so I spoke calmly as I stroked Jasper's neck.

FULL OF EYES: A REBEL BISHOP MYSTERY 49

"Did you spend money on him?"

"We done find him and feed him," Pecan replied. "Plus, he bin run an' gone an' we folk had to catch him up."

"You fed him grain?"

He giggled a bit at that. His voice was high pitched. Walnut smiled perceptibly but didn't say a thing. I figured him for a baritone.

"Ain't no grain round 'bout here, Cap'n, but that there grass be value. Gimme coupla coins."

They both pushed off from the door and balanced their weight. I decided that the new stance was immediately threatening, so I stepped toward them with my fists clenched. Both stood up, eyes opening. That hesitation gave me the chance to fling myself into the saddle. My sudden move caused spooky Jasper to raise up. He didn't exactly rear. He snorted and lifted his front hooves off the ground. It was enough to make the men step back a half pace and was the opening I needed. I whirled the mount and dug in my heels. Jasper took off running. Over the thunder of his frantic gallop, I could hear a high-pitched laugh split the sullen air.

I let the gelding run stretched low for a while, getting the edge of nerves worn off both of us. We were outside town, and it took a few wrong turns to find the pathways back by the time the gelding slowed. It was twilight as we came home in a walk. I knew I had skirted trouble by a whisker and wasn't anxious to set eyes on either man again.

I had already decided not to tell the tale of the confrontation to the bishop or to any other person. There was enough anti-black sentiment in this town already, without the intimidating tactics of two rogues adding to it. I told myself then, as I had many other times, that men who were brought up in filth and poverty were bound to become shiftless as adults. Maybe slavery itself was the cause of at least some of their tendency to minor criminal acts.

By the time I'd stabled the horse and washed up, supper had already been served. I tucked in to the cold bird and hot grits as Bishop Lynch waited patiently for me to eat so I could tell him what I had learned during the day.

He shook his head slowly after I had finished the meal and started relating my news. Once I'd told him Mrs. Chesnut's story, I asked, "What do you think of the situation, Excellency?"

He took off his wire-rimmed eyeglasses and pinched the bridge of his nose.

"General Beauregard was at St. Mary's for an early service this morning, and he told Monsignor Reed that he thought the federal presence on Ft. Sumter was an affront to his army and bad for morale. He fears what the men might do on their own if he doesn't act against the fort."

"So, you think war is a possibility?"

"I'm afraid that we've been pushed too far, Father Dockery. The South, God bless her, is ready to fight back."

CHAPTER 6

That night, it took me a while to fall asleep, despite the rigors of my day. Then I had a restless time of it, twisting in the bed sheets and dreaming of amorphous evils that glided through the dark room. One dream finally caught on, though, and pulled me awake with frightening power. I found myself sitting upright on my hard horsehair mattress, eyes wide open. The sky outside the window was still a night sky, dark and brooding with humid heaviness, but it held a paleness in the distance. Too early for dawn, it was, but just. I heard a clap of thunder and knew that's what had woken me in the first place. Somehow recognizing that it was not God's storm I was hearing, I went upstairs to an open window at the end of the hallway. It looked south from Broad at a good height, and I could see a definite light on the horizon across the harbor.

The thunder crashed again, and a streak bolted across the sky. Certain of what it must be then but daring not to verbalize it, I rushed back down to my quarters and dressed quickly without lighting a candle. When I made it back up to the first floor, his Excellency was waiting in the kitchen. He handed me a cup of steaming tea.

"Might as well have a cup, Tom. It'll be light enough to walk to the battery by the time you're done with it."

He smoked a pipe, seemed to be as calm as a man about to leave early to go fishing in the harbor. To his left, a dark shape appeared soundlessly in a white nightshirt and a lot of white showing in her eyes. She had a white cap on her head.

"Can I get you some breakfast, Bishop Lynch?"

"Don't bother yourself, Flora. We're going right out."

"What's going on out there, do you think?"

The slave was speaking in a stage whisper. The bishop answered in a matter-of-fact tone, but that didn't ease her anxiety. Her mouth was open, her eyes still wide.

"I think something serious is happening down at the harbor. We're going to find out. If you decide to dress and come along, please don't leave the house unattended."

"Yassuh," she whispered and was gone as silently as she appeared.

By the time we left the house, other people were up and about. A few Negroes we knew were waiting on the street outside the episcopal residence. Bishop Lynch and I nodded to them as we made our way down the front steps and across Broad. We walked quickly. The air was damp and cool. There were moving shadows everywhere. Not much noise, some hacking and spitting and the sound of shoe leather on the packed street dirt. Human forms materialized out of the air as the sky lightened. By the time we'd made the waterfront, a false dawn had broken, and our eyes had adjusted enough to the dim light for us to see.

We turned the corner at water's edge and came upon a sight that halted us in our tracks.

Shine-faced soldiers, some in confederate gray and others in the blue uniform Beauregard wore, worked around the cannon that lined the seawall. The men seemed to float in and out of the mist that drifted in from seaward on weak salted breezes. When a patch of it reached us, we could smell the tang of burnt black powder. The soldiers had been firing artillery.

FULL OF EYES: A REBEL BISHOP MYSTERY   53

"Y'all suppose this is some sort of training exercise?"

We all knew instinctively, even the man who asked it, that the question was gratuitous. These soldiers weren't training. You could tell by the looks on their faces and by the grim urgency with which they went about their business. I remembered Mrs. Chesnut's bleak forecast, and my heart felt suddenly heavy.

We started when a distant cannon went off and tried to follow the flight of the ball. It flew from the jut of land to our left, Fort Johnson by my reckoning, but was shortly lost in the sky. Our gazes were drawn out to the federal fort in the harbor. Part of it was burning.

"Good Lord, they're shooting at Fort Sumter."

The voice behind me filled the sudden silence after the cannon roar. It carried such pain on it that I turned to see who was speaking. Alfred Huger, the postmaster, was standing there, rigid, face drained of color. I immediately offered a quick, silent prayer for the poor man, for I knew what torment he must have been going through. He was a local man, an owner of plantations along the Cooper River in fact, but had been appointed to his present position by Andrew Jackson. Now the people of his city were apparently firing on Union troops. He believed right then that some line had been crossed, a line that we may not have been able to step back over.

I turned away from Huger, afraid to see in his face the bald, awful truth. The facts themselves, Americans shooting at other Americans in anger, was bad enough. I could hardly stand seeing the ugliness of it scratched cruelly into the man's skin. I looked instead out at the long land that lay on the sea, peninsular Charleston shadowed by the black vapors of artillery fire.

We were at war, and I didn't want to face it. Besides the momentous inference for life as we knew it, impending conflict also meant that I had precious little time left to find out who killed

Jamieson Carter. War would bring many more bodies to Charleston than that of one adulterous sacristan.

CHAPTER 7

The battle lasted all that day and the next. It was the constant background noise to our lives for those long hours, the anguish-driven beat of our battered collective hearts.

I wandered down to the harbor three more times myself, listening to the guns exploding and ducking involuntarily each time, although there seemed little chance of a stray artillery round causing civilians to be put in harm's way. All the chunks of lead seemed to be heading toward the fort in the harbor. If the Northerners were shooting back, they were confining their artillery aim to the Confederate forts on Moultrie and Sullivan islands. So the conduct of the opening battle remained civilized, but I was worried sick over the implications of this fierce new assault on our senses.

On my third visit, some thirty hours after the predawn attack had begun, the area was strangely quiet. Billows of gunpowder gas wafted away slowly in a grudging breeze and suddenly the fort itself came into clear view. The Stars and Stripes had been taken down. A white cloth, tattered and torn, fluttered feebly from the flagstaff.

Word spread. Within the hour a crowd had gathered, and we watched three boats flying Confederate flags sail across the water and land at Fort Sumter. We couldn't see exactly what was going on until old George Barkley arrived. He had commanded troops in the War of 1812. Slowly, he withdrew a long brass spyglass from inside his cloak and stood on the seawall. He twisted the barrel of the scope and squinted, all the while chewing on a great wad of tobacco that bulged his cheek. We all stood around him, watching him scratch his head and make juicy noises with his mouth.

He spit a stream of red-brown into the sandy grass. "The boys are taking Yankees into their boats."

We cheered. It was over. Still, the episode had been frightening for its ferocity and noise, and we knew that a barrier had been breached.

Once a boy made that first fatal step of stealing a piece of candy, he became a thief in his own mind. Greater and greater robberies were possible once that first moral obstacle had been removed from the conscience. The firing on Fort Sumter was that kind of obstacle to peace. We were past it now, as inconsequential as it was tactically, and bloodier battles were possible.

That evening after supper, I joined Bishop Lynch in his study for glass of port. He poured three glasses, and I was about to query that gesture when Flora escorted Father Antoine Gagnon to the door. He came in, bowed to the bishop, and smiled at me as if we had remained best of friends. He offered his hand, and I half-raised to take it. Bishop Lynch watched the two of us, saying nothing. Then, once we'd settled with our wine, he told us of a pastoral visit he had made to General Beauregard.

"The general assured me that they treated the Yankee troops with Southern courtesy, in his words, and no one on either side was killed in the bombardment. One soldier, one of theirs, died when a celebratory round set off a munitions cache at the fort following the surrender ceremony and some northern troops were injured from bits of flying metal and stone."

"What will become of the captives, Excellency?" Antoine asked.

FULL OF EYES: A REBEL BISHOP MYSTERY   57

"Well, that's interesting. You probably know that Beauregard was a student at West Point of the Union commander of the fort, a man named Anderson, who was wounded in the shelling, by the way. The two commanders worked things out amicably, it seems. The northern soldiers are being sent home on one of the ships that had sailed down here to rescue Fort Sumter."

"Sweet irony, that."

"Indeed, Father. A fitting ending to a war of noise and smoke. Let us pray that future battles will be as painless."

We had no idea, in our innocence, how bloody some would become. We did know that our lives had been irretrievably altered. That left us with a sense of nervous emptiness inside as we came to appreciate the implications of all our bravado about protecting states' rights and the Southern way of life. Suddenly, we were nose to shirt button with the bully, and it was too late to mediate, too late to run. We were committed to fight.

Not many Charlestonians would have been willing to admit this, but we were frightened badly by what we had done. The only certainty for the future was that violence would be a part of it. Maybe a large part.

The bishop interrupted our musings by clearing his throat with some delicacy. He asked if we knew anything more about the murder of Jamieson Carter.

"Well, sir," I said. "We are quietly looking into the affairs of the Reverend Andrew Quillery."

He raised his eyebrows, so I explained what Antoine had overheard through his parishioner's sitting room window overlooking an alley. The bishop asked if we had passed on our information to the police.

"I'm afraid that the police are not putting much effort into the investigation of the murder just now. If we find out something firm, we will turn it over."

He nodded agreement to that. "I hope this coming war doesn't make the police even less concerned with the violent death of a prominent Catholic, but I fear it will."

"I agree."

"Then you had better work fast, Tom. Find out who killed the poor man."

Nothing much happened in Charleston for the next few weeks, at least not as far as the War Between the States was concerned. The Confederacy grew in great leaps. Jefferson Davis, who had been snatched from his life of peace in February to become the first CSA president, began to exert his leadership. It was a dramatic and exciting time politically, but the guns were silent.

My life was anything but. A lot happened in our investigation of Carter's murder during those few weeks, and in the vexing conundrum of slavery that continued to etch away at the lining of my soul.

Bishop Patrick N. Lynch sang a solemn "Te Deum" in the cathedral the day after the Yankees in Ft. Sumter gave up. During the service, he stated that thanksgiving was being offered for the paucity of casualties in the attack. The Bishop of Charleston was grateful to God for that fact. He said so. Later, a New York journalist, Horace Greeley by name, recalled the liturgy as if it were a slight that he could never forget and excoriated the bishop in print for offering the "Te Deum," a praise hymn, for the Union surrender in Charleston Harbor. Greeley called Lynch "The Rebel Bishop."

The bishop responded with a gracious, civilized letter to Greeley's New York Tribune. He made the editor look like a bitter and puerile fool. But the opprobrium stuck. I don't think that Patrick Lynch was ashamed of being known as The Rebel Bishop, if the truth be told, and his reputation as an elegant Southern spokesman grew.

FULL OF EYES: A REBEL BISHOP MYSTERY 59

That was all much later, of course. On April 14 1861 we had just taken a daring and dangerous stride toward independence, and the delicious fright of it all kept the denizens of the Holy City in a state of high excitation for most of the next day. Nothing else happened in the immediate wake of the artillery battle, however, so the Charleston fever soon died down. We imagined that things were anything but quiet in Washington, where Lincoln and his advisors tried to make sense out of the attack—although most Southerners felt that he had provoked it deliberately—and formulate a response.

Two days after the attack on the fort rumbled to a close, and as we all were becoming accustomed again to calm spring nights on the peninsula, I stumbled across another form of violence.

I was strolling back from visiting Marybelle Donoghue, a staunch Catholic from the old sod who was battling her body's decision to shut down following seven decades of a hard life. She was fighting death with badly concealed ill-grace. The poor old woman's face was carpeted with wrinkles and hung on the end of a stringy neck that jutted forward at a right angle from her shoulders. Her back bowed between those sagging shoulders, mounded like a hump on a Brahmin bull. She rarely smiled, at least not in my presence, and her wit might have been slow, but it was also poisonous. Mrs. Donoghue poked her chin at whomever she was addressing, looking for all the world like a snapping turtle sighting prey, and let loose a stream of invective at every perceived slight.

Her rooms on the east side smelled of death. The odor was probably something to do with her failing energy level. She could scarcely get out of bed anymore, and her bitterness drove off the kind of volunteers who would otherwise have washed her and changed the linens. It smelled like death to me because I could see in her eyes that she was dying. It was the bright glow of the last ember in a cook fire.

One granddaughter cleaned the house and seemed to ward off the complaints from the old woman with good humor. She always smiled in a kind of fraternal way when I came to administer the sacraments, as if we both knew that the real Marybelle Donoghue was hiding somewhere in the pain of this old harridan.

Even with the young Colleen's warmth and help, a visit to Mrs. Donoghue was an ordeal for me and getting worse every day as she deteriorated further. She accepted communion but refused the Last Rites, reacting to my offer as if I was attempting to push her into a black hole in the earth, sliding her toward what she had to know awaited her but refused to accept.

After every weekly visit, I had to pray hard. I asked God to understand that my response to Mrs. Donoghue's bile was not a lack of charity, because it grabbed me instantly and without time to consciously will it. I was never ugly back to her, please understand, but my mind could not easily accept her mean spiritedness with equanimity. I always felt churlish after a visit and glad to be shut of her griping and whining, and that was precisely not the way a Christian was supposed to react to a person fighting hard with the Grim Reaper.

So I was walking along Calhoun Street on that Sunday night following the bombardment of Fort Sumter, asking God to forgive me and to grant Marybelle Donoghue peace, when something, some noise or vibration, broke through my thoughts. I stopped and listened. It was maybe nine in the evening and not a particularly dangerous section of town. But all cities were habitats for human vermin, as for other species, and that was especially true of Charleston now that war had been unofficially declared. People, some at least, had adopted a desperate attitude, as if the impending conflict was so threatening to their ways of life that any behavior was suddenly acceptable. It was as if the heresy of determinism had gripped them and offered them an excuse for vile behavior. If war was inevitable, they seemed to think, then what difference did it make if we dropped our endeavors at civility? Surely God would excuse some immoral behavior in poor people who faced cold steel and hot lead.

Those who didn't believe in God, of course, wanted to make hay while the sun shone, in a manner of speaking. It was dark as I was mulling this over, of course, and the dark side of human nature was at work in the slide toward war. Disbelievers thrived in that dark. They were simply enjoying all the licentiousness they could grab. But they drank as well and liquor made men mean sometimes.

So I was cautious as I quartered the street, listening for the commotion I thought I'd heard. When I had located the proper direction, I lay down my satchel of sacramentals carefully on the side of the road and took a firm grip on the walking stick I always carried when afoot. I was a big man and a former policeman, so it never occurred to me not to intervene if a disturbance was happening near me. I moved quickly but quietly down an alleyway. I could hear noises that seemed vaguely violent, but I could not interpret them. Still, they were not good, I knew that much, and my heart started to beat rapidly. I had to work some spittle into my mouth. It had gone suddenly dry. I raised the stick and moved farther into the darkness.

The lane cut to the left after a dozen feet or so, and when I got to the bend, I could see well. A tall house, in yellow brick, had two pitch lamps burning in front of it, on either side of the steps. Flicking in and out of the lamps' shadows was a man raised up over what appeared to be a fallen beast. As the beast attempted to rise up on his four legs, I could see that it was instead another man on his hands and knees, who was felled instantly by a kick from the standing one. The sound of the kick startled me into action. It thumped against the victim's chest, driving the air from him in a gust. A great gargling cry of agony burst from his mouth, along with a splash of dark fluid.

By then I was upon the pair unobserved. The beaten man's cry drove a bellow of anger from my own lips. As unworthy as it sounds

62   PAUL A. BARRA

for a man of the cloth, I must admit that I swung the walking stick
with evil intent. The attacker heard me at the last moment, for I had
yelled and swung at almost the same instant. He raised his right arm.
My stick caught his shoulder before it caromed into the side of his
head. The blow stunned him and threw me slightly off balance, so
that he toppled to one knee, and I had time to clear the red fury
from behind my eyes before I was in a position to hit him a second
time. During that short instant when I was out of position I managed
to hold my temper and not swing again. I did push him onto his
back, and none too gently, with the sole of my foot. I might as well
have been back on the savage streets of New York for a moment.
He sensed something of that and didn't move, so my righteous rage
cooled. When I saw who he was, however, my anger threatened to
return.

"Are you a police officer or a common thug, you filthy bastard?"

CHAPTER 8

Chief Gordon Becknell of the Charleston Police Department looked up at me, befuddled by the blow to his temple and, perhaps, by my vehemence. I might as well have been back in uniform for the moment. The chief stared at me and did not move. Shortly, I cooled and stepped back. He rose slowly, careful not to lurch in my direction. But lurch he did, anyway, and fetched up against the side of the house opposite the torches. Dark stains of blood showed on the right side of his face where I had hit him and on his knuckles when he put them to his mouth. He straightened.

"You—you struck an officer of the law, man."

"I thought you were a strong arm robber. I'm thinking maybe I still do."

"This is police business."

"Very doubtful, Becknell. If this is how you conduct police business, then perhaps a judge would like to hear more about it. Now, move off before I break this stick over your ugly face."

He pushed off the wall and staggered out to Calhoun Street, wobbling and holding a hand to the side of his head. I had no doubt that he would have a different reaction once he recovered from the blow, but my main concern now was the man he had beaten. He was still down, curled on one side but wide-eyed and soundless. His

PAUL A. BARRA

dark-skinned face was mostly in shadow, but as I helped him to his feet, he came up facing the torches. I got a good look at him then, and a tremor of recognition hit me. I knew this man, and from a recent encounter. As I cleaned his face as well as possible with my handkerchief, my memory whirred like a pinwheel. In seconds, it clicked into place.

This Negro was one of the two who had my horse tethered after he'd run off, the pecan-colored one who had brandished the knife. Here was the man who had threatened me, at least implicitly, and who had hoped to extort money by tactics of intimidation. Had I rescued a thief from the law? He was badly hurt, though, so I pushed all the questions to the back of my mind and took his arm over my shoulder.

"You're safe now, son, and we'll soon be among friends."

No one at either residence had appeared when the man was being beaten, so I assumed they would be of little voluntary help now. The man gasped as we started off but could walk with my assistance, although he sometimes dragged one foot and lay his entire weight on me. At times, he moaned, but he didn't try to stop or lay down in the street. I picked up my bag on the main road and set off for the bishop's house. It was a long, slow process, and I was tired when we finally arrived. We went around to the back where Flora answered my knock and immediately took on the burden of the injured man. When she set the kitchen light on the table to tend to his wounds, she drew in a breath.

"Why, it's Bones!" she cried.

I looked up from the washbasin where I was splashing my face. Was this the same Negro Antoine Gagnon had overheard in conversation?

"You don't mean your nephew, Bones Fletcher?"

"Yessir, Father Tom. It's Bones, all right. Looks a bit worse than last time I saw him, but it's him. Uh-huh."

FULL OF EYES: A REBEL BISHOP MYSTERY   65

Bones smiled at her, despite his obvious pain. He hadn't said one word besides the occasional grunt all the way home from the attack site. We had walked for twenty minutes, and his body was shiny with sweat. His eyes had the glassy look that indicated they were focused inward on the hurt he was enduring.

"I'll do what I can for this po' boy and put him up in the spare bedroom in our wing, if that's all right with you Father."

"Of course," I said.

Again I reined in my instincts. The slave was a criminal, but he was also a victim. I could not but wonder at the coincidence that had brought us together again. This man I had rescued was the same man who had seen Andrew Quillery leaving the scene of Jamison's death on the night of the murder. Surely the Lord had put him into my path for a reason. I found myself thanking Him for calling me away from the police force and into His service, for, otherwise, I might not have learned to show such a man mercy. God himself knew that I had not always been a merciful man, not when I wore the blue and gold of the New York City Police. There was many a low-life I had knocked about in my quest for justice, many a petty thief I had left slumped in a mud puddle of some nasty alley. My penchant for brutality was the one thing that sent me back to the Church, for I suffered the guilts whenever I let my passion overcome my conscience. But that was the past, I told myself, this time I had a murder to solve, and time was running out.

I went to bed and tried to assess what the night's activity meant and what it would precipitate. I was anxious to talk with Bones, to find out what went on between him and Gordon Becknell and also to question him about the supposed sighting he made of Andrew Quillery on the night of the murder. But I was enervated after the hard walk home, the fight, and the massive amounts of adrenaline it had consumed, so I soon fell into a deep sleep.

The next morning, Bishop Lynch was waiting breakfast for me when I returned from early mass. He knew about Bones, probably from Flora. When she came in with our food, I asked her how her nephew was doing. She looked as fresh and gentle-faced as ever, despite the fact that she had been up much of the night nursing a badly hurt relative.

"He not going to die, I don't think, but he gonna need a lot of rest. They's some damage inside."

"Tell him I'd like to talk to him when he feels up to it, please."

She nodded and left us alone. I told the bishop about the entire incident with Chief Becknell and his victim. Bishop Lynch mashed the red-eye gravy into his grits and ate them while he listened. He also consumed a strip of hard-dried country ham and a biscuit, about as big a breakfast as I ever saw him eat. Perhaps he was anticipating, as was I, wartime shortages of many of the things we had learned to take for granted. If that was the case, he didn't share any of his anticipations with me that Saturday morning.

"I suppose, Excellency, that we should send a message to the man's owner about this attack? Isn't he a servant of the Groves family?" I disliked identifying a man as property, but so the conventions were here. The shacks I had seen when I was retrieving Jasper were near the Grove's family property.

"I'm afraid that won't be possible. If you recall, Mr. Groves passed away last year during the fever season, and his slaves are now freedmen."

"You mean that Bones Fletcher is not a slave?"

"Indeed. The only Grove heir is a sister who had migrated to northern Ohio to settle near her husband's family. She never even visited Charleston to seek anyone's advice when she was informed of her inheritance. She just sent a rather ill-advised letter instructing the family lawyer to free the slaves. There were three or four of them."

FULL OF EYES: A REBEL BISHOP MYSTERY 67

I was momentarily confused. "I thought it was illegal to free slaves."

"Manumission is illegal in this state, as you say, but not in Ohio, and the law is poorly enforced here in Carolina. I fear the Grove sister thought she was doing her Christian duty to the slaves her brother owned. She hadn't thought it out, however. The four slaves were cast into society without a concern for their welfare and without a way to support themselves. I'm afraid poor Master Fletcher has had a bit of a time of it since then."

"How so?"

"Well, one of the great ironies of this whole issue has been the fate of freed slaves. You see, white people don't wish to hire them. Partly it's a reaction to their antagonism about the idea of freedom for brown-skinned people, and partly it's simple economics. It's much cheaper to own a slave than to hire a freedman. Manumitted slaves are left to their own devices, ignorant and destitute."

"Surely the Church has an obligation on both those fronts?"

"Bishop John England actually opened a school for freed blacks, right here, near this very house, but a swell of disapproval from Charlestonians forced him soon to close it. People apparently wish to keep their Negroes in ignorance, missing the pleasure of having an educated one like Flora around. But that very ignorance prevails against the African. The incompetence that issues from that ignorance is but a foretaste of what's to come for these poor beggars if we lose this war, and they are all set free at once."

He gazed out the window gravely. "Mark my words, Tom, the precipitous end of slavery will be ruinous for the South, to say nothing of the fate of the Negro. But will any of these Christian abolitionists think of that? Or will they be content with having made a grand gesture? How ironic, that men who own slaves often think more of the welfare of Negroes than their so-called advocates."

PAUL A. BARRA

Once again—I should have been immune to it by then—the Bishop of Charleston surprised me with the depth of his thinking. He was on record as being pro-slavery and could argue persuasively in favor of the institution, yet here he was presenting a fair assessment of the difficulties of the freed Negro. I wanted very much to engage the learned Bishop Lynch in a discussion about slavery in the Catholic Church of the South and suddenly realized that this breakfast was providing exactly the kind of entree I had hoped for.

"Is the war to come to be fought about slavery, then?"

He put his hands together at my question, just as the clock tower chimed, and I realized I had doubtless made him late for some appointment.

"Forgive me, Excellency, for my forward question."

"Not at all, Tom, not at all. I welcome it and all the others that are jumping around in your head." He smiled. "Now, will you hear my suggestion?"

"Sir?"

"Listen to my discourse at the cathedral tomorrow. It may not give you all your answers, but it will lay out for you my thinking, at least."

The bishop rose, and I immediately rose out of respect.

"I have to prepare that sermon for tomorrow, Father Dockery. I hope you will attend me at the ten o'clock service."

Dropping my napkin on the table, I told him that I would be honored to serve at the altar with him. Then he was gone.

Somewhat chagrined at the lost opportunity for a grand discussion, I was anxious for some sort of action.

I walked down to the city police station to see James Moseley. I found him laboring over some paperwork in a large room we called the Bullpen in my New York PD days. Rough desks were fitted throughout the room. Some were occupied by policemen, here and

FULL OF EYES: A REBEL BISHOP MYSTERY 69

there with witnesses or suspects. James was alone at his desk. He stood when I approached.

"Hey, Father Tom."

"Hello, James. I don't wish to take up your time, but I was wondering if there was any progress in the case of Jamieson Carter's murder."

Moseley looked embarrassed, ducking his head and folding himself back into his chair.

"I don't rightly know. The chief is taking charge himself."

"Are you not assisting?"

"No. Fact, no one seems to be. Maybe Gordon has something he's following up on and don't need help."

"Does he have any suspects?"

"Don't know. He did mention he was going to question some nigger boy who'd been causing a ruckus here and there, but I ain't sure if the boy knew anything about the Carter murder. And the chief hasn't come in yet this morning. Sorry."

I left him then. I didn't want to make him feel bad that nothing was apparently being done in the case, especially since he didn't know about Chief Becknell's wife being involved with the victim. Moseley's ignorance about progress in the killing, however, seemed to give credence to Bishop Lynch's theorizing about the cuckolded husband being a prime suspect.

I walked back home fast enough to raise my breathing and then eased away the frustration I still felt by preparing for the next day's liturgy.

CHAPTER 9

The war talk and worry drew a large crowd to the main Sunday mass at the cathedral. Perhaps Bishop Patrick Lynch had anticipated this. He seemed somehow tense during the foremass, as if he were waiting to go on stage or stump. Of course, a Sunday service was a performance of sorts for any minister, but I had seen this prelate at many celebrations of the sacred mass and was, in fact, his master of ceremonies at solemn occasions. He had never appeared anything but completely at ease before. This time, his mind seemed caught in a future trap, an athlete unaware of the present as he tried to imagine how the game would be played, how his role would eventuate. Significantly, I thought, Bishop Lynch altered the routine of the Sunday liturgy.

For one thing, he asked me to proclaim the gospel for him along with the epistle. He didn't actually tap his foot as I read from the ambo the Gospel according to Luke, but he may as well have.

Bishop Lynch was seated across the altar from me on his majestic carved cathedra. I could fairly feel the radiations emanating from him. The atmosphere affected me, and I was more dramatic than usual in the readings. My gospel presentation, however, paled in comparison to that which immediately followed it.

FULL OF EYES: A REBEL BISHOP MYSTERY

I read about the Roman centurion in Capernaum whose servant was dying and who sought the help of Jesus in curing him. It is the great story of faith that we have made a key part of our service, the breaking of the bread. The priest presents the consecrated host and calls it "the Lamb of God who takes away the sins of the world." Then we all tell the Christ that we are unworthy of receiving him into our homes, just as the officer of Rome spoke to Jesus. But the worshippers at St. Finbar—as the Cathedral of Sts. John and Finbar was popularly known—had scarce time to reflect on my dramatic delivery of the piece.

No sooner had I finished reading than the bishop rose and walked to the front of the altar. This was a major departure from the norm, for I had never known him to speak from any location but a lectern. He looked small in his heavy woven vestments as he adjusted his spectacles and looked out over the crowd. The bishop normally held good color in his fair face, but that day I thought he appeared paler than usual.

He cleared his throat, and I sat hastily. He started talking in a clear, loud voice. "In the name of the Father, Son, and Holy Ghost, Amen.

The Gospel reading is so appropriate to our situation today in Charleston, or for the entire Confederacy, for that matter. Isn't it amazing that we should have this particular holy scripture on this day, in Charleston, after what happened this week?"

He paused momentarily to let the question linger in our minds.

"The guns of war have shattered our fragile peace. Suddenly, the uniforms of fighting men are as commonplace on our streets as they must have been when Jesus lived, when Rome ruled the known world.

"At first glance, the healing of the centurion's servant is a story of faith, and how our Lord even said, "I have not seen greater faith!" It teaches us that faith is required for us to move the hand of God, in

72 PAUL A. BARRA

most cases. However, there is an auxiliary meaning to the story. One of love, one of compassion.

"It is obvious that this Roman soldier, this centurion, comparable to a captain in the Confederate Army, was a convert to Judaism. Even though he was a Roman soldier, a mercenary of the occupying army, he was sincerely admired by the Jews in the area. He had obviously heard about Jesus and knew that many miracles had been performed at his hands. Contrary to the opinion of many of the Jews in Capernaum, he knew that Jesus was special in the eyes of God.

"The statement of this soldier, so wonderfully rendered by Luke, that if Jesus spoke but a word another miracle would happen, is the very foundation of our faith in the Eucharist. This is why we repeat this scripture each time we receive the precious Body and Blood. 'Lord, I am not worthy that you should enter my house, only say the Word and my soul shall be healed.'

"Isn't it ironic that the most profound faith statement that we can utter as Catholics is to repeat the words of a Roman slave owner?

"Yes, that's right, fellow Southerners—a slave owner!"

The church was still, almost as if no living thing breathed inside the great walls except the man in the braided fiddleback vestments at the altar. Bishop Lynch's deep, dramatic words reverberated through the crowd like the very percussions of cannon. He paused now, as if to gauge the impact of his opening statement. I half expected some of the middle-of-the-roaders to walk out.

But no one moved. He had them. He had captured everyone's attention.

"This leads us to the secondary message of the scripture, the message that I believe is a providential word for us in South Carolina, this Sunday in 1861. Jesus did not point his finger at the centurion and say, 'Don't you know that it is a sin to own slaves?'

FULL OF EYES: A REBEL BISHOP MYSTERY 73

"From my theological studies, I can assure you that what Jesus did not say is every bit as important as what he did say.

"Just this week we have been attacked once again by the abolitionists. One of my brother bishops from a northern diocese has managed to break the news to The Charleston Mercury that owning slaves is a sin against God. I have no idea why any newspaper would print such an article, other than once again the southern press had the opportunity to slander Roman Catholics in the Holy City. And they never seem to pass up such opportunities, do they?

"It must have seemed a supreme irony to the editors of the paper to have a prominent Catholic, the Archbishop of Cincinnati no less, take the position so relished by the anti-Catholic abolitionists. Perhaps the temptation was too great for them.

"The piety of our abolitionist brothers and sisters is commendable in that they are zealously pursuing what they believe. That is the definition of the Gift of the Holy Ghost, 'Piety.' However, piety becomes HERESY when we are pursuing something that is against God's wishes or desires!"

The bishop fairly bellowed the last words, then stopped suddenly for effect. His nostrils flared, and his face had been transformed into a shining beacon. He had removed his glasses as he spoke. He had waved them in wild gesticulations and held them high now. Gradually, his arm fell. I could see people in the pews following the spectacles down.

The Bishop of Charleston continued in a soft voice that had the flock craning their necks forward to hear. I fear that I was as caught up in this incredible defense of slavery as the next person.

"The idea of owning slaves as being sinful is contrary to scriptural and Church teaching. How as learned a man as my colleague Archbishop John Purcell could contradict nineteen centuries of Church teaching is not something I find easily fathomable.

74   PAUL A. BARRA

Perhaps he made the mistake of reading one of the abolitionist tracts that the mail service delivered to his house."

That was greeted with a few titters at first. General subdued laughter followed when most worshippers saw their bishop's smile and realized that levity was being permitted to ease the tension of the sermon. It was highly unusual for laughter, even quiet laughter, to grace the solemnity of such an occasion, but it worked.

Bishop Lynch let the relief play through the church. When he started speaking again it was in a lecturing manner, an expert teacher instructing his pupils. If I had not been so mesmerized by his performance myself just then, I would have realized, as I did later, that I was witnessing a master dramatist at work.

"In sacred scripture, brethren, slavery is not a subject that is ignored or even merely tolerated, but a subject that is specifically addressed, many times. The laws for buying and selling slaves are contained in the Book of Deuteronomy. It instructs the Jews to offer each of their slaves, male or female, freedom at the end of six years of slavery. It even says that if the slaves desire to stay with their owners, then they would remain slaves for life.

"The scripture in the New Testament which most directly approaches this subject is in the little known book of Philemon. Here, the Apostle Paul is writing a letter to Philemon, one of Paul's disciples, and is informing Philemon that he is sending his slave Onesimus back to him. It appears that Onesimus had stolen something from his owner and then run off.

"Somehow he wound up in the same cell as Paul. The apostle converted him to Jesus and is sending him back to his owner as he writes this epistle. Paul even says that he would like to keep him as his own slave, but could not do that since he belonged to Philemon. He writes, 'Perhaps he—Onesimus—was gone for a while in order that you may have him forever.'

FULL OF EYES: A REBEL BISHOP MYSTERY 75

"An interesting consequence to this scripture is that many scholars today believe that this slave matured into none other than the great Bishop Onesimus of Ephesus.

"We all know that it has always been Church teaching that we are to be good stewards of the things that the Lord provided us. Unfortunately, we all also know of slave owners, right here on the Charleston Peninsula, who are committing grievous sins in the way they treat their slaves. It is those people who give fuel to the abolitionist movement."

Voice and spectacles rising again, Bishop Lynch thundered in righteousness, "They will receive a severe judgment for these sins! Scripture tells us that when it comes to Christians living in sin, that we are to 'have nothing to do with people like that.'

"I urge each of you this morning to make a resolve to restrict yourselves from doing business with these kinds of slave owners, and not to have any kind of social contact with them.

"I know that boycotting cruel slave owners may cause financial and social difficulties for some of you, but we have no choice in this matter. We as Catholics must stand up for man's rights, whether it be for the free or the slave, regardless of the cost.

"In the Name of the Father, Son, and Holy Ghost, Amen."

We sat there in abrupt silence. He let us think about what he had said for a few minutes before he went on with the creed. I forced myself to concentrate on the rest of the mass, but my mind kept sliding back to my bishop's homily. He had actually defended slavery, and on scriptural grounds. In public.

I processed out of church that morning singing the Salve Regina and feeling in my bones that new ground had been broken. I wasn't the only one with that feeling in mind.

As I stood outside greeting parishioners after mass, I could hear, as usual, the many voices of worshippers just released from the imposed silence of the church service. Behind me, Negroes flowed down from their balcony pews in a torrent of lively talk.

"That was something, now, wasn't it? You ever hear about slavery in church before?"

"Not never. De bishop start somethin' heah."

"The man said our masters ought to treat us right."

"He gonna hear about that, now. White folk don' talk about slaves like that."

She was right, I thought, as I crossed over to the stables to give the horses some Sunday sweet feed. Christians simply did not talk about owning slaves and how to treat them, especially not in church, not even when they were blaming the North for trying to infringe on the rights of states to govern themselves. Slavery was a part of that governance, but not an issue that was raised intentionally. Only Northerners, abolitionist Northerners, did that. And only then if they were rude types who had never learned the brand of gentility that held sway south of the Mason-Dixon.

I doled out the oats and sat listening to the animals munch contentedly, letting my passion from the liturgy subside. The stack of newspapers I sat on were old diocesan issues, used by the chancery staff for cleaning tack and windows. When I rose from them to go in for our big meal of the week, I recalled that a good bit had been written about the issue of slavery in the newspapers of the nation.

In The United States Catholic Miscellany, the first Catholic publication in the nation and the newspaper of the Diocese of Charleston, slavery had become a taboo subject once Bishop England had written his definitive word on the subject. John England, the first Bishop of Charleston and the founder of the Miscellany in 1822, also taught at the seminary where Bishop Lynch took his formation in the faith as a young man, before he went off to Rome for the rest of his formation. I expected that the great man's influence would be reflected in Bishop Patrick Lynch's convictions.

FULL OF EYES: A REBEL BISHOP MYSTERY 77

Bishop England published a series of letters he wrote to John Forsyth, the United States secretary of state, in 1841 and 1842. Bishop England wrote in response to Forsyth's interpretation of a papal bull condemning the slave trade by profiteers. The first Bishop of Charleston didn't agree with the barbarous slave trade from Africa either and probably would have preferred that slavery itself not exist. Since it was a problem for which he could see no immediate solution, Bishop England was content to tolerate it until it died a natural death.

But the abolitionists would not wait. Once South Carolina took the lead and seceded from the Union just before Christmas, the editor of the *Miscellany*, James Corcoran, wrote a famous column explaining a name change. *All we could do*, Dr. Corcoran wrote, *was to expunge those two obnoxious words, which being henceforth without truth of meaning would ill become the title of the paper...*

The two obnoxious words were *United States*, so *The United States Catholic Miscellany* became *The Charleston Catholic Miscellany*, a clear indication to me of the political loyalties of Catholics in the Deep South. But slavery was still not mentioned in the diocesan newspaper, despite the name change. I knew it had to be an embarrassing subject for the Catholic Church. Bishop Lynch was not alone in owning slaves. Catholic colleges and religious orders like the Jesuits owned them, and many other individual Catholics in the South. For the South's most prominent Catholic to suddenly raise the subject publicly and at mass was a major surprise. Now, at last, I had been presented with the opportunity to discuss with the bishop the concerns that had been festering in my mind for months.

I was not sure of the timing of his sermon on slavery but had the distinct and uncomfortable impression that the prism of the impending war had reflected and colored his decision.

I also thought that, as an offshoot of his sermon, he may have been inviting that very discussion with me that I both anticipated and feared. How could I compete with a man as knowledgeable as he? Or as dedicated to a cause?

I didn't have long to wait or wonder. Over the dinner which followed that Sunday mass, with Antoine Gagnon in attendance, the man himself broached the subject.

"How'd you like my homily, Tom?"

"It was a masterful performance, Excellency. Certainly one of the most moving sermons I have ever heard. You could have heard a pin drop in church."

"I fear our friend is begging the question, Father Gagnon."

Antoine's mouth was full of new potatoes just then, but he made a polite question mark with his eyebrows, and Bishop Lynch continued.

"I defended slavery, you see, and my performance had less to do with reaction from the faithful than with the content of my speech."

Then the bishop turned to me again and said nothing, inviting my comments. I knew that the time had come to confront the issue, at length and in the open. He had to know how I felt about it.

"Excellency, I must tell you, with all due respect, that I cannot accept in comfort the idea of one human being actually owning another. Slaves are bought and sold as if they were farm animals. It's un-Christian."

"What in particular do you object to, Tom? What sin is committed by ownership?"

"Well, for instance...How can a man exercise free will, a God-given right and obligation, when someone else creates the rules of his existence? A slave is not free, and so he cannot live freely, cannot make the kinds of choices that he would make were he free."

"Ah, not to worry. Imagine, if you will, the structure under which some of our brave boys will soon begin to labor in the Army of the Confederacy. Rules about when to get up, what to wear, how to address others, when to defend yourself, when to run, possibly. Do

FULL OF EYES: A REBEL BISHOP MYSTERY   79

you think that any slave lives under tighter controls? Yet the soldier has the choice, at every juncture, to be a good soldier or a bad soldier. The bondsman has the same types of restrictions under some owners, but not nearly so rigid. He has plenty of freedom, freedom to be a good slave or a bad one. Free will is natural to mankind. No bondage can remove that."

The bishop took a swallow of water and continued, "The Jews of the Old Testament are a perfect example for a young scholar like yourself. Reread some of it, especially Isaiah, and recall how the Jews maintained their faith and their free will in the Babylonian exile. And Genesis 9, when Noah curses his son Ham for his contempt for his father, so that the Canaanites descended from Ham became slaves. The Hamites are today's Africans, as you know. You also know the Lukan gospel you just read at mass. The centurion wanted Jesus to cure his slave. Not the act of a man who would take away the free will of a person he owned."

He looked at me with a serious but benign cast to his features.

"Now, do you have any further objections to slavery that we can discuss, Father Dockery?"

I shot a glance at Antoine, certain that my face had reddened enough to blend neatly with the roots of my hair. He was grinning on both sides of the pork- laden fork he had stuffed into his face with his left hand, like some aristocratic Englishman. It irritated me that he was being so cavalier and not coming to my defense, and that made me intent on continuing the argument, such as it was so far.

"Well, sir. Didn't Paul say that for Christians there was no distinction between Jew or Greek, male or female, free or slave? That we are all one in the sight of Christ?"

"Indeed he did," the bishop replied.

"If we are all one, it follows that we must be all equal as well. Each of us has been created in the image and likeness of God. God gave us dominion over the birds of the air and the beasts of the land, but He never said anything about one human race having dominion over another. Slavery is contrary to God's wishes."

The bishop pushed away his plate and drank the last from his wine glass. He tilted the rim of the goblet at me.

"Do you not think, Tom, that some people are naturally in a service class? I'm not talking about us priests, who serve mankind and Mother Church. I'm talking about men and women who are disposed to serving another human."

"I quite agree, Excellency. Not all men can be leaders. Some must follow and seem content to do so. But working in another's employ is a lot different than being owned by him."

"If it is, it shouldn't be."

We sat there as Flora and Mrs. Ryan came into the dining room to clear the table. I was wide-eyed. Antoine looked to be at ease, as if this were just another Sunday dinner discussion. The bishop did not wait for the servers to leave before he went on.

"What I am saying is that slavery, as envisioned by the Church, must be a sort of symbiosis in action. Master and slave should work together for the betterment of mankind, or at least for the betterment of each other. The two are almost in partnership. Each has rights and obligations. The slave owner's obligations, for instance, are to care for the slave and his family, and to treat them with dignity. That's why we have permitted slaves to join our congregations and why we have built schools for them. We are even contemplating commissioning St. Peter's, a Catholic parish for Negroes right here in the Holy City, are we not? The problem is one of viewpoint. We all should look upon slavery as a form of noble service."

The bishop referred to Charleston as the Holy City, a local construct that was popular because of all the spires that grew from the fertile soil of Lowcountry congregations. I wasn't thinking of holiness, though, when the man conflated slavery with noble service.

FULL OF EYES: A REBEL BISHOP MYSTERY   81

"How is that possible, when slaves are beaten and sold, families broken up, women taken as playthings for a master? Slaves are not treated as if they are human."

"Those are abuses of the system, I agree. It is unconscionable. In fact, the Catholic Church forbids her members to sell or otherwise break up family groups, under pain of excommunication. We must hear their confessions and witness their marriages. Slaves must be treated with dignity and respect, they must be cared for properly and supervised as if they were the slave owner's children."

"But they are precisely not children. They are adult, capable human beings!"

"When they are freed, Father Dockery, they are cast off like poor Bones in there or like Uncle Williams, incapable of running their own lives. At least as slaves, they are cared for from birth to death. Our obligation as good Christians is to work within the system and improve the lot of slaves, not try to tear the institution down. God help us and them if we lose this war, and the Negro has to govern himself."

We concentrated on our dessert and coffee for a few minutes after that. The bishop was a persuasive speaker, and I was afraid that I had done about as badly in the argument as possible. What he said might be true, but improvement of the lot of slaves seemed restricted by the very system that he thought to preserve. Real educational opportunities were the only way the Negro could work himself up to the position where he was capable of governing himself, but slavery in the South did not permit that. Even our own schools were geared down when they were for slave children.

Two mulatto brothers named Healy, born into slavery, had been ordained into the holy priesthood in the late 1850s, however, so maybe advancement was not entirely impossible. Rumor was that no one knew the Healy brothers—there was a third studying for the priesthood—were Negroes when they first applied for priestly formation. They managed to make it through seminary. But it took a rare and extraordinary person, a Father Healy or a Frederick Douglass or a Robert Smalls, to rise above the quicksand that slavery represented to our dark-skinned brothers.

Bishop Lynch looked again at Father Gagnon before I could say more and asked him his opinion on the issue.

"As usual, Excellency, Sunday dinner at the episcopal residence has been nourishing to body, soul, and mind, and I am grateful for the invitation. I fear that my opinions of slavery, however, are less inspired and more pragmatic than either yours or Father Dockery's. It seems to me that we have no choice just now. We are Southerners, and if we expect the Catholic Church to be accepted in the South, then we must act as Southerners. We must be true to our heritage and stick together in our common cause. Especially now, when our very way of life has been so grievously threatened. We have no choice but to defend the institution of slavery, just as we have no choice but to defend our homeland."

"But after the war, Father," I put in quickly, "by then, we must have made a decision so that we can act when we are again free to do so."

"I am afraid that, after the war, the issue of slavery will have been decided for us, my friend."

The bishop and I looked at the Louisiana Jesuit. Deep in our hearts, knowing the odds against victory for the rural South, we were afraid that his bold assertion was correct. Our voices were hushed as we excused ourselves from the table and drifted off.

CHAPTER 10

Antoine Gagnon and I repaired to my rooms on the lower floor. I always thought of it as the basement but, of course, basements were unheard of in Charleston since the city sat at sea level or below. The main floor of the episcopal residence was really one flight of steps above the street. In order to enter my floor directly, a visitor had to come in through the back of the building.

Antoine and I walked down to my rooms through the inside staircase.

Usually, I regarded a conversation with my colleague from Louisiana with a cautious outlook. He was, after all, a Jesuit with a superior way about him. On this day, we were both fairly bursting with internal energy that needed the release of discussion. The world as we knew it was changing with dizzying speed. As leaders of the church community, we had to be prepared to offer direction in the midst of what would surely be reigning confusion in the months to come. I was beginning to see some validity of Bishop Lynch's pro-slavery arguments and wondered about Antoine's reluctance to engage in the argument at dinner. Surely he wasn't in favor of keeping other humans in bondage? I wanted to know his opinions, especially since mine seemed so feeble in the face of the bishop's.

Antoine, of course, surprised me as he so often did. He lit a cheroot and asked about my rescue of Bones Fletcher, with never a mention of slavery or of our conversation in the dining room with the bishop. Or of the war and the southern states that were now following South Carolina's example and seceding one atop another.

I surprised myself by telling the tale of Bones and Gordon Becknell with animation. Since my mind had been consumed with the moral issue of slavery and with the question of how good Christians could not only own slaves, like most white families of any substance in Charleston, but defend the practice, I did not anticipate that it could be so easily diverted. But one query from Antoine and I was off. I talked for five full minutes before stopping, partially from embarrassment at having dominated the conversation and partially from a need to slow down my train of thought. I didn't want to run off the track completely.

Antoine, for his part, seemed fascinated by it all. "You mean, Thomas, that you struck the chief of police and then threatened him with further bodily harm? How refreshingly quaint."

"I'm afraid that I was angered to the point where I lost perspective for a moment."

"Do you want to confess?"

At first, I thought he was being his usual snide self. He wasn't, so he put on one of my stoles and heard my confession. He went on, afterward, as if the sacramental interruption had never occurred.

"Well, what's happened since? Has Gordon Becknell been around to redress his grievances?"

"No. As a matter of fact, I'm a bit surprised that he hasn't made an issue of it. Perhaps he's realized that he was totally in the wrong and is too ashamed of his behavior to face up to it. Maybe he's going to let the whole thing ride and pretend he doesn't remember."

FULL OF EYES: A REBEL BISHOP MYSTERY 85

"Or maybe he is merely waiting and biding his time until the opportunity for revenge presents itself. Have you thought about that?"

"I've thought of little else, to tell the truth. He has demonstrated his..."

"Propensity for violence?"

"Yes. Thank you. So, I consider myself at risk, to say nothing of Flora's nephew. Also, we have to consider Becknell a suspect in the murder of Jamieson Carter."

"Thomas, really. Beating the tar out of Bones, an impecunious colored boy with a nefarious background, hardly qualifies the chief of police as a suspect in the murder of one of the town's most prominent citizens. When I mentioned revenge, I was thinking more along the lines of police harassment. Please don't overreact."

"I'm not, believe me."

"Then you must know something you're not confiding in me."

He stated it as a fact, but he raised his eyebrows as he looked at me for confirmation. I hesitated. I needed a partner to help in the investigation. Reverend Gagnon certainly had the contacts to help, and the logical brain. And for all his faults of demeanor, he was a brother priest. He gossiped, true, but not in a malicious fashion as far as I knew. I wondered what the bishop would think of enlisting his help.

"Will you kindly wait here for a moment, Antoine? I'll be right back."

He nodded, and I jogged up the stairs to the main floor. I found Bishop Lynch in his study, sipping the one French brandy he allowed himself each week. He invited me in, and I broached the subject of confiding in Father Gagnon.

"I'm pleased that you brought the subject up, Tom. I have feared for a while now that the two of you were not particularly close in your friendship."

He breathed in the cognac fumes from his snifter, rolling the brandy around in the bottom of the bulbous glass. Now he lifted his face out with an odd little half-smile on it.

"He's your age and priests need one another, you know. It can be a lonely life without a family of your own—although I consider you family to me, a valued son if you will. Still, you need the company of peers, too."

The cognac had flushed his face a little, and perhaps the gesture of love as well. Men had such a hard time expressing feelings for one another. I thought it well worth the temporary embarrassment when we occasionally use our voices to communicate what is already in our hearts.

His fatherly statement had the effect of lifting my spirits to an extent that surprised me. I knew that he cared for me, of course. After all, I dealt with him every day and had given him ample opportunity over the past few years to show any dislike toward me. And I readily admit that the feeling of affection was mutual. Still, his expression of it buoyed me immensely, and I assumed he meant for me to confide in Antoine. I took my leave and fairly bounded from the study. So it happened that I came upon Flora rather more suddenly than usual. She was walking up the broad hall in her peculiar gait. I put out my hand and hipped to one side, thinking that I might run into her, and apologized for my haste. She noticed the smile Bishop Lynch had generated with his paternal sentiments still on my face and was the embodiment of graciousness.

"Don't think nothing of it, Father. Sure you got every right to move around your own house any way you want."

"Yes, of course, Flora. I just ought to be a little more careful when I'm feeling my oats."

She grinned hugely at that and patted my hand that still touched her sleeve.

FULL OF EYES: A REBEL BISHOP MYSTERY 87

"When you're happy like that I don't care if you do knock me down."

We both laughed.

"I was looking for you anyway, Father Tom, 'cause my nephew says he ready to talk to you anytime you're ready."

"I'll come to the kitchen in ten minutes."

That gave me just enough time to brief Antoine on my investigation so far and ask him to accompany me to the interrogation of Bones Fletcher. I knew he was excited at the prospect, but he never dropped his studied casualness. Nevertheless, he was right on my heels as we walked upstairs to the kitchen.

We found Flora's nephew sitting at the scarred table that doubled as a chopping block when Flora or Mrs. Ryan were preparing meals. He was alone. He sat up straight and stopped drumming his fingers on the tabletop when he saw us walk in. Father Gagnon moved to the table first and sat opposite him.

I couldn't help but be struck by the contrast between the two: the priest, thin and very pale, with delicate features and a prim mouth; the Negro youth, much darker and strong-featured with a full set of lips. One was dressed in tailored black cassock, the other in mended, rough clothes. I spoke up, both to break the tension I felt boiling between the two contrasting men and to set the tone for what I hoped would be a gentle interrogation.

"Good afternoon, Bones. You're looking a lot better than the last time I talked to you."

He nodded at me, saying nothing. He cut his eyes to Father Antoine as I took a seat next to him. The priest smiled at the Negro, trying, no doubt, to put the young man at ease. I imagine that Father's ghastly attempt at a companionable grin had the very opposite effect, especially since it was accompanied by a stiff and unwelcoming posture. Antoine sat bent away from Bones, as if he was afraid of getting too close to the Negro. I tried to reassure him anyhow.

"Father Gagnon is a friend of mine, Bones. He has agreed to help you as well."

The smile died on Antoine's face as I imagined he tried to recall actually having offered to help, but Bones Fletcher looked somewhat relieved. He still said nothing, however. His facial bones were molded in sharp planes under his buttery skin, but his facial musculature seemed less tense after my offer of help. His eyes were dotted with red and appeared to be floating in their sockets. There were scabs on his face from the beating and some puffiness still over one eye.

"How are you feeling?"

"Well nuff."

We were silent for a few seconds before he added, "Thank you now."

"Can you tell us why Chief Becknell was beating you?"

"He been after me for a, a ting. Said ain't no sense waste de jail cell. Gonna teach this po' boy a lesson, he say."

"What sort of thing?"

"Some ting I did."

"What something?"

"Wasn't nothing much."

"Bones, you are going to have to confide in us. We're not the police. We're not going to tell anyone."

"You gonna whomp me with a stick like you did that po-liceman ifin I don't tell you?"

That struck me dumb momentarily. Didn't Moses hear the same reaction to violence when he killed the Egyptian guard who was beating a Jew? Surely this man Bones couldn't be afraid of me. I was a man of the cloth. Was I becoming something else under the strain of the unresolved murder in the cathedral? Or was it the looming war

FULL OF EYES: A REBEL BISHOP MYSTERY   89

that was already beginning to color my moral landmarks? I looked almost frantically at Bones, but he didn't seem physically afraid of me. Something else was bothering him and making him reluctant to tell us what he knew. Then it dawned on me what might be bothering him.

"We're not going to tell Flora anything you tell us. Promise."

"She does be a good woman and don't need no more trouble."

"Agreed."

"All right then, mister man, I goin tell you what I done." He sat up when he spoke, and the planes of his face hardened. "I show my knife to some boy in he goat cart and took some he groceries. Tings is hard. Nobody want to hire me out. We got to eat."

He was a sudden mixture of arrogant tough guy and whining beggar boy, hooligan and victim at the same time. I saw none of the malice he had presented to me the day I went to rescue Jasper from the grassy patch in front of his shanty. Perhaps that display of fearsomeness was just a ploy to extract money from me. Perhaps I had been a mite hasty in leaping on the horse and tearing away. Perhaps that's why his high-pitched laughter followed my escape. He must have been enjoying the effect of his dramatic acting. The idea made me even more acutely embarrassed about my behavior then, but I figured a few humbling experiences here and there fit in nicely as necessities of a priestly vocation. So I put it away in the recesses of my mind and concentrated on how to convince Bones to open up to us.

I had an idea of how to handle him and do my Christian duty at the same time, but I was unsure of how to decipher truth from fantasy if he agreed to my offer. Still, it was probably worth a try.

"Bones, I think I can help you."

"You already has."

"Thank you. I can help some more. Look here, you need money for food, and we need information. Let's do a trade.'

Bones looked doubtful, one eye squeezing almost shut, but he said nothing.

"I'll give you, let's say, one dollar if you answer our questions truthfully. You tell us something, and it turns out to be true, then next time you find out something, I'll pay you for that too."

"What I know can help you?"

I glanced at Antoine, and he took over the questioning smoothly.

"On Tuesday night, you were walking past that red house on the lane between Pinckney and the old slave market. The one that runs down to East Bay? You were chatting with an older Negro man as you went along."

Bones seemed to search his memory for an instant and then nodded.

"Early. Just gone dark."

"Correct. I was visiting old Mr. Farr. His housemaid had opened the window to air his bedroom, and I heard you and the other man talking. I was supposed to be hearing Mr. Farr's confession, but he went quiet for such a spell that I swear he fell asleep. When he came back to consciousness, he acted as if nothing untoward had happened and went right on where he'd left off. Had I asked him he surely would have denied going off."

He said this to me with a bemused look on his face and then turned back to Bones. This odd interrogation technique did not appear to bother either one of them.

"Anyway, Mr. Bones, I overheard you and the other man talking. Can you tell Father Dockery what you were talking about? I don't mean everything, but the part about someone you'd seen the night before."

"You mean when I see de wild preacher man?"

Antoine nodded and smiled in encouragement.

"I seen him, all right. I been telling Harold 'bout it 'cause the man done act funny and put me off some. I been tinking when I

FULL OF EYES: A REBEL BISHOP MYSTERY   91

seen him come out to Queen Street off de alley Tuesday night that I might come up to him. You know, ask him for de penny or some ting."

The brown youngster looked at me quickly. I was thinking that Bones probably had been planning to flash his knife again and extort some money from the man he'd seen Tuesday night, like he tried with me and my horse and like Becknell caught him doing to some youngster in a goat cart. I could tell by his look that he knew what I was thinking, too. But I just inclined my head at him, and he went on with his story.

"First off, I din know who he be when he turn off of Queen. He wear de toboggan over he head, cover up most de hair, and he be scrunch up some. I done come see who he be bare in time."

Antoine looked perplexed, so I explained that a toboggan is local jargon for a soft wool hat, the kind that a person might wear in snow country or a sailor might wear at sea. Seamen called them watch caps. Andrew Quillery was a painfully thin man with white hair that stuck out from his head when he ranted, which was apparently often. He was fairly tall and looked even more so since he held himself rigidly upright. He seemed to go straight up. His eyes were flinty, and he used them to accent his fiery ways. No one crossed Reverend Quillery, no one risked his wrath. He was reputed to be the owner of a brutal and quick tongue. When he scolded Africans, which was his main claim to fame, they looked as if they had been beaten physically. A lot of people thought he represented either the devil or God's dark side. When they referred to him as the wild preacher man, everyone knew who they were talking about.

"I seen who it be, I quick jump back in de shadows. When you hear me, I been tell Harold 'bout that close call. We was laughing. It be funny dem time, but it sure enough wasn't funny that night before."

"Are you certain it was Andrew Quillery you saw?"

"Yeah. Ain't no mistake that man. The moon catch he eye, and he nose look like de hatchet for chicken. It be him all right. No mistake. Nossir. I done get de nerves just tink bout how close that be."

"Why do you say that he was acting funny?"

"He be bent over, heah, holding some ting to he front. He look bigger and not so tall that way, so I din know who he be first look."

"What was he holding?"

"Doan know. Some ting."

"Did it seem heavy?"

"Doan tink so. It might be bunch de onions. He grow de patch near his church I been tole, and they's coming up now, dem tin ones. I couldn't see dem, but they din seem too much burden for de man. I mean he not been struggle or breathe hard or nothing. Or he could just as easy been carrying a log, or a...a...roll up blanket. But he done held it close, like it be worth some ting, y'know?"

We acknowledged that we did indeed know what he meant. Both of us were thinking the same thing, that the carved statue of Mary could easily have fit the bill. If the wild preacher man was really carrying the statue that had been used to brain Jamieson Carter, the possibilities were intriguing. The day was right for the murder of Jamieson, but the timing was off. If my estimate of time of death wasn't too inaccurate, he was killed early in the morning of Tuesday. Bones said that he had seen Andrew Quillery skulking about in the evening on Tuesday. He mentioned the moon, and I knew from my daily reading of the almanac that moonrise was early most of April, when the sun was still up, and it was gone from our sky by eleven p.m. Daylight was starting to fade, and roads in the city were darkening by seven o'clock in the evening. So the earliest Bones could have seen Quillery would still have been some sixteen or seventeen hours after the murder took place. Quillery was heading toward the cathedral, to boot, not away from it.

FULL OF EYES: A REBEL BISHOP MYSTERY 93

I gave Bones Fletcher a silver dollar. He grinned hugely, and he went off to find Flora and say his goodbyes. Antoine and I thought about what we knew so far.

"You believe him?"

"I don't know him like you do, Thomas, but I tend to think he was being truthful. If he didn't concoct some lie to cover up the reason Becknell was beating him, I doubt he would have done so about Quillery."

I agreed with him. Then I invited him to come back for supper after his sick call rounds. Sunday evening and Monday were Flora's days off, but she would leave cold plates in the icehouse for us. The bishop was planning to visit kin who were in the army down at Fort Morris near Folly Island as soon as he awoke from his postprandial nap. His family, including his father, the formidable Conlaw Lynch, was from Cheraw, a six-day trip inland. They occasionally vacationed at the coast, though, and were down now to work out what the bombardment of Ft. Sumter might mean to soldier and civilian alike. The meeting at Ft. Morris sounded like a tribal gathering, the kind of council we heard that the Indians out west were fond of holding. I imagined that many an extended southern family was engaging in just such a council about now. There were plans to be made and advice for enlistment-age young men. And there was news to be shared. His Excellency would be full of war news when he returned.

Since Mondays were quiet around the chancery, he was going to stay the night at Folly rather than risk getting caught by darkness on the ride home. Flora had already left for her one night away from the house that week, which meant I'd be alone in the big house. I'd meant to forestall that bleak possibility by extending the supper invitation to Father Gagnon.

I had begun trusting in him more since the murder in the cathedral, even though his Jesuitical ways were often annoying to a simple parish priest, which was what I considered myself. I enjoyed

94   PAUL A. BARRA

my duty of service to the bishop but eventually hoped to serve a parish. Antoine, it seemed to me, would never be happy unless he took the miter. Still, our conversations were of interest to me, and I hoped for another good one that Sunday evening.

Antoine begged off, though. He had other plans himself, although he didn't say what they were. And, of course, I wouldn't think to question him about them. So I was left alone.

I said goodbye to the Jesuit and saw him to the door. He stopped just inside, in the foyer, and turned to me.

"Take care of yourself, Tom. If Gordon Becknell really was involved with Jamieson Carter's murder, he now has more than one reason to get you out of the way. You are the best chance to find out the killer, and he knows that. And he'll want revenge for knocking him around and saving Bones. Be careful, hear?"

Antoine walked away into the spring day, dusting pine pollen off his sleeve with a studied nonchalance. He walked, nay strolled, as if he had all day to get home, but then Hasell Street where his residence lay was a fair walk, and he was probably only pacing himself for the distance. But his nonchalance didn't fool me. He was worried about my safety, and so was I.

The bishop departed an hour or so later. Since he was comfortable atop a horse and had many miles to Folly Beach, he took Jasper, the fastest of our house mounts.

"I want to get there in daylight and think the exercise will expend some of his energy and ease his rambunctious nature, don't you? I don't wish to end up on the side of the road if the horse decides to get fractious. It may be a long time before a Samaritan comes that way."

"I agree, Excellency. Jasper can use the work, and he's agreeable enough when he has to make an effort. Once you get down to the sand roads on James Island, you'll be able to canter most of the rest of the way."

FULL OF EYES: A REBEL BISHOP MYSTERY 95

The day passed quickly after both clerics left. Mrs. Ryan also left the house, without a word to me, and I was finally alone. I began the next week's sermons. I read and loafed and ate bread and cheese on the second floor balcony, watching the gloaming steal over the city and the lamps outside the Baptist churches begin to glow. Those folks went to church most of the day on Sunday, including an evening service. The mere thought of such a day tired my mind, so I went to my rooms on the lower level. I was reading and succumbing to lassitude with the lack of activity when I thought I heard a sound overhead. I laid the book—a volume of the collected works of John England, compiled by Ignatius Reynolds, the second Bishop of Charleston—on my lap and listened intently. The big old house was silent except for the usual creaks and groans of a settling structure. We had stopped burning wood in the fireplaces once the nights turned mild a week before, but Flora had opened all the windows to air the house before she left in the morning. As the day's warmth began to leave in the late afternoon, I had closed them up, so the house was comfortable enough.

Later, I heard a scratching noise and then a window rattling in a draft of breeze. Each time I stopped reading and listened. This sounds ridiculous for a grown man who did most of that growing in the streets of a major city and who was a trained police officer, but the emptiness of the place made me nervous. Of course, Antoine's reminder that Gordon Becknell may try to prevent me from solving the mystery of the murder in the cathedral also had me a bit on edge. I appreciated the real possibility that the chief might not want me poking around in the case, especially if he had been involved in it. I also appreciated that one's imagination in a big, empty house on a dark night could play on one's nerves.

By the middle of the nineteenth century, Americans had gotten so used to living with other people that being alone now made them uncomfortable. Some trappers and shepherds still spent months at a time alone, but most of us lived in family groups and worked with crowds. As a former denizen of a city teeming with humanity, I was hearing things in the emptiness that weren't there and fancying movement in the darkened rooms all around me.

By nine, I was ready for bed. The reading had gone poorly, and I was tired of trying to concentrate when my imagination kept getting in the way. I knew then why people kept a dog in the home. Even a small animal would have provided companionship, and that lack was probably at the root of my anxiety.

Finally, though, the weighty style of Bishop England's prose dulled even my fantasies, and I began to drowse in my chair. Easing myself from that chair, I shuffled upstairs.

I moved slowly around the main floor, carrying a single unshielded candle, intending to check the locks without driving away the groggy sense of peace that had invaded my inner body. I was ready for bed and wanted to stay that way.

As I rounded the bend in the corridor that ran past the kitchen, I felt a cool draft at my feet. Still slowed by sleepiness and only mildly curious, I looked up the hall. What I saw froze me in my tracks, popped my eyes open, and drove my heart rate to a pounding wakefulness. The back door was ajar.

CHAPTER 11

I stepped back automatically and blew out the candle. Then I forced my will upon my mind. *Think*, I said. Mrs. Ryan was gone from the house. Neither Flora nor the bishop would leave the house without securing the door. I myself had let Antoine out through that same door hours earlier. But had I checked to be sure the latch had caught? My mouth had gotten dry, and I had to swallow. I could hear the pulse racing in my ears.

The inescapable conclusion was that someone had gained entry to the big house, maybe through a window or the back door itself. He must have been frightened off when he heard me approach. The question was, had he slipped into the house to hide or had he left before he got caught? The smart thing to do was to leave myself, immediately, and summon help. My mind whirred through that possibility, bleated out into my consciousness that the chief of police was the most likely identity of the intruder, unless, of course, it was a common thief. I couldn't very well call the police to protect me from their chief, could I? Besides, I hardly had enough proof to call for help.

But an open door was proof enough for me to proceed cautiously.

Priding myself on my ability to think straight in stressful situations and remembering that discretion was indeed the better part of valor, I turned abruptly and headed for the front of the house. I didn't want to summon the police, but I would go out to Broad Street and find someone to assist me with a look through the dark house. I moved purposefully toward the front of the house. I didn't get very far.

The back door slammed behind me, and I immediately darted without thinking into the kitchen to the right. Still working on instinct, I ran past the stoves and the table where Bones had been seated that very afternoon and fetched up against the plank door to the root cellar. I stood there in the dark, trying desperately to listen for sounds of pursuit and cursing the thudding of my heart. I hadn't gone very far, but my breath was coming fast already. My belly felt like it was pushing up into my chest, filling with air itself, and restricting the capacity of my lungs. I willed my body to relax.

Maybe a half-minute of silence slipped by, and my eyes became accustomed to the dark. The early moonshine painted silhouettes of hanging pots and shadowed the branches of trees outside the windows. The branches started to whip around, and I heard rain tingle against the windows. The smell of raw onions came to me and, had I time to dwell on that peculiarity, I would have assumed that Flora had hung some in the kitchen. It was the season for them. I watched for movement in the kitchen—the only thing I could hope to discern in the kaleidoscope of light and dark in the big room. When I saw a shadow move, I dropped the candle and turned out of the kitchen. The shadow muttered and pots rattled behind me. I pounded down the hallway toward the front door.

I ran like the demons of hell were chasing me, and I knew I had to calm down, but it was too late. The shadow was no more than a few steps behind me. The door didn't open when I got to it and pulled frantically on the knob. Mrs. Ryan had locked it. The intruder

FULL OF EYES: A REBEL BISHOP MYSTERY 99

followed me instead of going back out the rear way. That could only mean he was determined to harm me, not make his escape. I struggled to throw the bolt as footsteps closed in on me. The lock gave as time ran out. At the last second, I twisted to meet the intruder just as he gripped me around the throat. We crashed into the door and went down.

My head struck the doorknob on the way. The pain was sharp and temporary, but it drove out the panic that had begun to take over my actions. It made me angry. Why was I running like a rabbit in my own house? If the intruder had meant to kill me, I would already have felt his steel or have been clubbed senseless. That knowledge revived hope in me and a sense of valor returned, even though he had me by the throat with one hand while he pummeled me with the other. He was strong, but by squirming I had avoided any telling blows so far. Accuracy in punching was difficult in the half-light of the hall.

I lashed out with a straight right. It bounced off his covered head and caused no apparent damage. I drove my knee up. Air burst from him when it struck between his legs. His grip weakened momentarily. I rolled him over but his fist caught me above the eye, and we fell apart. He grunted as he tried to throw another punch. It missed low, and I gained my knees. We faced each other in that posture and both rained blows. I had the advantage at that and thought I could keep it, but he twisted away from a hard left hook, and I banged it off the doorsill as it missed. Neither one of us could get decent purchase, so our blows were arm punches mostly. Still, it hurt when I hit the sill. I was on top of him now, but the pain in my hand prevented me from hitting him for a moment.

He twisted out from under me, and we both scrambled to our feet. My left hand felt numb. I winged a right at him, but he went under it and threw me back with a great shove. I realized then that he was a powerful man but anger had taken over my consciousness, and I launched myself at him as he tried to escape by jerking open the front door. I grabbed a handful of coat collar and banged his head against the jamb. We were both outside on the small front porch suddenly, in a wet breeze. He threw me off with another burst of strength. I stepped back to gain leverage and found only air beneath my foot. I had been pushed to one set of steps that arched up to the front door from the street below on either side. My front foot slipped on the wet porch floor as the rear one missed the second step. My momentum carried me backward. It seemed to be a slow fall, but I could not stop it. I noticed the cold rain stinging my upturned face. I hit hard, bounced once, then saw a burst of brilliant white before everything turned to a sudden and complete blackness.

CHAPTER 12

I was never sure afterward if it was the hard ground or the soft voice that brought me back to consciousness. I lay on the marble sidewalk that fronted the bishop's house, dressed only in a sodden undershirt and pants, no shoes. The rain had stopped, but the air still smelled of it. I opened my eyes, realized that my cheek was in a cold puddle, but was afraid to move. My head felt soft and fragile, the pain making me fearful of how badly I'd been damaged in the fall. The voice came again, vaguely familiar. My head hurt too much to worry about deciphering it just then. I'm afraid I must have groaned aloud. Instantly, warm breath kissed the side of my face, and I could smell a hint of rosewater and fresh air.

"We have to get you in the house, sir. Can you stand?"

That voice again, whispering. I looked up. Her face was close to mine, looking pale and muted through the fogged vision caused by the ache in my head. Worry lines creased her forehead and ran a crack between her eyes. Gretchen Becknell knelt next to me, her hair pulled back and glistening with tiny droplets of mist. I closed my mouth and eyes and hunched up into a kneeling posture, head hanging low and throbbing unmercifully.

After a minute, during which I inexplicably started to pant, the pain eased enough for me to rise fully. I swayed. Gretchen put her arm about me. I wanted to lay down again, but her arm tightened. Both of us knew that I couldn't very well sleep in the wet street in front of the episcopal residence. The very idea made me smile slightly, and she took courage from that.

"Come on now, let's go on up the steps."

She still spoke as if she might be afraid of disturbing the neighbors, although I heard no indications of anyone else about and there were no lamps lit that I could see. I responded to her arm pressure, and we slowly ascended the same staircase I had fallen down brief moments ago, appearing for all the world like a woman assisting her dead drunk husband, if anyone cared to look.

The main problem with that scenario was that priests were celibate, and women were not supposed to be helping drunken men into the bishop's house. That house was located on a main street not far from the commercial downtown of Charleston, but I was too dazed to care about perceptions of impropriety just then.

Gretchen followed my slurred instructions to the staircase and got me down to my sitting room. Parts of the journey were a blank to me, still are. I didn't recall walking down the stairs or reaching the couch. The next recollection was reclining on my back as Gretchen patted my forehead and lips with a wet cloth.

"The doors—"

Her face was close, and she barely breathed her reply. "I've already locked both and have had a look around. I think we are quite alone."

The room was brightly lit by three oil lamps when I awoke the second time. Instantly, I recalled our intimacy in the darkened room as Gretchen Becknell had soothed my fevered brow, so to speak, with a cool cloth after having rescued me from the street. Feverish or not, my mind flashed back to her scent near my hot flesh earlier in the night, her softness as inviting as it was threatening.

It may as well have been imaginative, considering the atmosphere of the room now.

The woman had hung her cape from the hat rack and sat primly on the hard chair I used at my writing desk. I raced through my memory to assure myself that nothing untoward had happened between her and myself. I remembered a sense of closeness between us, but it had all been innocent, surely. Of course, my fall and the injury to my head may have contributed to my own moral resistance. I thanked God quickly for the grace that had sustained me even so. That grace did not dissolve the effect of her gentle charms, however. When I looked at Gretchen sitting there with a concerned expression on her face, I was taken by a sort of warm feeling, as if my skin was glowing. Considering what I'd been through that night, it was a perplexing response.

It was high time, however, to return to reality and try to make some sense of the evening's events.

"Do you know what time it is, Mrs. Becknell?"

"I believe the clock in the hall struck midnight not long ago."

My God, I thought, *after midnight and I'm alone in the bishop's house with an attractive woman. I have to escort her home immediately.* When I tried to move, though, my head protested, and I was not quick witted enough to prevent a moan from escaping my lips.

She was at my side in a flash. "Please don't try to move yet, Father. You've sustained a serious blow to the head and may well be concussed."

"We—We have to get you home, Mrs. Becknell."

To maintain the proper distance between us, and to reestablish a formal relationship between a cleric and a laywoman, I had decided to use her married name. She didn't see things that way.

"Please, call me Gretchen. After all we've been through together, that's the least you can do. Besides, there's a problem with getting me home, as you say."

I stared, nay gawked, at her around the throbbing of my head, breathing noisily through my nose. What in the world had she meant by "after all we've been through together?" And then what else had she said? My mind was losing its grip. I felt myself falling back into the darkness and decided it would be easier if I just let go. Maybe the situation would be improved with the passage of time.

I felt my eyelids flutter. The edges of my thoughts seemed to darken as I let go, feeling somehow safe and secure in this room with this gentle woman.

The next time I awoke, things were indeed better. My head hurt considerably less than it had, for one thing, and the blonde woman was back on the straight chair a goodly distance away from the couch. She leaned forward but did not rise as I swung my feet to the floor, and so I made it to a sitting position without so much as a whimper.

"May I ask what time it is now, madam?"

"Perhaps one thirty or so. Are you feeling better?"

"Yes. Very much so. Thank you."

"You seem afraid of me. I can't imagine why. I've never done anything to you."

"I assure you, Mrs. Becknell, it is nothing personal. I am committed to a celibate life and am not used to dealing with women, so things sometimes come out awkwardly. You never have done anything to me and have been the very soul of courtesy and gentility. To say nothing of having saved my life back on the street there—"

"Oh, no, I didn't save you. The man you were fighting with ran off when you fell down the steps."

"Perhaps he saw you approaching, do you think?"

"Yes, perhaps."

"Then you saved me." She opened her mouth to protest, but I forestalled it. "Let's give it the benefit of the doubt."

Gretchen sighed. "If you insist."

FULL OF EYES: A REBEL BISHOP MYSTERY

"I insist. Also, dear lady, I insist that I escort you home this very minute. Your reputation, to say nothing of mine, is at stake."

"Father Dockery, my house is a dangerous place just now."

"How can your own home be dangerous to you?"

"When I left, by the back door, someone came to the front door. My husband let him in. Then before I could effect my escape, more men came. Soon the downstairs was full of men, maybe a dozen in all. They were drinking rum and looked prepared to spend a full night in their...deliberations. Now I don't for a minute think that my husband's friends, even fired up on liquor and war talk, are a threat to me, but for a man walking me home...well, that's another matter."

I was beside myself with questions, especially the one which would be answered by an explanation of her nocturnal sojourn, but I held my tongue. After all, it was not my business what a woman did on her own time. And I was afraid, from what I did know of her relationship with the deceased sacristan, that I would not be happy with the answer. Still, as I knew from personal experience, the streets of wartime Charleston were not safe.

"Well, there can be no question of you walking home alone at this hour, dear lady."

"What can we do then?"

What indeed? If only Flora were at home this evening. She could accompany us, take Gretchen to her door while I waited out of sight and, best of all, I could rely on her complete discretion. But it would be an egregious imposition to ask a lady to leave her home in the middle of her one night off, so to save a friend some embarrassment. On the other hand, of course, Flora was a slave and was probably accustomed to much more cavalier treatment at the hands of previous owners. She had told me once when I was mentioning how impressed I was with Bishop Lynch's handling of some diocesan matter, that he had purchased her for the unlikely sum of $800. It was an act of charity, Flora said, saving her from an unkind owner. I said that she had turned out to be a bargain for the bishop, causing her to honor me with that sweet smile of hers. With that conversation in mind, I knew what I had to do.

"Please lock the door behind me, Mrs. Becknell, and do not answer it unless you are certain it is me returning. Under no circumstances. Is that an agreeable precaution?"

"Yes. Yes, of course."

I went out to the stable and got out the Cleveland Bay, a big mare with a plodding disposition. We called her Betty Lou, and she acted as if being called to duty in the black of night was as natural as a bowel movement. She was the third horse we owned. I rigged her to the Dearborn, a light boxy vehicle the diocese kept on hand for special occasions such as funerals. Bishop Lynch and I both preferred to ride horseback whenever possible, and none of the house servants went anywhere on normal official duties that required anything more than the use of shank's mare. The carriage was black and nondescript. Rather thin curtains covered the open windows, and the broadcloth seats were showing little signs of wear too, but I thought the rig would suit perfectly for the incognito adventure I envisioned. It was a common enough buggy in Charleston and bore no coat of arms or seal to mark it as a diocesan vehicle.

Jasper would have wanted to go along for the nighttime drive if he were not already at Folly Beach, but I reckoned him to be too skittish for the job at hand and was happy enough with the Cleveland. Quiet was desired more than haste on this journey. The other diocesan horse, an aged gray gelding, clattered about in his stall a bit and neighed plaintively when we left, but I knew he'd be back asleep in minutes.

I drove over to Flora's house in the slave quarters the diocese shared with a few other downtown firms. The horse clopped through the empty dirt streets and the occasional cobbled one, splintering the dead silence of the night and parting the mist that had begun to form as the night air cooled above the sun-warmed ground. I couldn't see Betty Lou's hooves. Occasionally the mist rose and whispered around the buggy. Still not fully recovered from my fall and tired that late in the evening, I was affected by the eerie circumstances of the quiet and the ground fog. My mind slipped back to my last big case with the NYPD. I didn't want to recall it, but the circumstances and my still enfeebled head rendered my resistance moot. The memory flooded back like a rip tide, black and nasty.

I was afoot then, in November of 1854, down along the East River. The air had a cold bite to it, and the fog rolled in from the sea, absorbing sound and obscuring vision. I shivered in my greatcoat every time I stopped to look and listen. My rounds had been quiet up till then, but I was cold enough and tired enough to want something warm to drink. So I was looking for a lighted window among the row tenements that housed shops on their lower floors, hoping to spot an eatery or even a grog shop where I could procure some coffee. Just then I heard what was to become "the sound of horror and blind terror" in the National Police Gazette's coverage of the crime. Someone screamed. The cry, which was horrifying all right, came at me and seemed to fade as the fog lifted and then returned. I was disoriented. The more I strained to peer into the fog and determine the location of the sound, the more confused I became. At first, I thought the scream was coming from one of the houses along the waterfront. Next, it seemed to be coming from the water itself. To make matters worse, the scream ended suddenly, in mid-voice. I had to do something. I ran down to the piers that I knew jutted into the black river. I gripped my truncheon tightly but could find nothing to use it against, nothing alive to question or chase. I ran up and down the piers, clumping loudly and calling out "Police! Police!"

Soon I felt warm and frustrated. I stopped for a blow. The scream made my skin jump when it began again. It was close, and this time I knew it was to my right. I also thought it was a woman screaming. Again, it stopped abruptly. I started off toward what I thought to be the location of the scream cautiously and quietly, so I heard the splash clearly. It sounded like a heavy object hitting the water. Could it have been the screaming woman? I took off running again, down First and left on the Twenty-Sixth Street Pier. A fog bank washed over me. I was lost in its gauze, so I slid to a stop on the water-softened boards. I was afraid to run into dense fog. I didn't know exactly where the end of the pier was and didn't want to become a second victim in the winter water. I moved ahead slowly, all my senses sharp. Suddenly, I heard footsteps, coming hard and fast toward me. A man burst from the fog and barreled into me. The impact spun me around, but I didn't go down. My assailant did, though, and I didn't let him regain his feet. I clubbed him with my stick as he tried to heave himself up from his hands and knees. He moaned and fell to the pier surface. He made a noise like a fish landing on deck.

The next few hours were grueling and confusing. I manacled the suspect, who turned out to be a young man, and whistled for the constable on the adjoining foot beat. By the time we arranged for a paddy wagon to pick up the suspect and organized a more thorough search of the riverfront, it was near to morning. We found nothing. The suspect said nothing. He held his head and wept, but he would not tell us what he was doing on the pier or why he had run at me. The whole ordeal exhausted me. When I got home, it was full light out. I slept until afternoon. So it wasn't until I went to the station house for my watch at four that I found out early fishermen had recovered a body from the East River. It turned out to be the remains of the suspect's fiancée. The coroner ruled that she drowned, probably after entering the water in an unconscious state. Her throat

FULL OF EYES: A REBEL BISHOP MYSTERY   109

showed signs of strangulation. Her purse was never found, but her corpse was wearing a ring and missing a necklace.

It was a depressing scenario, one that produced the final nudge toward the priesthood for me. I had been convinced long before that I wanted to spend my mortal life in service to others. That was why I entered the police department, in spite of having earned a baccalaureate degree at the University of the City of New York—later NYU. I was known by the nickname "Books," fondly by my fellow constables, derisively by the sergeants. The trouble with police service was that its justice was prescribed by law and was not always just. I had a bad feeling about the Twenty-Sixth Street Pier case, for instance. The city claimed that the suspect strangled the girl after a lovers' quarrel. The man himself finally rose from his depression and admitted they had argued and she left in a huff. He had walked away, he said, determined not to give in to her fit of pique.

"Beatrice was a spoiled young woman," the young man said. "She got what she wanted from me by refusing to speak to me or by walking away when we disagreed. I was going to teach her a lesson this time."

He ended up sobbing at that because he realized later what a dangerous position he let her walk into. The waterfront was a place where romance blundered into misery with alarming speed if you ended up in the wrong section. Twenty-Sixth wasn't the rat's nest of crime that some other places were, but it could pose some danger for a girl alone. When he heard her scream, he was already heading back to find her. He had the same disorientation difficulties that I experienced, he alleged, and was frantic by the time he heard her scream the second time. He crashed into me in his haste to save her. By knocking him out instead of joining forces with him in a search I had allowed her to drown, perhaps. If he was telling the truth.

A jury of his peers exonerated me from blame and convicted the young man of Murder Two. In New York that was homicide without the planning aspect of Murder One. He went to prison after the trial. I went back to the seminary where I had enrolled under the auspices of the New York archdiocese before the wheels of justice moved forward enough for the case to be adjudicated. I was unconvinced that the jury was right. What had happened to her necklace and her bag? Neither was ever found. Did she really run afoul of some thief in the night as the defense claimed? I could imagine a girl refusing to give up her valuables, especially if she was used to getting her own way. Was the suspect running to her aid as he claimed? He was a banker with a promising professional future, according to a witness, and had no previous record of any kind. The couple had been engaged for six months and had arranged for a church wedding in the spring. It was a perplexing enigma, and it preyed on my mind for years. It became a sort of purgatory for me, an unhappy time that ended in joy. The Twenty-Sixth Street Pier case pushed me into the priesthood.

As Betty Lou and I plodded along the streets of Charleston that fogbound night in 1861 on the way to Flora's home, another episode in my police career that left a lasting impression on me, although of an entirely different nature, inveigled itself into my thoughts. I had been assigned to guard a funeral in 1853. A black man named Pierre Toussaint was being buried out of St. Peter's Church on Barclay Street and the crowd that had assembled was much too large for the church to accommodate. About two dozen of us uniformed officers were on hand to maintain order. We needn't have bothered. The mourners, as many white as Negro, were too soulful to cause any disruption. Toussaint was a former slave from Haiti who became wealthy in New York. All of us who worked downtown knew of his charitable work among the city's Negro population, and so did hundreds of others apparently. Our boss man thought that Toussaint's abolitionist writings might have stirred up some resentment, but we saw none of that. One man told some of us after the funeral Mass that the pastor of St. Peter's had called Toussaint "God's reflection in ebony."

Almost eight years after the funeral and seven after the case that ushered me into the priesthood, I was supposed to be investigating another death, this time in Charleston under the threat of impending war. Instead, I was off in a fog bank trying to arrange to smuggle a woman home when I should have been sleeping soundly and dreaming of angels on high. I hoped that my impression of Flora was correct, that she held as much charity in her heart as did the late Pierre Toussaint.

CHAPTER 13

Our noise was muffled when I drove the rig onto Lagare, a dirt road. The rhythm of the steady walk on soft ground lulled me briefly and a prayer technique I had developed eventually eased out of my mind the awful uncertainties that the Twenty-Sixth Street Pier case occasionally brought to the surface. Betty Lou and I soon arrived at the complex where Flora lived with her sister and other relatives. At least, I thought they were relatives. It occurred to me then, as I peered into the gossamer darkness, that I knew little about Flora's personal life, despite living in the same house with her six nights a week for longer than two years. I had dropped her off at her quarters on two rainy Sundays, however, so I recognized the place, even in the fog.

It was a dismal, uneven shanty, unpainted, with a roof that was down in the center and surely must have leaked in the frequent Lowcountry rains. Other homes, in similar states of disrepair, tilted and canted on both sides of Flora's, as if they had been fighting a gale at sea and had been congealed in place.

I could smell decayed wood and mud carried on the mist, along with wet dog and the unmistakable, if faint, odor of a pig pen somewhere off in the darkness.

FULL OF EYES: A REBEL BISHOP MYSTERY   113

I reined up and climbed down. No sooner had I turned from the buggy in the suddenly intense silence than a candle flared in the front window of Flora's house. I waited. The horse blew once and shook the harness. Then it was quiet again.

The door to the house creaked open, and an old man stepped out. He carried a candle in a tin cup to one side of himself, so that I could see part of his face while the other half remained in darkness. He did not speak but looked at me with a question in his eye. His thick neck was bent toward the candle, and his back slumped, as if he was carrying something heavy on his shoulders. He must have anticipated that nothing good could come from a late night visit from a man in a black carriage.

"I'm Father Dockery from the cathedral, sir. I'm very sorry to disturb you at this hour, but I must speak to Flora."

The old man bobbed his head, saying nothing, and went back into the house. I waited and the enormity of what I was about to do struck me, the imposition I had already made on the woman's family, waking them hours before they would have to work all day, probably frightening them with the unusual nature of a nighttime visit. Would I have done all this to another friend, or was Flora's slave status what made my boldness possible? Did I argue against slavery yet take advantage of it at the same time?

Moments later, Flora appeared. She was dressed to travel.

"Flora, I'm so sorry to bother you, especially at this ghastly hour, but I didn't know where else to turn. You see—"

"Why don't we get in that there wagon, Father? No sense in wasting time. You can tell me about your problem as we drive."

So we did, and so I did. Flora made no comment, not even a cluck of disapproval, as I explained what had transpired at the episcopal residence. She didn't ask why I couldn't escort the woman home or complain of being called to duty on her night off. She acted as if she saw her Christian duty and was bent on performing it. Her voice was neither begrudging nor obsequious. Always, her temperament was implacably steady, that much I knew. I hadn't realized before that she wasn't just accepting my imposition, and many others I imagined, as a burden to be borne because of her lowly status. In her mind, her status was not at all lowly. I could see that clearly now in the black of the night. She held a responsible position in the home of a distinguished prelate, and she performed her duties well. She was willing to help me out of my predicament because she could. She wanted to do good things for people she considered good. I felt blessed.

Flora had a suggestion about the trip to Gretchen's house and agreed with the general plan I had formulated on the way over so that, by the time we arrived back on Broad Street, we both knew what we were going to do and say on our adventure.

I went in to get Gretchen, who didn't answer my knock until I identified myself. Then she opened the door so suddenly that I realized she'd been leaning against it waiting to hear who was rapping. Her eyes were wide, but she asked no questions as I led her down the steps and helped her up onto the carriage seat. Flora nodded to her and took up the reins.

As I hunkered down in the back, I could hear the women talking briefly after we'd been underway for a few minutes. I couldn't understand what they said but assumed they were confirming the plan. I could also detect the comforting tones that Flora used sometimes. She may not have known about Gretchen's grief over the loss of Jamieson Carter, but she did know intuitively that Gretchen was in some emotional pain because of her husband and the associates he entertained in their home. She consoled this stranger just as easily as she agreed to help me.

Before long, the carriage slowed and tilted backward as we came to the rise that led to the Becknell's neighborhood. I slipped out of the cloth-covered doorway and let the momentum of the buggy

FULL OF EYES: A REBEL BISHOP MYSTERY   115

carry me forward until I came to a sizable tree. I stopped myself with my arms, finding that I was now in a small wood that had not been cleared by the builders of the cottages on Partridge Lane. Flora never slowed the horse nor looked back to see how I had done on my moving dismount. In minutes, the buggy had moved out of sight and sound into the thickening mist. I shivered and waited in the dark.

Perhaps twenty minutes passed, and I approximated the time to be about three a.m. Some slight sound up the road reached me, and I strained to hear. At first, it sounded like a horse, until I realized that the clumping of hooves was too quick in succession to be less than three or more horses walking. I pressed myself closer to the backside of the pine tree and waited. Presently, I could make out the sounds of men talking over the sounds of their mounts. As they rode abreast, I could understand snatches of their conversation. Afraid of giving away my hiding place, I didn't look out to try to identify them, although that would probably have been a useless endeavor in the thickening mist anyhow.

"...damn odd hours to keep, if you ask me."

"I believe she'd be grateful ol' Gordon already packed it in, now."

Laughter. Then the voices were opposite my tree, the nearest not three feet from where I stood. I could smell the oiled leather of their tack, a slight horse smell, and something else wafting along on the heavy night air: liquor.

"You don't reckon Gretchen or that nigger lady heard nothing?"

"Nah. We was about done by the time they got there."

"Good thing, too. Wouldn't do to have Andy's name bandied about tan town now, would it?"

"Not any more than it is already."

"Well, them colored folks is so frightened of him as it is, they probably wouldn't say nothing anyhow."

More laughter followed and faded as they moved out of earshot. Four men, I made it, judging from the pitch of the voices, but it

PAUL A. BARRA

could have been more or less. Not that it mattered. What was that about an Andy? Andy. Could be the nickname for Andrew Quillery, unlikely as it seemed that a man with such a reputation for sternness would have a diminutive name among friends, or that Reverend Quillery would have friends such as the lot that spent the night drinking and talking politics with Gordon Becknell. Strange bedfellows, it seemed to me. Since the murder of our sacristan in the cathedral was at the forefront of my mind, I also wondered to myself what connection, if any, this revelation might have to one of our suspects, Chief Becknell.

In another five minutes, Flora came driving the buggy down the same road, moving more slowly than the riders had. I slipped out of the woods and into the seat next to her. Neither horse nor slave so much as flicked an ear at my sudden appearance.

"Everything go okay, Flora?"

"Wasn't no trouble. Master Becknell was already gone off to bed, and them men was just leaving, time we got there."

"You hear anything about the murder?"

"Nossir. They was speechifying about the Know Nothings or something that sounded like that when we pulled up, but then they heard us and shut up. They was passing around a bottle. They tipped their caps to Miss Becknell but didn't say nothing to us. As I was driving off, I heard her tell them men that she was visiting someone sick. They must of left right then too, 'cause they passed me 'fore too long."

"You know what the Know Nothings are, Flora?"

"I know they don't like Catholics none."

"Actually, it's probably more the Irish they don't like, although for practical purposes, it amounts to the same thing. It's a sort of defunct political party that tries to keep men from voting unless they're native-born. That effectively eliminates most Catholics."

"Say nothing of slaves and women."

FULL OF EYES: A REBEL BISHOP MYSTERY 117

I looked at her rather quickly, but she kept her eyes on the big mare leaning into the harness ahead of the buggy. I thought I saw a flash of teeth in the vaporous air.

"I believe one major difference is that these nativists will probably not be successful, ever, Flora. Socrates once wrote in Plutarch, 'I know nothing but my own ignorance,' but these characters got their name from another source. Their political organization, once known as the American Party, was supposed to be a big secret. The members got their nickname by claiming to know nothing of what the party was up to. I thought it was passé, but maybe guys like Becknell and that crowd are keeping it alive."

I was more or less talking to myself, but the Negress nodded. I believed that she understood all that I ever talked about, and that was why I refused to talk down to her. Her formal education was limited, of course, but Flora had learned how to read and was often a source of information for the diocesan staff. She still used the cadences and accents of the Gullah dialect a good bit in her language, Gullah being a musical creolized mixture of West Indian dialect and Elizabethan English. It didn't surprise me that she was fluent in it, since she had been raised in that coastal African culture and was probably proud of her upbringing.

We drove for a while in silence. I was trying to decipher who the Becknell guests meant by Andy. I tried not to imagine what was going on in Flora's mind. God knows what she thought of bigots like those Know Nothings, or of my recent nocturnal activities, for that matter. She must have thought I was up to something devious and immoral, if not downright evil. I'm afraid I supplemented those ideas by recommending, as she reined in near her home. "I was thinking, dear Flora, that it might be better all around if we kept this little...er...midnight sojourn to ourselves. What do you think of that idea?"

"That do seem a prudent thing to do, Father."

With the flash of a startling white grin, she was off and gone into the night. I drove home slowly, wondering at the marvels of human nature. Wondering also what the adventures of the night meant.

CHAPTER 14

Having sworn Flora to secrecy, I wasn't sure how to handle revelations to Antoine when he visited the next day. I had agreed to confide in him generally when we decided to work together to solve the Jamieson Carter murder following my conversation with the bishop about the Jesuit. The pact between Father Gagnon and me had brought us closer together more quickly than I was sure I was comfortable with, but a commitment made must be observed, in my mind at least. If I expected him to partake of the efforts and potential dangers of the investigation, I would certainly have to be forthright in revealing activities that occurred in his absence. On the other hand, I knew that one of my weaknesses was that I tended to trust people too easily, had tried every so often to tie a little skepticism to my character and pretty much failed in the attempts. I honestly wanted to trust Antoine. So I sat in the episcopal residence undecided.

Bishop Lynch was presumably breaking fast in Folly, so I was alone when the Jesuit found me in the dining room, sipping tea after the morning liturgy. I felt desperately the need to discuss last night's events with someone, especially with someone who might offer some sort of analysis. For all Flora's goodness and sense of charity, she could not be expected to know enough about our investigation to help me with it. I had no intention of discussing the ripening intimacy between Gretchen Becknell and myself with anyone other than my regular confessor, to be sure, and maybe not with him either. After all, I had successfully fought off the temptation, hadn't I? Plus, I swore I would never allow myself to get into anything even resembling a similar situation again.

Forestalling any further self-imposed questions about the temptations of the flesh, as we Catholics so quaintly refer to the natural drive to copulate, I thought instead about how to break the story of the attack on my person most efficaciously to Father Gagnon. Surely it would prove to be germane in our investigation of the murder. I needn't have bothered. As it turned out, he barely gave me the opportunity for a civilized greeting.

Certainly, he wasted no time on inconsequentials. He started right off engaging my mind with his own eclectic and spirited one. Before I could entice him into an evaluation of the drama of the previous night, he caught me up in a subject he had passed on last time around. It was almost as if his intellect worked in cycles.

"Who is the most famous American bishop thus far, do you think, Thomas?"

"Why, uh, I would imagine that to be our own John England. Possibly John Carroll of Baltimore, since he was the first ever, I mean, and he did some big things. But, no, I think I'll stick with the first Bishop of Charleston. John England certainly had the most influence. He started the first Catholic newspaper, dined with presidents, addressed congress—"

"To say nothing of writing the first pastoral letter in the country, opening the first southern seminary and—" Father Gagnon paused theatrically. "—he was the first American bishop to ordain a Negro priest."

Antoine sat there looking smug while I had to admit to myself, and to him, that I was impressed with his knowledge of the arcane.

FULL OF EYES: A REBEL BISHOP MYSTERY   121

He explained that Bishop England had been in charge of Haiti, as well as being the ordinary of the Carolinas and Georgia, such as the diocese was composed at that time. In the 1830s, England went to Haiti and ordained George Paddington, a colored man and a native of Dublin, remarkable as that sounds. Father Paddington had been evangelized by Pierre Toussaint, whom I knew from his work in New York and my assignment to crowd control at his funeral. That event probably solidified my tendency toward abolitionism, which was now being tested by the persuasive arguments of Bishop Patrick Lynch, so this news from Antoine Gagnon stoked me with energy. My adventures of the night before and the woeful shortage of sleep I enjoyed because of them seemed to suddenly whisk away, like the nocturne mist when the morning breeze blew in from the sea. This was intriguing news to me. But my colleague was not done yet with intrigue.

"Do you also know, Father Dockery, that the good first Bishop of Charleston tried to justify slavery?"

"If you mean his letters to John Forsyth, he was only defending Pope Gregory from the label of abolitionist. I hardly think that qualifies him as an apologist for slavery."

"I'm afraid you're wrong again, my well-intentioned friend. Bishop England actually defended slavery on scriptural grounds in those arguments to Forsyth. He set the tone for Catholics in the South," Antoine went on. "The Irish-born bishop wanted badly to be a true American, you see, and I think he felt obligated to take the side of the people who counted in his society, which was, of course, both Southern and aristocratic. Dr. England's friends owned plantations and needed slaves to maintain their way of life. And as brilliant as he was supposed to have been, he must have appreciated exactly what he was doing."

"Antoine, you're making much of very little. I hope. Bishop England was a great man. Look at all he did for Catholicism in this young nation. His whole attitude about the Church, the notion that she belongs to the people, made him a man who will go down in history as the great prelate of nineteenth century America. And his conciliatory attitude toward Protestants! Why, he spoke of our common humanity and how we should never let what he called 'mere religious differences' separate us all. Can you imagine what courage and foresight that kind of thinking took? How could one reconcile what you've told me with his reputation? With his legacy?"

Antoine shrugged eloquently. After a minute, he said. "All humans are complicated children of God, friend."

"Did Bishop England own slaves himself, do you think?"

"Yes, I believe both he and his successor Bishop Reynolds owned at least one slave each. England was reputedly to have remarked privately that he found the concept of slavery reprehensible. He apparently believed the Catholic theologians who made a sort of fine distinction between what they called chattel slavery, where the slave has no rights, and ameliorated slavery. That's the kind we're supposed to tolerate. It's a benevolent type, and according to Bishop Auguste Marie Martin of my own precious state, there are some Catholic slaveholders who do recognize the rights of their slaves."

"Well, that's something, at least."

"The only problem is that chattel slavery is the kind being practiced most commonly in the South, not ameliorated, although I believe as does Bishop Martin, and pray, that Catholics practice ameliorated slavery on the whole. At least we know that the official Catholic Church does."

We sat in silence for a few minutes. Antoine reached over and picked up a biscuit. He munched abstractedly, a crumb falling to his black cassock. I cleared my throat, but he spoke up before I could speak.

"Slavery is an intrinsically evil concept, *n'est-ce pas*? Even though it was accepted as normal in classical Roman Catholic theology.

FULL OF EYES: A REBEL BISHOP MYSTERY   123

Slavery is mentioned often in the Bible, yet it is never condemned. Not even by the Lord himself. Christians here, and in my own beloved Louisiana, I might add, say that owning slaves is okay if you but treat them humanely, as if they were your children—"

"The Catholic Church has severe rules about the treatment of slaves, Antoine. The bishop spoke of them Sunday. You can be excommunicated, for instance, if you knowingly split up a family by selling siblings off or selling a husband and keeping the wife. And so forth. Bishop Lynch defends the practice as a sort of benevolent paternalism. Besides, he says the South can't survive economically without slaves to work the plantations. Certainly, no farmer could afford to hire all the workers he'd need to make a living on cotton."

"Your master is simply wrong about that. We don't need slavery to survive, only to get rich. The institution itself fosters mistreatment by putting the slave owner above the law. By the very nature of the beast, by putting some people as God over others, slavery almost has to result in serious abuses. Church laws, even if they were universal, cannot protect a race with no rights. It is virtually inevitable that some landowners will treat their slaves as they treat their other holdings, brutally or negligently. And what might be worse, by not caring either way."

I found myself nodding in agreement. Turned around yet again by this Jesuit.

As I was cogitating, I became aware of someone standing close to my chair. I looked up with a small start. It was Antoine. He was holding a piece of paper in his hand. I took it and began to read. Neither of us said anything.

The sheet contained a single poem. It was called A Prayer for Slaves.

Dark, the cry of the poor,
wheedling wind through the narrow straits of life,
gull-screeching though obscure

124 PAUL A. BARRA

and unholy tremblors shaking with strife.
Spare these needy mankind.
Douse all the flames that char their souls to dust,
cool the hot storms that blind
and winnow away their cries and mistrust.
Ease their pain to one side.
Shoulder a portion of their heavy load.
Soften the stony tide,
the sharp pebbles and shards on their long road.
Lighten the crush above,
the crackling cold and the wolf's molten breath.
Look at them with Your love,
gray and hollow, tall, handsome, bleak in death,
wallowing in pity,
suffocating in chains, no place to rest.
To the Golden City
how can they survive from here to Your nest?
Grace them from the surfeit
earned by Italy's Francis and our own
Irish England and yet
give them peace in the face of war homegrown.
Grant them succor from blight
as it descends and water vapors sail
under black powder might.
Whisper psalm strains in the violent gale.

I sat in wonderment when I had finished reading the prayer. I thought it was beautiful poetry. I wanted to study it later. This little prayer might be the sign I was looking for to settle in my mind the value of slavery or its abolition, a way out of the purgatory of my soul. It seemed to speak to that soul, somehow tugging at my innards with its quiet power and imagery. It described all sides of colored people in America and intimated at the changes the impending war could bring. Especially the wheedling wind phrase, which reminded me of the noise the cannon balls made as they flew into Fort Sumter that frightful dawn—was it but three days ago?—and also of the sounds Bones made when Becknell was beating on him. Two different sounds, to be sure, but it described both. At least for me. I needed time to think.

"Are you going to memorize it, Thomas?"

"Wha—No, no, sorry. I'm afraid to admit that this...er... prayer has affected me rather more than I expected."

"It's just a romantic bit of doggerel, after all, my friend."

"No, Tony, that's not true. It's quite strong and...er... apt. I think it's beautifully done, too. Who wrote it?"

"Anonymous, I'm afraid."

I looked carefully at him, but his face betrayed nothing more than a bland sophistication. I had my suspicions about the author of the poem, but I let it be, for now. Antoine had the look of a poet about him, and I'm afraid that his countenance may have colored my suspicions. His face was pale as marble, long, and carried up to a high forehead. He never seemed to need a shave, despite his French heritage. The fine dark hair on his head was longer than was fashionable, at least in the cities of the south, and his fingers were long and elegant. I thought he might have buffed his fingernails. He was thin, ascetic, and his brown eyes seemed to burn or glow when he became excited. But looks were no substitute for the raw talent required to pen such powerful poetry, so I decided to wait until a more opportune moment to probe the authorship of the slave prayer.

Instead, I just assumed that he had been the author, so I was doubly distressed at his next piece of news.

"My pastor is himself a slave owner," my brother priest blurted out without preamble. "I'm afraid he's somewhat of a zealot about the issue. He knows my views and took the opportunity last night to berate me about them. In public."

126   PAUL A. BARRA

"Tony, that's terrible."

"It gets worse, my friend. Two of the priests in attendance at my disgrace were visitors from Baltimore. Monsignor Reed advised the world at large, or at least the world within earshot, that opposition to slavery by a consecrated man placed one in the camp of the hated abolitionists and outside the fold of the faithful Church in the South, if you can believe that."

Antoine was acting as if this were just one more naughty tale being related by an urbane and dispassionate raconteur, but I could see that he had been deeply hurt. Accusations in front of representatives of the archdiocese, the only one in North America at the time, could have a devastating effect on Tony's chances for making the short list for bishop. He dearly wanted to be a bishop. He wanted the responsibilities of the office more than the trappings, although I had no doubts that he would fit perfectly into the lace and miter. I believed that Antoine Gagnon wanted more to lead Catholics in the new land, especially in the South, where our numbers were few and our influence minimal. If Bishop John England could have a major impact on society in the 1820s, then Bishop Antoine Gagnon could have one in the 1870s. If his own pastor did not support him, however, how seriously would Rome take his qualifications?

"What can you do about it, Antoine?"

"Nothing short of abdication, I don't suppose."

"What do you mean?"

"Well, Father Reed has assigned me to give the Pentecost sermon in six weeks' time. It is one of our best-attended services at St. Mary's. He further instructed me to discuss in that sermon the Southern Christian's position in this impending War of Northern Aggression, as he's taken to calling it. Clearly, it is my opportunity to straighten my stance on the issue of slavery in full public view."

"Whatever will you do?"

FULL OF EYES: A REBEL BISHOP MYSTERY 127

"Well, I'm not a political idiot, am I, Thomas? Besides, I am a born and bred Southern boy, even if I am from a papist state. What can I do?"

His rhetorical question ended that conversation, although I made a mental note to pray hard for Antoine, pray that God gave him the strength to do what he had to do on Pentecost.

To fill the strained gap of silence, I told my colleague about my adventures of the night before. He didn't betray any disappointment at the change of subject and pretended not to notice as I tucked the slave prayer into the pocket beneath my cassock. I didn't mention what had transpired between Gretchen Becknell and me in the bishop's house, in the very room we now occupied, in fact. Not that anything actually had transpired, short of my fainting away once or twice. Did I protest too much? But I told him everything else. Including the way Gretchen happened by after I'd knocked myself silly falling off the porch and how Flora and I had sneaked her home. I also related the conversation I'd heard among the men who were riding away from the Becknell cottage, when they were talking about the mysterious Andy.

The narrative seems theatrical to me even now when I think about my adventures that night, but it had the dramatic power to energize Antoine. He had seemed pensive after telling me about his pending appointment with destiny on Pentecost. Plus, he was such a caring man, despite his airs of arrogance, that he immediately focused his attention on my plight.

"Gracious me, Thomas. You are attacked by a deranged killer in the home of the ordinary of the entire diocese, and you sit there listening to me babble on about cultural issues and my own insignificant problem. How could you ever contain yourself? Never mind. Let's get right to it, as they say on Broadway. Who attacked you, and why? Could it have been a common thief, surprised when you came upon his forced entry and determined not to allow you

128   PAUL A. BARRA

to identify him? Or was it someone intent on harm to your person? Someone trying to warn you off or something? What do you think?"

His eyes could have lighted a shipping channel.

"I don't believe he was a thief. I could never have identified him from what I'd seen, not at first, so he'd have been better off escaping than attacking. That would have been especially true had he not engaged me in fisticuffs. Had he run from the house when I discovered the door open, I would have had no idea who he was. And I don't think he wanted to kill me either. He had no weapon, as far as I know. He certainly did not use one when he had ample opportunity. I haven't the foggiest what he was after. But I do know who he was, I think."

"How in heaven could you know that? I thought you never got a look at him."

"I have been brewing this over for hours now. The intruder was almost certainly Andrew Quillery."

I put my palm up to him, to hold off his questions or protests.

"I never did see him clearly, as I said. At least, not his face. But I got a good description from my other senses. He was tall, almost as tall as me, and wiry, tight, not a bit of fat that I felt. His nose pushed out the wool cap that he had covering his face, a sharp nose, not flat like a Negro or short like an Irishman. He was strong, though not fast. I actually outran him to the front door and got my blows off first a few times. So I think he was not young, not a youth, at any rate. But the big thing was his smell. He smelled of onions on his clothes and hands. Bones said that Quillery was raising onions this spring and might even have been carrying a bunch of them the night he came upon him up the road a ways. By compiling my observations, I have concluded that the intruder was the preacher man."

"That sounds like good deductive reasoning to me, Officer Dockery, although I was assuming that the parcel Quillery carried was the Madonna statue that proved fatal to Jamieson Carter. The question begging for an answer in my mind is why. Why would a fundamentalist preacher sneak into the home of a Catholic bishop and attack his young aide de camp? You could have been badly hurt. That fall could have cracked your skull, had it been delicate like this fine continental one of mine instead of the thick Irish cap you lug around all day."

"I don't think in retrospect that he meant me any serious harm. If Mrs. Ryan hadn't locked the front door again, I would have been out in the street yelling for help rather than fighting him off. And the tumble I took was my own fault. And the rain. I can't answer your question, however."

"Maybe we'll have more success," Antoine said, "if we analyze the intelligence you got from Becknell's visitors. They may well have been talking about the same person who went after you, if the mysterious Andy of their conversation is indeed Quillery. I admit to being mystified as to why a man of the cloth, a poorly qualified Congregationalist or not, would espouse the holdings of the Know Nothings. If he is going to proselytize for his church, he would not want to exclude all foreign-born folk. Besides, I thought the Know Nothings had died out a decade ago. They've certainly not had many successes of late."

"True enough, what you say. Maybe these friends of Chief Becknell are throwbacks," I said. "Maybe they can't find it in their blackguard hearts to let the concept of nativism die. Once you get outside of Charleston proper, you realize what a tolerant city this really is. I wouldn't be surprised to learn that open antagonism toward Irish people and Catholics in general is thriving in the country."

"No, you wouldn't. I rode up to a country place called Moncks Corner a few weeks ago, to serve a few dozen faithful in a little church up there that was started by some Irish railroad workers. A few people nearby made rude noises as I rode past and one young hooligan had the effrontery to wing a pecan at my horse's rump. The animosity was so overt that I was actually frightened. I insisted on an escort for the way home and traveled without my dog collar, I can tell you. Some of these rural folk are positively uncivilized indeed."

He spoke with some vehemence. I thought that his anger was directed more at the very idea of fellow pilgrims disliking someone before they knew him than at the fear he must have felt for his safety. We were all of us Americans, not that long free from the yoke of Great Britain, after all. It was a hard country we inhabited, as hard as the souls of some men who trod across it and wrested a living from it.

"Well, I'm sorry for the diversion," he said quietly. He acted as if his vehemence had completely evaporated in the few seconds it took to compose himself. I shook my head in wonder, but he made no remark about it and said instead, "Let's assume that the Know Nothings still do ride the night airs in the Holy City as you think. The question remains, why would the Reverend Quillery get involved with that sort?"

There was no answer to hand, of course, but we agreed to assume for the purpose of argument that my interpretation of the sentient facts I observed while being abused and frightened last night were true. Those facts must have had some relationship with the murder in the cathedral. What could that be? We decided, sitting there in the shafts of sunlight in the sitting room of a mansion, that we had to pay a call on Andrew Quillery.

CHAPTER 15

We walked out into Charleston, into the incipient heat that was beginning to steam the ocean air already in the day and already in the spring. I strode purposefully, reengaging my police persona, and Antoine Gagnon kept pace. I knew I was running through my mind how to confront Quillery, and imagined that Father Gagnon must have been doing the same. For a fact, neither of us talked until we arrived in front of the preacher man's residence on State Street, just off Broad and not far from the business district. I was surprised to notice that the neighborhood was rather more elegant than I would have imagined for a Protestant minister. Then we were shocked into further silence.

Quillery opened the door to my knock. He was in a shabby robe, and his hair was flattened against the top of his head and thrusting out from the sides like a wheat field after a storm. His lips were pressed together in that characteristic flatness of a man not wearing his false teeth. His eyes pinned us to the stoop, and no one spoke. Then the preacher slammed the door in our faces.

Antoine and I stood there, open-mouthed. We looked at each other with questions, silent questions, darting between us. We had about determined that we had been rudely turned away, when the door opened again, and Reverend Quillery nodded us in. He was dressed and had brushed his hair. He pushed past us in the dark hallway that smelled of fried fish and walked into another dim space, a sitting room to the right. He sat in a rocker, and we took the sofa opposite him. The furniture was surprisingly fine, glossy well-cut hard wood and butter-soft leather.

A portrait of Quillery as a young man hung over a marble fireplace. It looked like a William Harrison Scarborough, an artist whose work I admired myself. He had emphasized the chiseled features of Quillery's face and had made him into a handsome man.

The man himself had not asked us to sit, had not spoken one word yet. He had teeth in his mouth now, and he worked his lips constantly, as if they were a poor and painful fit. I wondered if he had his teeth in when he attacked me last night.

"Did you have your teeth in when you attacked me last night, Reverend Quillery?"

I stared straight at him, emboldened by his odd social behavior and by an anger that threatened to escape now that I was in his company. I felt rather than heard a sharp intake of breath from Gagnon to my left. Quillery kept working his jaws. A trace of drool glistened in one corner of his mouth. He opened that mouth to speak, but I bore right in.

"Don't insult me by trying to deny it. I have to assume that a man of the cloth had a rationale for his actions, and I am prepared to listen to your explanation."

Quillery opened his mouth again, but no sound came out except a faint stutter. He wiped his lips with a handkerchief he pulled from his sleeve, cleared his throat, looking at the plush carpet under his slippered feet.

"I...er...did not realize it were you, not until it were too late, lad."

He rolled his Rs. His voice was a flat and grating burr.

"Who in God's name did you expect to find in the bishop's house? Did you wish to attack the Bishop of Charleston?"

FULL OF EYES: A REBEL BISHOP MYSTERY   133

"I wished to attack no one, ye must believe me. I panicked, in the dark and all. Thought you was trying to lock me in after the wind slammed the door in back. I just wanted out then, believe me."

His eyes finally reached up to mine. They were bright but not the piercing lights of his reputation. Nor was he ramrod straight, preaching fire and fear. He was bent and pinched, a gray and white crone in a dead still rocking chair. I slumped back on the couch and sighed. I had never been able to cultivate a killer instinct. Would have made a mediocre boxer. An unsuccessful lawyer.

"Whyever did you want in, in the first place?" Antoine's voice was drawled out, languid, almost insolent.

Quillery snapped up at that, a brief fire darted through his eyes and died out.

"I—I thought the house were empty. I wanted to see if—er—something had been left there. Accidental like. Didn't reckon nobody were to home. I'm sorry, lad," he said to me. "I hope you weren't hurt when ye toppled off the porch."

Antoine answered for me.

"Father Dockery is obviously recovered from your unprovoked, and illegal, assault, Reverend Quillery. What were you looking for in the bishop's house?"

"That I cannot say. It involves an innocent person."

"Bollocks."

Quillery sprung out of his slouch at that, betraying the musculature of his core. A flash sparked and snapped in his eyes.

"Don't ye dare use profane language to a man of God! Yer in me own home, man, have ye no respect for age at least?"

"Your actions hardly encourage respect of any sort, Reverend. One might expect a common thief to attack an innocent person in the dark, not a man of God. Now, what were you hoping to find?"

"I cannot say. I'm sworn to secrecy, for the love of God."

Quillery slumped back over. Antoine looked at me, and I raised my eyebrows in resignation. The priest spoke again, this time in a low voice. "Who are you trying to protect, Reverend Quillery?"

"I cannot say. I cannot say."

We were quiet for few moments after that, and the older man seemed to collect himself. I told him we were leaving but had no intention of abandoning our investigation. He stood with us. He stopped working his mouth long enough to crack it in what must have been an attempted smile.

"Before ye go, would ye take some spring onions for yer kitchen? I've a lovely crop in the back garden."

Bishop Lynch was an active listener. He asked a quick question now and then. He grunted, smiled, frowned, and either nodded or shook his head as you talked to him. His pale eyes peered at you, widened when you gesticulated, crinkled when you joked, narrowed when you growled. He sighed at injustices and whistled soundlessly at superlatives. I expect he would take up his pectoral cross by the bottom if you blasphemed. There was never any doubt that he was listening to and hearing what was being said to him. Whether or not he was interested was another question entirely, but the speaker at least thought that he or she had the bishop's interest piqued.

This time, I was sure of it. He absorbed my tale of Andrew Quillery's perfidy and my experience with Antoine Gagnon at his house. When it became his turn to tell a tale, he gave as good as he got, for his verbal sketches of the war talk at Folly were fascinating. Young men from Cheraw and the other hometowns of the Lynch clan were already signing up to fight for the Cause. Women were sewing and knitting uniforms, and God help us, bandages. CSA quartermasters were buying and beginning to stockpile grain and salted meats. Army wranglers were inspecting local horses. And flag officers were plotting a Southern strategy.

FULL OF EYES: A REBEL BISHOP MYSTERY 135

One dashing Southern gentleman who knew the name of the Revolutionary War champion Francis Marion told guests of the Lynch tribe that he was figuring on evening the odds against the Yankee numerical superiority by hiding his troops and horses in the swamps and striking out like summer lightning when the men in blue least expected it. Just like Marion himself had done in South Carolina when the British held superior numbers and equipment. The bishop grinned hugely when he told of reactions from some of the younger women to the bold talk from the dashing cavalry soldier who wanted to become famous as the Swamp Fox of modern times.

"He's a wealthy young man, self-made they tell me, the son of a blacksmith or something. His name is Nathan Bedford Forrest," the bishop said. "His friends called him Bedford."

"Generally, though," the bishop said, "the war talk had a sobering effect on the people gathered at Conlaw Lynch's summer home. There was plenty of emotional patriotism displayed and bravado too, if the truth be told, but there was also enough real strategic blueprinting going on to make the guests, young and old, realize clearly that the South, at least, expected imminent war.

"Plus, Abraham Lincoln, whose election I daresay provoked the secession of this fine state, has issued a call for seventy-five thousand volunteers. Border states are protesting the draft, and that, in itself, will probably lead to further separation between north and south.

"Northerners are insulted, one businessman told my cousin, by our attack on Fort Sumter, if you can believe that effrontery. We have a foreign army garrisoned in our own harbor, and they get insulted when we chase them off. Imagine!"

Then the Bishop of Charleston sat back and sighed aloud. He seemed to let the Lord's peace enter so that I could see his body visibly relax. We were sitting on the second floor porch or piazza, as Charlestonians called them, as we talked, a light breeze lifting our hair. Our porch overlooked Broad Street so that we could see what

136 PAUL A. BARRA

are known as single houses fronting the alleys that lead down to the harbor.

The weather had cooled overnight, so the full sun was pleasant on our shoulders and had a salutary effect on our souls, harrowed as they were with threats to peace and the cares of the diocese. A few Negroes were out hawking their wares on the streets below us, thin onions—mine from Reverend Quillery's garden were even now being chopped by Flora in the kitchen below—and overwintered collards, baskets of oysters, eels and fish.

We could hear their cries and the bursts of stout laughter that seemed to accompany so many purchases or negotiations in the city. Wagons clattered and creaked their way up Broad every so often, scattering pigeons and the occasional brood of chickens.

Off in the near distance, gulls screeched, and a line of elegant pelicans glided low over the water, searching for dinner with studious aplomb. We could smell a tang of salt on the breeze and the bouquet of honeysuckle vines that clung to the brickwork and balustrades all around us. Across the street, the big houses were afloat in yellow ponds of daffodil.

We both felt the need to grab onto brief moments of tranquility in this setting, so our conversation became slow and desultory, despite or perhaps because of, the nature of our news. We paused regularly to let nature's peace come over us, knowing it would be a precious commodity in the future.

I had to work at accepting peace just then, there seemed to be so much on my plate that needed cleaning up. I knew something had to be done about the murder of Jamieson Carter and about my own inner turmoil, burbling with doubts and questions, as well as I knew that I needed moments of serenity to soothe my soul. At this very time, in a Charleston spring with the guns of division silent for a while, this verandah was as good as the cathedral itself for quieting souls.

FULL OF EYES: A REBEL BISHOP MYSTERY   137

After the bishop's sigh, I knew from the tone of his exhalation and the timing of it that the hour had finally come to get down to business. We both sat up, almost in tandem, and had a hard talk then, discussing the preacher Quillery's revelations, our options and responsibilities and speculating about the murder. Lynch's sharp mind probed, uncovered a question or two I wished I'd asked of Quillery or of Gretchen. The sun was behind the house before we finished. We were glad to respond to Flora's bell, because both the enervating talk and the falling sun had sucked the warmth from us. Her catfish stew, a Negro specialty that we had adopted for ourselves in the bishop's house, was the perfect antidote to the chill that had taken over. It was peppery and rich, served hot with slabs of cornbread.

That night I heard things I didn't want to hear and saw things I knew could not exist. I blamed Reverend Quillery's onions in the soup, but surely my own saturated mind must have had its say to its subconscious.

CHAPTER 16

The horror began when a great gust woke me in an alarmed state. It was well after midnight. A cold wind banged the shutters in dissonance as it charged in through the window. Wisps of what seemed to be a red and green miasma slipped into my room with the breeze. Afraid to breathe in the bizarre fog I got up quickly, with a groan of foreboding, and went to block it from my room by locking the shutters. The colors on the breeze, I thought, must be the remnants from some dream or nightmare, or an aftereffect of the spicy stew. I shook my head, rubbed my face, and reached for the shutters. I stopped dead with both hands on the two handles when I saw what lived outside my room in the packed dirt of the path to the stables. A man dug in the soil, grunting and clawing with his hands. Clumps flew from the hole he was digging, and the colored air swirled about him. He stopped suddenly and looked up, directly into my eyes. His own were a certain frightening and empty gray, as if they harbored no life behind them, and his chest heaved with labored breathing. His lips flapped and his cheeks sunk as he blew and sucked air. He continued to lower his vacant stare at me as he sat back on his haunches, shoulders slumped until his breathing eased. Then he jerked his hands out of the hole and raised up what he had

FULL OF EYES: A REBEL BISHOP MYSTERY 139

been unearthing, a fiendish, almost maniacal grin outlining his black, toothless mouth.

He held aloft a vision so gruesome that I wanted to turn away. I felt gizzard bile rise in my throat and I gagged. But I did not vomit, could not wrench myself from the impossible scene beneath my window.

The man in the dirt was holding the severed head of a Negro. Its eyes showed only white and its tongue dangled from its mouth. The head was muddied but not bloodied, and I could detect no smell on the peculiar green and red air. I could not help but notice the anguished expression on its face, however. It stared at nothing, begged for mercy in silence. Wet dirt slipped off the head with tiny plopping sounds. Neither the monster below nor I moved or uttered a sound of our own. We were frozen in a tableau of horror, him grinning like a brainless maniac and me white-faced with shock. Then he began to laugh.

It was wild laughter, shocking in its inappropriateness, terrifying in its madness. I found myself with a sudden and fierce case of the shivers just then, more from the eerie scene in the street than from the cool night. Only as I pulled my nightshirt closer to my neck did I recognize the face of the severed head beneath the dirt that clumped on its eyebrows and stuffed its nose. It was Uncle Williams.

I knew I had to do more than stare in dread. I reached for my robe on the bedpost behind me. When I turned back to the window, both the man in the dirt and the detached head he carried were gone.

I managed to stuff my wooden feet into a pair of slippers and pull on the robe. I felt absurdly clumsy and stiff. Breathing in quick gulps through my mouth, I hurtled upstairs, and before I knew my destination, I found myself tapping rapidly at Flora's door.

Maybe the house slave thought that early morning calls in the dark by the associate pastor were destined to become part of her life in the bishop's service, because she was robed herself and out the door in seconds with a burning oil lamp held in front of her.

Flora wore a flannel nightcap that under saner circumstances might have looked comical to me, but this time I was so glad of the company and her lamp that I hardly noticed the cap.

"There's something outside you must see."

She didn't answer, although her head may have bobbed. It was hard to tell with the lamp flickering as we padded quickly to the front door. There was no one outside. I looked up and down the street for a retreating figure, but there was nothing to see and not a noise to be heard. The breeze had died off, leaving no trace of the red and green air I had seen. It was a clear night and cold. It took with it the atmosphere of my room. I felt awake, alert. The stiffness and sense of unreality seemed to have gone with the colored vapors. I realized I had rousted poor Flora for nothing. I rubbed my forehead with the side of my forefinger and turned to offer an apology. She was staring at the road. I turned back to follow her intense gaze and saw it myself. There was a hole in the path with a pile of dirt next to it.

Flora stoked the embers and made coffee. We shared a cup in the kitchen as our muddied slippers dried near the wood stove. As my shivering got under control, I told her what I had seen. After a minute, she spoke for the first time.

"I expect you'll see Uncle Williams at church in a couple hours, Father."

I nodded, staring blankly into the cup. Neither of us mentioned the hole outside the front door.

After a few more minutes, Flora broke the embarrassed silence by telling me about Uncle Williams. He was a proud man, she said, who managed his conversion to Catholicism by turning quiet as he aged.

Most slaves, most Negroes, took a more flexible approach to Christianity than that offered by the universal Catholic Church.

"We like preaching men who can raise our feelings some. This here Catholic Church is too formal, y'know, for most niggers. Though, Lord knows, that bishop can raise some feelings now."

Uncle Williams, she said, was a farm manager for a large plantation after an early career as a farm hand. He was delegated the duties of arranging for the sale of harvested crops and the purchase of seed. Flora said it was a trusted position that took him a lifetime to obtain, even though he never touched actual money, everything being arranged on credit. The credit system worked because southern gentlemen were scrupulously honest and trustworthy, traits that proved remarkably absent when Uncle Williams grew too old and stiff to function adequately. He was still shy of sixty when that happened, the hard work of a lifetime wearing his body down. First his master gave him an apprentice to learn the trade and assist the older man, according to Flora. Once that apprentice knew the ins and outs of farm management, however, he was promoted and Uncle Williams was set free. Set free when he was too old and decrepit to make a living on his own.

He came to see Flora, because he knew her from both their extended families, extensions that were far too complex and convoluted for outsiders to comprehend. Flora arranged for the old man to do some odd jobs around the chancery and cathedral. In return, she fed him and found him lodgings in her morass of slave quarters up on Legare Street. The arrangement was not approved formally by me or the bishop, nor even by Mrs. Ryan, but everyone gave his or her tacit approval by not commenting on it. We never noticed the difference in our accounts and, before long, Uncle Williams was just another part of our world. He was always around, quiet and self-effacing, doing anything asked of him and never asking anything of us. He rarely came to the house, and never in it, but he became a fixture in church. We were kind to him and sort of accepted him as part of the diocesan establishment. I don't think any of us

142

PAUL A. BARRA

ever spoke to him about personal things, although I suspected that Bishop Lynch may have done so. Uncle Williams was particularly fond of him.

Eventually, the old freedman converted to our faith. I never knew if his motivation was sincere or if he was merely responding to earthly salvation by joining the church that provided him a means to grow even older without begging. The bishop had received him into the church before I arrived in Charleston. I made a silent vow, as I listened to Flora's story of Uncle Williams' trials and tribulations, to make a point of getting to know the man better.

Flora fell silent and began to move around the kitchen quietly, getting the space ready for another day. I roused myself to action. I knew it would be futile to go back to bed. Dawn was no more than a few feet below the horizon by then. I apologized for waking Flora, but she waved it off, saying that it was near time for her to get up anyways. I went back to my room and dressed. I wrapped a wool scarf around my neck and left the house as quietly as possible. There was no sound from the kitchen.

I looked down at the hole again. It looked fairly shallow in the pre-dawn darkness, and even if I couldn't see clearly, I imagined that it could scarcely have contained a head. There were signs around it, of digging and footprints. I imagined I could detect lines where fingers had scraped soil away from the insides of it. It was still too dark to see if any of the moisture in the dirt was blood. The hole smelled of damp and worms and death.

I walked quickly down to the Battery. I sat on a bollard and watched the sky turn light. A spray of pink cloud flumed from Sullivan's Island across to Fort Sumter. A bell tolled from a buoy that rocked when a gull landed on it. Otherwise, the sea was quiet. After a while I imagined a tiny figure raising the Stars and Bars out at the fort. It was too far to see without a glass, and if reveille played, I couldn't hear it.

FULL OF EYES: A REBEL BISHOP MYSTERY 143

I prayed in the silence, in my own outdoor basilica, and began to think about the contrast between the beautiful Catholic cathedrals and the plain churches of our Baptist neighbors. It's not only the sacramentals and other external trappings that distinguish us from our brothers in Christ who dwell in protest. Some values, rules of behavior and practices are startling in their contrasts. Douglas Deas once told me that he and other Baptists find their religion to be overly serious and humorless, and enjoined on me to tell him a Catholic joke, since "you Catholics don't seem to mind having a drink or two and enjoying life." I know that Doug was hoping I'd tell a bishop joke. Baptists cannot imagine how pastors can manage to function as free Americans under the thumb of a local prelate, to say nothing of the authority of the pope.

I told him the story about Father Edison, an upper New York parish priest who was always at loggerheads with his bishop over the administration of his church. It seemed to the priest that the bishop was hidden from reality in his big house on the hill and did not appreciate the many minor and major afflictions that attended to the operation of a small parish. Finally, one sunny summer day, Father Edison screwed up his courage and journeyed to the see city to have it out with the bishop once and for all. They would settle the contentious issues that stood between them, even if it meant reassignment to a rural parish at the Canadian border for the priest.

When Father Edison knocked on the door of the bishop's residence, he was met by a red-eyed housekeeper who informed him that the dear bishop had passed away in his sleep that very night. The priest bowed his head and walked slowly away.

An hour later, however, he was back asking for the bishop. The housekeeper, thinking he must have misunderstood the first time, told him quite clearly that the bishop was dead.

Still, before noon, Father Edison was back yet again knocking on the door and asking for the bishop.

"Are ye deaf now, Father? I've already told ye twice before that the bishop is dead. Can ye not understand me?"

"Aye, Mrs. O'Brien, I understood you the first time. It's just that I love to hear you say it."

I smiled, even now, thinking of the effect it had on Doug. After he finished hooting and then catching his breath, he averred that my joke proved his point. Sometimes I think that telling it to my friend was wrong, a scandal of sorts, but then I remind myself that life is serious enough as it is. Surely God expects us to lighten our load when we can.

Sitting there at the seaside in the cool dawn, I tried to wrench my wandering mind back to the business at hand, prayer. I gazed out at the still, gray water of Charleston Harbor and talked some more to my Lord. I said an Ave and asked the Blessed Mother to enjoin upon her son to grant me a measure of peace. The events of the past fortnight had brought a tenseness to my innards and a fear that my mind was slipping ever so slightly toward madness.

I realized then, after my entreaties to the Almighty, that it was time for me to investigate the vision that had torn me from my sleep, so I rose quickly and walked back home. In the clear early light I could see quite easily that the hole had been covered up. Someone had even brushed the dirt smooth over where it had been. There was nothing to see, no evidence, no sign. I squatted anyway. I sniffed the soil and peered at it from a few angles, but there was nothing to smell or see. I got up and went in to breakfast.

The bishop was saying the seven, so he wouldn't eat for a while yet. Flora was cooking and serving, but Mrs. Ryan was bustling about getting ready for the day. Finally, she went outdoors to fetch flour or something, leaving Flora and me alone.

"The hole was filled in when I got back from taking a walk, Flora."

"I know, Father. I done it myself."

FULL OF EYES: A REBEL BISHOP MYSTERY   145

I looked at her and must have displayed some of the surprise her statement had engendered in me.

"I knowed it was worrying you, what you saw last night, and I figured it was best if that hole wasn't around no more."

I nodded and went back to my grits and butter. I couldn't very well accuse Flora of covering up or disposing of evidence, could I? I made up my room and answered some church correspondence at my desk until Bishop Lynch returned from mass. I hurried upstairs and found him finishing up grace before breakfast.

"Morning, Tom."

"Good morning, Excellency. Do you mind my asking, sir, was Uncle Williams at church this morning?"

"What an odd thing to ask, under the circumstances. I had to dress the altar myself this morning because Uncle Williams was not present. I can't remember the last time he missed mass." He looked up at me. "Is there something you know about him that I don't?"

"No sir."

The bishop nodded at that and went back to his food. I turned to leave the room and saw Flora standing in the dining room doorway and obviously having heard our brief conversation about Uncle Williams. She was holding a teapot and looking as if she'd seen a ghost.

CHAPTER 17

I drove out to the country, to Catholic Hill near Ritter, to say Mass at a little church that attracted the faithful from area plantations. It took me more than four hours, but the weather was fine and the countryside refreshing and peaceful. And quiet. Not surprisingly, since interrupted night's sleeps were becoming rather more common than I liked, I nodded off more than once with my face to the thin sun and the rest of me swaying with the gentle motion of the cathedral buggy. It was a pleasant journey along a plantation road that meandered past the confluence of the Combahee and Ashepoo Rivers. I had plenty of opportunity between naps to continue my conversation with our Heavenly Father.

At Ritter, I heard confessions—some of the slaves were speaking Gullah, and I had a time understanding everything, although the converse was apparently not true—and celebrated mass before a large crowd. That was no wonder since a priest didn't get out that way regularly. I guess the plantation owners gave the day off, or at least some time off, because the church was filled with slaves. Most Negroes in South Carolina were not Catholic, as Flora had said, but this church was full of them. I guessed the plantation owners did

FULL OF EYES: A REBEL BISHOP MYSTERY   147

a good job of catechizing them and I blessed them in my mind for their work at teaching the faith.

I was assisted by a church elder who was dressed out in an alb and a hand woven cotton sash, although I had my doubts that he was ever ordained to the diaconate. Still, the pot-bellied old man was a great help to me. He solemnly directed the congregation and led them in the prayers they were used to, and he kept my own social constraints from spoiling the fun that was part of the slave religious experience. Their prayers were structured so that the people responded to a call. The elder would shout out, "Our God be good! That right?"

The people would answer, "That right! Amen!"

"Our God be gracious. Yes?"

"Yes! Amen!"

"Our God done helped us?"

"Yes! Amen!"

"Helped us walk this lonesome valley, hear?"

"That right! Amen!"

The stern-faced elder read the Gospel like a storybook, kept it pretty much authentic but entranced the listeners with his theatrical manner. I thought the whole liturgy was moving, and legitimate, but I was worried about my own participation. By the time I got up to deliver my sermon, I thought I could never entertain like they were used to, and I was afraid I'd be poorly received as a stiff-necked white man who could neither release his emotions nor evoke those of the worshippers. I wanted to make my visit as lasting as possible, especially since so many had turned out in what must have been a special occasion for them. So I decided to try to reach their emotional level.

I spoke about faith and the courage it takes to sustain it in a country that was at the same time free and fearful of the Latin mystique. The colored folk murmured assent at some of the things I said, and some even shouted out Amens after more passionate statements. It was unnerving at first, but gratifying and infectious, even seeming to release some of my inhibitions. And I found that the concept stuck with me even when I was back preaching at predominantly white churches. The bishop might have wondered about how spirited my homilies became after a while, but it was pure pleasure to liberate so much energy in preaching.

The whole liturgy was a joyful episode for me, since the slaves in Ritter loved to sing and the little wood church was filled with voice music. Two white families sat in the front pews, one on each side of the aisle. They maintained their decorum during the emotional service, although I noticed the children and a couple of the women swaying to the gospel singing. After mass, they gave me some money and a ham.

"That was a lovely service, Father," a patrician-looking older man in a linen suit told me. "It was good of you to travel all this way, especially for the black folk. We all get into Charleston every so often, but they are generally restricted to the plantation."

"Do you worship at the cathedral when you're in town?"

"We do indeed. We've heard the distressing news of Jamieson Carter."

"Was he a friend of your family, sir?"

"An acquaintance, more like. One of my children knows his daughter, Annie, quite well. She actually is a bit concerned that Annie will now have to drop out of school to manage Carter Chandlery."

"I can see where that would be a shame. Is the girl mature enough to run a business, do you think?"

"In my mind, that's another cause for concern. I always think of her as young and impetuous, but that's how old folks think about the young."

The young of his family came up to thank me and ask for a blessing just then, so that ended our brief conversation. I wanted to inquire of the white folk if one of them might have been either Susan or Harriet Bellinger or Mary Pinckney, the three grandchildren of Edmond Bellinger, who was given a huge land grant in the Ritter area by King James II. The women started St. James when they converted to Catholicism in the 'thirties. They also financed the conversion of the building we had just worshipped in, since the original church burnt down in 1856. But I did not get the chance to slake my historical curiosity. The white families nodded pleasantly to me and stepped into their carriages. As they rolled out of the courtyard of the little red church, I could see them smiling as many slaves crowded around me to shake my hand and leave presents of sweet potatoes and baskets full of winter greens.

One woman gave me an elaborate woven cross that smelled of sweet grass and asked me a curious favor. "Please use dis cross I make when you pray in de big church down yonder, heah? It gwan bless us out in de field."

An old man gave me a carved image of a man I took to be Jesus. I was moved almost to tears by this unexpected display of affection. I hardly knew these people, but they loved me because I represented the Church. To them, I was the voice of Christianity. That realization filled me with an overwhelming sense of responsibility.

I gave my silk stole to the elder, showed him how to wear it like a sash so he wouldn't be mistaken for a priest. He laughed in his big, booming voice when I told him that. I suspected that he was the priest to these people most of the time.

The ladies had prepared food, and everyone ate and visited. Many of the faithful came up to me and told me stories of how Jesus or God or one of the saints had helped him or her earlier in the year, got him through a bad week, made the fever fade in her little boy. I was astounded by their faith. Long after the white folks had gone off, the slaves gave their witnesses. When one talked, the rest listened. Sometimes they murmured in assent, sometimes they moaned in sympathy or shouted with joy. It was an amazing experience. All I could do in response was to thank them and bless them. I did both dozens of times.

Finally, as the sun began to tail off, they helped me load the buggy with their gifts. I was glad I didn't ride Jasper as I had first intended for I would have had no way to carry all they gave me, and I wanted badly to accept what they offered. The black folk sent me on my way with waves and shouts. The elder, still wearing my stole, began singing in his basso profundo just as I started down the wagon path through the tall pine forest that reached to the coast. Soon the dozens of slaves who stood in front of the church were singing. Five minutes into the speckled gloom of the woods, I could still hear faint strains of "Nobody knows the trouble I see."

I sighed. The hymn haunted me for a while. I didn't know their troubles, but I had no trouble of my own imagining what it must be like to be enslaved. I wished then that we had more Catholic priests in the Carolinas to minister to these slaves. Although I was uncertain about some of their masters, I felt then that Negroes would make good Catholics, after all.

I thought back on the liturgy in the little wooden church in Ritter and felt a kind of glow start up in my breast. I had been part of something good today, I thought, and now had a long ride home in the cooling day to cherish every moment of it. It didn't seem right to be so content. Deep in my viscera, I knew it couldn't last for long, but I enjoyed what I could of the serenity. When it ended, it ended abruptly.

About a half hour into my journey home, I saw the stolid mare suddenly prick up her ears. Betty Lou had been plodding along like a four-footed metronome, all but asleep in motion with me in tune to her drowsy beat. She heard something I didn't and was suddenly alert. I looked to the left, in the direction the horse turned her head.

The undergrowth was heavy in the treed area fronting a cotton field we were passing, but in the adjoining woods that we were coming up on no ax had ever been laid to the trees. They were thick and gnarled and their tops knitted together to blot out the sun, leaving the ground beneath them in shade. Growth on the floor of this old forest was sparse. The fat trees sucked up most of the available nutrients and light, so little other plant life could compete. The forest floor was a carpet of rotting pine needles. I could see nothing as we creaked and jangled along. The horse threw her head up and blew. She quivered and stared at the woods. Then, in the sudden quiet, I could hear someone running. The footfalls were heavy, no deer or bear this. Maybe it was someone from the Catholic Hill church was my first thought, but then I realized that someone trying to catch me would sing out my name or something to make me stop. The sun was low now and behind the big trees. Its absence gave me a shiver. I knew, suddenly and without a doubt in my mind, that the person in the woods was not a friend.

I looked around desperately. There was nothing suitable as a weapon in the buggy. I saw a stout branch on the side of the path and, without thinking twice, pulled up Betty Lou and jumped down to snatch it up. It was a good size and did not appear to be rotted through. I stepped into the woods and half crouched, hefting the log.

The footfalls through the woods came closer. They thumped along at a steady pace, occasionally cracking a twig. Without warning, they stopped. It was not warm in the forested shade, but I felt my blouse sticking to sweat at the small of my back. I swore I could feel someone staring at me.

The horse blew again and nickered. That made me start. I scurried over to the shelter of another tree. It got quiet again for a half minute, then a sudden piercing scream stopped my heart. The mare bolted. My heart started in again, racing wildly. A creature ran from the woods and started down the cart path chasing the

152 PAUL A. BARRA

stampeding horse, waving its arms and screaming. A couple of sweet potatoes bounced from the careening buggy and then something else. It was light and flew backward, into the path of the wild thing in the wagon's wake. The creature stopped, stopped running and stopped screaming. It stooped and picked up the fallen object. I could see then that the creature was a man, and but a medium-sized one at that. Still, I did not move to confront him but stayed crouched behind the tree.

He dropped the object—nay, almost threw it from him—and then ran into the woods. Within seconds, he had disappeared from view. Moments later, his footfalls faded out. None of this happened quickly enough for me to fail to recognize him, however. The screaming creature from the woods was the man who had been holding up Uncle Williams's head beneath my window in the morning dark.

I stayed where I was, alone, cold now and, frankly, afraid to move. I didn't think of myself as a fearful man and had faced dangers in the past, but this mysterious creature, and the circumstances in which he appeared, unnerved me. A few long minutes later, I imagined I heard hoof beats, muffled by distance, but was never sure of that. Eventually, my leg and back muscles began to cramp, and I stood up slowly, like an old man. I did some waist twists, and arm raises and the warmth of the blood that began to course again through my limbs took some of the primordial fear from me. The creature that had so frightened the mare and me was only human, after all. He was crazed perhaps, but not likely to be immune from a swat with the small log I still held tightly.

So I started down the road at a quick pace. In a few minutes, I came to the object that the man had thrown down. It was the grass cross the slave woman had given me. I pitched my log to one side and picked up the cross, somehow feeling instantly more secure. Then I set off again at a more reasonable walk.

FULL OF EYES: A REBEL BISHOP MYSTERY   153

I kept at it steadily for about twenty minutes before I spotted my horse and wagon. The mare was grazing on the grassed berm of the road. She stopped to watch my approach with eyes wide and nostrils flaring. I began to croon to her as I got closer. She never dropped her head for more spring grass, but she did begin to chew what remained in her mouth after a while. I talked to her and rubbed her between the ears until she acted as if she wasn't about to run off again.

Then I got back into the buggy and headed her southeast. She was spooky for another hour, until the drive began to tire her a bit.

I gave her a good rubdown and some dried oats when we finally made it back to the chancery gardens.

The bishop strolled out to the stables just as I was putting up the tack.

"Have you seen a ghost, now, Tom?"

I stood dumbly. How could he have known such a thing?

"Your hair is everywhere, Tom. That's all I meant. You're staring at me as if I've looked into your very soul. Are you all right?"

"No. No, Excellency, I'm not. I have indeed seen a ghost. Or something like it. Do you have a minute to hear a wild and improbable tale?"

"Yes, of course, man. Please unburden yourself."

I told Bishop Lynch the story of the man beneath my window and the hole in the dirt street, the red and green vapors, the head of Uncle Williams, and the screaming creature from the woods in Colleton District. It sounded so bizarre that I was hesitating in my speech as I finished up. What must this learned man think of his hallucinating associate?

"I think someone is trying to unbalance your mind, Tom."

"But how is it possible for these things to happen? I know what I saw, Bishop Lynch. I had taken no medicines of any sort nor had I drunk even any wine. I was clearheaded at both times, when both these incidents occurred. Perhaps it worked."

154   PAUL A. BARRA

"Eh? Whatever do you mean?"

"Perhaps someone has unbalanced my mind."

"I hardly think so. The things you've seen can be explained. The colored air, for instance, could be no more than gases released by some chemical reaction. Check with the pharmacist, Doctor Brown, will you?"

I nodded assent. The bishop put his hand on my shoulder and patted me, smiling his fatherly smile.

"The head of Uncle Williams was made of clay or cloth, no doubt. After all, it was the middle of the night. The streetlights were already extinguished by that hour, and the mood of horror had been set by the vapors floating about. And make-up, from a theatrical agency. Heaven knows, we've plenty of dramatists and theaters in Charleston these days. The madman digging in the street could have been an actor, made up for the stage. The same could easily be the case for today's fright. He apparently did not see you leave the buggy to pick up the branch and thought you were in it when the mare bolted."

Of course, the bishop was right. Someone had successfully unhinged my mind, if only temporarily. To answer the question why, however, was the crux of the mystery. It must be that I was alarming the killer of Jamieson Carter with my attention to the case, and these incidents were designed to throw me off the scent, as it were, to divert my attention from the investigation. I said as much to Bishop Patrick Lynch.

"My suspicions exactly," he replied. "In fact, I sent around to the police department today for a status report on the murder of a cherished parishioner, citing a worrisome security breach at the cathedral, and received a reply that can best be translated as 'we know nothing more and are doing nothing to find out more.' At least, that's my interpretation of Chief Gordon Becknell's barely literate note. Your prying is the only serious threat to the identity of

FULL OF EYES: A REBEL BISHOP MYSTERY 155

the culprit, I believe. Someone doesn't want you learning anything more. Someone is creating diversions."

Could the ministrations of the lovely Gretchen Becknell be part of that diversionary plan? Before I could fret more over that possibility, Bishop Lynch went on. "I fear for your safety more than your sanity, Tom. We may have a moral obligation to the memory of Jamieson to continue our probe into the circumstances of his death, but once the person or persons who are trying to divert your attention realize they have failed to do that, then the next step may very well be attempted violence to your person."

"But aren't we getting ahead of ourselves, Excellency? These persons trying to keep us from concentrating on the murder in the cathedral may already have committed a violent act."

"You allude to the strange disappearance of Uncle Williams, do you not?"

"I do indeed, sir."

"Yes. And he is still missing, Tom. No one has seen him, and it is now bedtime. I submit that finding him might better be your first order of business on the morrow, although I hate for you to forgo any more sleep. I'll ride over to the west of the Ashley community and say the mass there in the morning. It'll be a treat for them to see their bishop—" He smiled when he said that. "—and saying mass in the fresh air will do me good. That will free you up to do some more checking. But for the love of the Lord, be careful, Tom. May the Holy Ghost go with you."

He gave me his blessing as I genuflected before him. Then I was alone in the dark.

It was still dark eight hours later when I awoke. After early mass in the lower church, said without the services of Uncle Williams, and breakfast, I counseled a young couple planning to marry. She was on her way to work as a nanny in an East Bay mansion and him to his cavalry unit garrisoned in the Citadel, so we perforce finished up while it was still mid-morning. When the couple left, I saddled Jasper and left the episcopal compound heading for the Devil's Hole.

CHAPTER 18

The Devil's Hole was the common appellation for a place without a formal name. It was named after a roadhouse hard by Town Creek on the upper outskirts of Charleston itself. The Charleston peninsula continues a long way inland beyond the creek that slithers in past Drum Island, but populations were thin after one left the district that housed the eponymous Devil's Hole. Many citizens of Charleston, especially the white minority, hardly considered the Devil's Hole locality as part of civilization. It was a dirty complex of mud-daubed shacks with open sewage ditches draining into the creek. The smell was bad as I rode in, though conditions were not nearly as fierce as they would be in a few more months when the air turned thick with heat. Mosquitoes, sand fleas and bluebottle flies would add to the misery of the hellish place in the summer months. When a serious outbreak of yellow fever hit the people there in 1859, not one white doctor would go to minister to the sick and dying. They claimed there was nothing to be done for the disease victims anyway, and there was no use carrying the sickness into other areas or endangering their own lives. Everyone knew the haze of odors that emanated from the wetlands that fed off Town Creek were carriers of all sorts of diseases, including typhoid, break-bone fever, and the dreaded smallpox.

The yellow fever epidemic nearly wiped out the residents of the area around the Devil's Hole bar. The population soon rebounded though, made up, reputedly, of runaway slaves and destitute freedmen. A colored man could virtually disappear in this jumble of hovels and distrust. If Uncle Williams wanted to disappear for some reason, this was the place to do that.

I hoped that my clerics and the Negro's normal respect for clergymen might help me in my search for Uncle Williams. I stopped first at the roadhouse inside the entrance to the Devil's Hole, thinking that it might not be too crowded yet this early in the day. A man with skin the color of cafe au lait dozed in the sun on a plank bench out front of the unpainted building. It was a tall-sided place with small windows. The upper ones were mostly broken out. The railing around the porch was also mostly broken, the posts canting up here and there like rotted teeth. The growth out front was untended. I left Jasper tied to a tree with his bit out, hoping he'd find something edible in the mess of weeds.

There were a dozen or so people in the dark, dank interior. It smelled of the beer that had spilled and dried in the moldering sawdust on the floor. Most of the patrons were hunched over glasses or bottles at tables, even though it was not yet noon. One man sat talking to a standing woman at the bar. No one was behind it. I walked up to the couple.

" Moanin', Reverend. You lost or somethin'?"

The woman smiled broadly as she greeted me. I returned her smile. The man on the barstool turned his head and squinted up at me. He said nothing.

"No, ma'am. I'm looking for a friend of mine."

"You got some mighty strange friends if he likely to be in this here place."

Her chuckle rumbled up from her belly. It was surprisingly deep for such a wisp of a figure. Her teeth and the red bandanna that covered her head stood out from the glossy ebony of her skin. She was so dark that I could not see the features of her face at first, not until my eyes fully adjusted to the dimness of the bar. She looked to be clean and well cared for, shiny black as wet bark. If she wondered what I was doing there, I could have reversed the query myself. She looked well above the rest of the clients of the Devil's Hole Road House. She had teeth and didn't smell that I noticed.

"I don't know that he's here, but if he is, he would only have arrived yesterday or perhaps the night before. He's an old man, wears a beard, a gray one. He's not very tall, but he's stout and strong enough for his age. Would you know if anyone like that has suddenly shown up here?"

"This here friend got a name, rev?"

"Of course. I'm sorry, he is called Uncle Williams. His Christian name is George."

"He a Christian man, then?"

"Certainly. In fact, Uncle Williams is a devout Catholic."

"Then if he is here, he the only one. Far as I know. Ain't no one else ever own up to being one. Henry," she shouted into the darkness, "you know a new nigger in town who say he a Catholic?"

From the depths of the cavernous barroom came a scratchy disembodied voice. "Old man, down by Beulah Mae's. Ain't said much. Did say that."

Before I could figure out who had answered the woman in the red rag, she was giving me directions to Beulah Mae's house. I thanked her and handed her a few coins.

"Please buy some supper for these good folks."

She chuckled again and bit down on one of the coins. Then she flashed her brilliant smile and nodded at the window behind me. Jasper stood there.

"Mind your horse around here, even down Beulah way. He worth a lot of money."

160 PAUL A. BARRA

Heeding her advice, I stayed mounted a few minutes later when I came upon the shanty that I thought belonged to Beulah Mae. Three youngsters, none older than ten and barefoot, came through the door opening. There was no actual door . They stood looking up at me. The youngest squished mud through her toes as she waited on bare ground. I could hear and smell bacon popping in a frying pan from inside. The children said nothing, looked up with wide eyes and closed mouths. I was about to ask them about Uncle Williams when a woman came out, pushing one of the youngsters gently out of her way. She was holding a big black pan and shaking it slightly to keep the meat from sticking. Her eyebrows went up when she spied my Roman collar.

"Who you looking fer, Reverend?"

"A friend of mine named Uncle Williams."

"You got a name?"

"I'm Father Tom Dockery."

She nodded at that then pointed her pan off to the left.

"You might could find him over yonder."

She turned and went back inside with her bacon. I said, "Thank you ma'am," to her back and got out of the saddle. Leading Jasper, I walked over to a broken down pigsty. As I got near, I realized that the shed didn't smell of pigs, it smelled of filthy human detritus. I would have preferred the pigs. Even the kids who followed me over didn't walk up to the low opening but stayed a few feet distant. I couldn't see into the shadowy interior and knew I'd have to go in. I looked at the oldest child.

"Will you please hold my horse?"

She didn't answer but held out a small hand for the reins. She looked at me with her forehead wrinkled in curiosity as I took a deep breath with my nose in the air and then ducked down and stepped into the sty. I tried not to breathe, but the stench was overpowering anyway. A dark figure was outlined against a backdrop of putrefying

FULL OF EYES: A REBEL BISHOP MYSTERY   161

straw, snoring lightly through an open mouth. I moved closer with the stench making my eyes water, and thought I recognized Uncle Williams. I reached down and grabbed the front of his denim coat in a fist and hauled him out to the fresh air. He was not a lightweight, but I had a strength born of desperation. I had to get away from that stink.

He woke up and was beginning to claw ineffectually at my hand. I let go of his coat once we were back in the sunlight, and he staggered, almost going down. If he hadn't stumbled into Jasper, he might have. His hair and whiskers were almost white with age. He smelled badly enough of dried sweat and urine that the youngest two children waved their palms in front of their noses. When he realized he was leaning against a horse, he pushed off and stood straight. The old man—he was probably past fifty and adults who survived childhood diseases were living an average of fifty-five years in most parts of the nation—stood like that, glaring at me and weaving involuntarily once in a while, blinking and coughing. For all his grimy visage, I knew immediately that it wasn't Uncle Williams.

"What the hell—"

He blasted out a string of vile epithets, most directed at me for bothering him. His breath was a wet blast of vinegary vomitus that forced me back a step.

"I'm very sorry, sir. I thought you were someone else."

He coughed up some phlegm, spat and mumbled unintelligibly, then growled and wiped his mouth with the back of his hand. Starting back toward the hovel I had dragged him out of, stepping in imaginary postholes with first one foot then the other, the grizzled man continued to make guttural animal noises. He reeled backward one time. I reached out quickly to steady him, and he shrugged me off violently. The movement toppled him. He landed on his seat and stayed there in the dirt for a minute. Trying to roll over and get to his feet he landed instead on the side of his face. He did not try to

162 PAUL A. BARRA

break the fall. I took him by an arm and heaved him to his feet. He spat dirt out of his mouth. Then he shook off my hand and aimed at the sty again, leading with his head.

A female voice sounded from behind me. "You done got the wrong old man, Reverend."

I turned to see the woman from the doorless house, who I assumed to be Beulah Mae and the mother of the three children, none of whom had as yet uttered a sound. She was standing behind us wiping her hands on an apron she wore around her substantial middle. She flinched and scrunched her eyes closed just as I heard the sound of the old drunk drive his head into the doorway lintel of his shed. Fortunately, the wood was soft with rot, and he didn't knock himself out. He did land on his seat again, though. I reached him in two strides, righted him once more and directed his progress into his sleep hole. He pitched into the sour straw and began snoring almost before I backed out of olfactory range.

I tried not to grimace when I addressed Beulah Mae again. "God bless the poor man. How can he stand it?"

She cackled back that he was used to it and so drunk most of the time that he didn't know any better.

"His mind done gone from him, mister. He rather sleep in that crap—excuse me, hear?—than in the house. Don't nobody bother him that way. Till you come along, 'course."

The very idea of me bothering the drunken slumber of the foul wretch brought forth another cackle from the woman and the kids tittered a bit too.

"I thought you indicated that Uncle Williams was in the shed."

"I pointed down de path. Never occur to me that you wouldn't have the sense to avoid that hellhole, you being a preacher and all. Come along, I show you your friend."

We walked around the sty and into a patch of pin oaks and skinny pine trees, the children following and leading Jasper. We walked slowly, but the woman was puffing loudly before we'd gone a hundred paces. We stopped by a small creek, swollen with winter rain, and she leaned against a tree with one hand, wiping the sheen from her face with the other. I waited until she caught her breath and was drying her hands on the apron again.

"Are you all right, madam?"

"Yeah. Yeah." She drew a large inhalation. "I just got a touch of de pleurisy or something. Let's go sit by that there rock."

There were no rocks in coastal Carolina. Antoine told me one day that the whole coastal plain had once been underwater and the rocks had been ground to sand by the action of the sea over the centuries. I didn't know enough to contradict him, so I believed the theory. Our destination was in reality a chunk of concrete and bricks that looked like it may have been part of a chimney in an earlier life. By the time we got to it, she was perspiring and panting again. Beulah Mae rested there with her bare feet in the water. The children watered Jasper in the creek and spent the wait time combing his mane and tail with their fingers. I didn't know what we were waiting for exactly, because we stayed even after Beulah was breathing normally again, but decided there was no way to rush things along. Before I started getting anxious, however, what we were waiting for stepped out of the woods on a footpath to our left.

"Uncle Williams!"

"Aye, Father Dockery. It good to see you."

I looked the short old man over carefully as we shook hands. He had a pinched sort of expression to his eyes and mouth, but physically he appeared in good shape.

"Are you feeling well?"

"Okay."

"The bishop missed you at mass yesterday morning and was concerned."

He averted his eyes and scratched at his beard. I didn't want to stare him down or do anything that might be construed as intimidating, so I looked around, noticing that Beulah had slipped over to her children, and had done it quietly indeed for a big woman. They had tied Jasper to a tree and were lounging around him, probably too far away to hear our conversation.

"I bin needing to get 'way for de time, Father."

"Good idea. It helps to get away once in a while."

"Yeh."

"I do wish you had told someone, though, so your friends wouldn't worry."

"Yeh. I sure shoulda done that there."

"Where are you staying, Uncle Williams?"

"My cousin, Beulah Mae, she bin take care of me. I does okay."

"I believe it. You look fine."

He nodded at that. He still had not smiled and had not looked me in the eye. He was not as clean as he usually was when he showed up for church services every morning, but I could understand that if he was living in the Devil's Hole.

"Them young'uns is my kin. They enjoy a visit once in de while."

"I'm sure they do. They seem like nice children."

"Yeah." He smiled for the first time, looking over at the children and their mother. "They sure enough a good bunch. I tell 'em stories, specially at night 'round de fire. We bin have de good time, for sure."

He fell silent, and the smile slowly slipped from his face. His eyes went blank again. He looked worried, and afraid.

I decided to try a shot in the dark. "Do you ever tell them any true stories, Uncle Williams?"

"What you mean?"

"Stories about yourself. Why you came to this place without even telling your friends."

"Don't get you."

"Did somebody tell you to take some time off and get away?"

His head snapped up and his face contorted in a flash, as if I'd prodded the wrong part of his brain. Spittle flew from his lips as he shouted his answer. "Nobody told me nothing, heah! I just bin wanting to get 'way for some time."

Then Uncle Williams turned and stomped off on the path into the woods. I stood there for a minute, immobilized by his unprovoked outburst. I had never heard Uncle Williams raise his voice before in the years I'd known him. I wiped my hand down my face and turned away from the last I'd seen of him. Beulah Mae and the three kids were watching me.

When I got closer, the woman shook her head and clucked her tongue. "I swanny, I never seen him act like that 'fore. He bin strange since he bin coming here last night. It bin late then, and we wasn't 'specting him, hadn't seen him for months, not since we went down Charleston way for Christmas."

"He a relative of yours, Beulah Mae?"

She gave no indication of surprise that I would know her name.

"Yeah, he kin to me, all right. George my momma's sister's first boy. Actually, he the second but de first die early on, I hear. He so much older than my family that we always call him Uncle, y'know?"

I motioned for her to mount Jasper for the walk back, and she didn't protest. Her children walked alongside of her, and I led the horse back slowly. As we passed the pigpen, I imagined I could hear snoring from within. I helped the woman off the horse at her front doorway, noticing that a curtain covered the opening now.

"Have you had this lung problem for a long time, Miss Beulah?"

"It come and go. It don't bother me if I go easy. Look here, we butchered de hog 'round Christmas time, and I got some bacon ready. How 'bout a meal 'fore you leave off?"

I hated myself for it, but I told her I was in a hurry. I didn't want to go into her house, and I was afraid to eat anything in this town, even though I had missed my usual big lunch and was hungry enough for some bacon and biscuits. She smiled and took no offense, leaving me wondering who of us was the better bred after all. I thanked her for her assistance and asked her to take two dollars for the care of Uncle Williams. She took the money without comment. I gave each of the children a coin. The two girls curtsied, and the middle boy said thanks.

"Well, you can talk, can't you?"

All three giggled at that, hands flying to cover their mouths. Then I got on Jasper and rode off. When I got to the main dirt road leading out of Devil's Hole, I put the big gelding into a fast canter. I wanted to get out of Devil's Hole and never come back.

CHAPTER 19

Distance riding was a good opportunity to cogitate, and I had been doing just that on the return from the Devil's Hole. It so happened that Chief Becknell was part of my cogitative processes.

I knew that Uncle Williams was lying about something. He was too nervous and defensive, for one thing, and no one who was not under some serious threat would choose to hide out in a dismal place like the Devil's Hole. Not when his habitual environs were the cathedral and its campus. Gordon Becknell was the obvious choice, to me at least, as the principal in this drama most likely to threaten a Negro, especially one with ties to the Catholic Church. Since the police leader was a prime suspect in the murder in the cathedral, I wondered what Uncle Williams knew that Gordon Becknell did not like. I suspected that Becknell was up to mischief. It turned out that my suspicions were correct, although I didn't find that out for a while.

Even so, the chief of police was still on my mind when I walked down Hasell Street to call on Father Antoine Gagnon after morning duties on the morrow after my visit to the Devil's Hole. It was cool and damp early in the Charleston day, and I enjoyed the brisk walk. My legs needed stretching after all the riding I had been doing lately,

168 PAUL A. BARRA

and it was a learning experience every time I ventured among the people of this gracious southern city.

Even though Charlestonians were invariably polite and friendly, I could not but fail to notice the subdued aura around them all that morning. We all knew the inevitability of war with the North by now. Our state had led the push to it as a matter of fact. But the people of Charleston felt almost predestined, perhaps like Presbyterians, as if the choices were being made for them. The fighting in Kansas and John Brown's polemic broadsides against slavery and the rhetoric of Lincoln supporters. It was as if the way of life enjoyed in the South, even by most slaves if the truth be told, was being run over by a stampeding herd of northern aggression. And what Southerner believed, objectively, that thirteen poor farming states could stand alone against the industrial might of the Union?

Hence, the quiet and polite pessimism, the soft smiles of seminal melancholy I met on the way to St. Mary's that April morning in 1861. The women looked like young wives supporting the imprudent business schemes of their husbands, hoping for the best, knowing the plans could never work. The men wore hardened faces. It was they who would be facing federal lead and steel before long. In the young, misted forenoon, the heat of patriotism had yet to flare into flames in their hearts. They looked at the future in these vulnerable moments of the damp morningtide, and they were afraid of what they saw there.

I prayed for Charleston and the South as I walked and nodded and tipped my biretta. I blessed myself in front of St. Mary's. The Diocese of Charleston may be the largest slaveholding diocese in the world, but the people who populated the two states of the diocese were generally good and kindhearted.

I looked at the venerable columns supporting old St. Mary's Church, pictured the interior, the colored balconies where the slaves worshipped, and I blew out my cheeks. I thought about poor Father

FULL OF EYES: A REBEL BISHOP MYSTERY   169

Gagnon and the ultimatum he was working under. How his pastor, in all righteous conscience no doubt, was forcing him to choose between a moral belief and a future of promise.

The melancholia of the early townsfolk was infecting me. I could not afford it. I had a murder to solve and a shrinking amount of days in which to do it.

Antoine Gagnon found me out front of his parish church and launched into a minor soliloquy about the venerable place.

"St. Mary of the Annunciation parish, the oldest in the diocese, formed even before there was a diocese, was one of the main reasons that Bishop John Carroll requested a Diocese of Charleston in the first place, don't you know, Thomas?. He was too far away in Baltimore to oversee individual churches with any hope of managing them properly, so when the laity of St. Mary's essentially took over the parish, Bishop Carroll decided it was time for a new see and for a new bishop in the area to deal with the overzealous trustees. Bishop England did just that admirably, I must say, treading a fine line between accepting active lay participation in the affairs of the parish and maintaining the authority of the pastorate."

By 1861, St. Mary's was fully back in the fold, and Antoine Gagnon was pleased to have been offered the position of assistant pastor under Reverend Monsignor Raymond F. Reed. Father Gagnon was still incardinated to the Diocese of New Orleans, but had his eye on a permanent change. He liked the pioneer spirit of the Carolinas, he said.

Antoine ushered me into his study, a small, dark, book-lined room illuminated mainly by the beaming countenance of the Jesuit from Louisiana. His outward appearance held no indication of the turmoil he must have been going through as his big speech on Pentecost drew ever nearer. We drank tea by the light of a single small window high in one wall as I filled him in about the goings-on since we last talked and then he told me the story he had heard from one of his contacts about Gordon Becknell. The priest, whom I considered my friend by that time, spoke with a particular richness of expression that morning, almost as if he knew that I would be writing about our adventures one day. The police chief had gone down to the waterfront on the east side of town the night before, Antoine said. It was dark, just gone suppertime. I was probably still on my way home from Catholic Hill at the time, in a wagon being pulled by a spooked mare and laden with gifts from St. James Church.

"The wharves on the Cooper were busy with shipping, mostly from Europe and England," my Jesuit friend said. "Please picture the place smelling of mud flats and tar. Gulls who wheeled and cawed overhead by day sat on pilings with feathers fluffed against the sea breezes. Despite the cool air, the faces of ten or twelve Negroes glistened in the shimmering light from pitch torches as they unloaded bales and boxes from a single freighter at Temple Wharf. Overlooking the wharf and the channels that led around sandbars and between forts Sumter and Moultrie to the sea was a large, sturdy building, Carter's Ship Chandlery, Limited. You get the picture I'm trying to paint, Thomas?"

"I do indeed. You are being most poetically descriptive. Please continue."

Antoine raised his eyebrows at my reference to poesy, but he made no comment about it—and did not ask for his slave prayer back. Instead, he continued his colorful narrative. "Becknell made his way to the chandlery past the workers, paying them as little mind as he would if they were mules. They, for their part, did not sing or shout as they worked. The only sounds were the labored respiration of the slaves and the lapping of river water against the ship's side. Even those undershot background noises were cut off abruptly as Becknell stepped into the chandlery building and closed the door behind him."

FULL OF EYES: A REBEL BISHOP MYSTERY 171

He paused then and smiled at me. As if he'd finished making prepared statements, Antoine took a breath.

"Everything else I am going to tell you is conjecture that we'll have to verify. You do understand?"

"Yes," I replied. "Can you tell me if your source for this information was one of the slaves working the docks there?"

"I could tell you but I won't. I promise my sources that I will never reveal their identities. Otherwise, they would never dare talk to me about anything. Nevertheless, here's the story as I understand it..."

Guided by the misty remnants of a lamplight some distance removed from the main entrance, Chief Becknell must have made his way through the storefront retail room of the business and down a short corridor to an open office, moving as silently and swiftly as a bear on the hunt, Antoine said. The Jesuit himself had actually gone into the business to see what it was like inside after hearing the story of Becknell's nighttime visit. In the warm, overstuffed office a lamp hung from the ceiling, throwing everything in the room into acute relief. That included bundles and barrels of shipboard provisions smelling of creosote, slabs of fatback in rock salt, boxes of canned goods crammed into every available space and tools piled on rough wooden shelving. It also included the person behind the thick oaken desk.

"That woman was Annie Carter, Jamieson's eldest child. She has apparently taken over the business on the death of her dear departed pater," he said.

"Has she enough experience to run a big business like that, do you think? I would have thought her mother would at least be guiding her."

Antoine shook his head at my naivety. "Cynthia Carter is that kind of Southern belle who lives only for society, Thomas. She has no head for business. At least, that's undoubtedly how she thinks of herself, as a way of rationalizing her ignorance. I wouldn't be surprised if she had some trusted slave do even the household accounts for her. No, I'm afraid it is now up to young Annie to keep the family enterprise alive."

"Well, what was Chief Becknell doing visiting young Annie, as you say, in the middle of the night?"

"I can't say with any certainty. All I know is that they were speaking seriously together and that Annie seemed afraid of the thuggish Becknell. At least, that's what my man was telling me until he had a little...er...mishap and could tell no more."

"What happened?"

"My man tipped over the bench he was standing on to spy through the window and alerted the two inside the premises of his presence. Becknell was already moving by the time a startled cry jumped from Annie Carter's mouth. He went to the window in two strides. My man had scurried away like one of the wharf rats that live around there, he told me, so that Becknell saw nothing but the dark and the flickering lights from the wharf. Becknell turned and ran through the store the way he had come in, knocking over a barrel of rope and a crate of hooks in his rush. He threw open the door with a great dramatic roar and ranted at the slaves like a wild man. Scared them all to stammering gibberish, no doubt. My man was so afraid of getting caught that he was sweating like a donkey, he said in his quaint but theatrical style of speaking, and afraid he wouldn't be able to talk sense. But Becknell had cast the rest of the workers into that same kind of condition, so he got nothing out of them. My man appeared no more afraid than the rest."

"How ironic that Becknell's aggressive behavior spoiled his chance to find out who was spying on him."

"Don't you wonder, Thomas, how Gordon Becknell ever solves any crime at all with his bull-in-a-china-shop technique?"

"I daresay he frightens confessions out of suspects," I answered Antoine. My thoughts, however, were far away from my words. What had Annie Carter, daughter of the murdered man, and the chief of police been plotting that Antoine's spy had seen? If my idea that the police chief had threatened Uncle Williams was correct, what did that poor freedman know that made him a threat to Becknell's plan?

"I hate to intervene in your ruminations, Detective Dockery, but I do have another tidbit of information."

"You do? Please tell me."

"Well, two tidbits. One is that another merchantman is scheduled to tie up at the pier alongside Carter's Chandlery sometime in the next week, maybe even tomorrow. The dockworkers are awaiting that ship once they finish unloading the one already there. And two, Chief Becknell was seen earlier in the day going into the New Town."

"What is the New Town?"

Antoine Gagnon grinned at my question with that superior cant to his eye I've become used to.

"It's a warehouse, my friend."

"A warehouse?"

"I'm not stuttering, am I? Or speaking in a foreign tongue?"

"What in the world does a warehouse have to do with all this?"

"I would venture to guess that the answer depends on what's in the warehouse, n'est pas?"

Within the hour, we were riding slowly out to the commercial district inland from the docks. Our plan of action enjoyed, to our minds, the very beauty of simplicity. We started at one end of the long row of warehouses. We were wearing our clerics and carrying collection baskets. Two priests were entirely in character here, so I wasn't worried about subterfuge. In fact, I felt happy to be doing something active to try to find the murderer. Instead of relying on other people's information, we were going to find out something on our own.

"We're collecting for Tom Shandy, a warehouseman who was injured on the job and unable to work. He has no way to support his family any longer."

We made the pitch to any white man who would listen, assuming slaves would have no money to offer. Sometimes we talked to a small group, other times to individuals. We walked into warehouses, some named for reasons lost in time, some merely numbered. Our mission was based on fact. Shandy had lost a leg on the docks. He was not a Catholic, but we intended to turn over whatever we collected to St. Michael's Episcopal Church, where a fund had been started for the poor man. It was six months ago when a pallet of pickled fish had fallen on him and crushed his left leg, but we assumed that his familial needs were as great now as ever before.

Some men dropped their pennies in the basket with a nod. Some turned away when we approached. One cock-eyed man splattered tobacco juice at our feet and another spit out "Papists!" as he walked away. Generally, though, Antoine and I were pleasantly surprised with the largesse from these taciturn laborers. They barely made their own keep as strenuous as their work was and they probably did not often have the opportunity to give to someone in tougher straits that they themselves were in.

Eventually, we meandered down to the New Town, begging as we went. It was mission work and it took a strange sort of hold on me, so much so that I was not at all nervous about the real reason for our effort by the time we came to stand outside the target warehouse. The New Town was closed up. It wasn't the only one in that condition, however, so we did as we had done at the others and went in through the workers' door at the side.

FULL OF EYES: A REBEL BISHOP MYSTERY 175

It was dark in the cavernous interior. The only light stole in from chinks in the siding and from one open window on the far side. Our footsteps and voices did not echo as they had in the other storerooms. Two men met us near the door. By the time we had made our pitch and they dug deep for a penny from one and a shrug from the other, our eyes had adjusted to the gloom. We could see large bales of cotton stacked three high and wrapped in linen sheeting. There looked to my unpracticed eye to be enough at least to fill the holds of two merchant ships.

We went outside and finished our canvass of the strip. I was bursting to talk but held it until we had emptied the collection into one of Antoine's saddlebags—$1.12—and mounted up. It was past dinnertime and the road in front of the warehouses where men had been pooling in small groups here and there was now deserted. We rode back the way we had come. Once we cleared the first warehouse we had approached ninety minutes before, I turned to Antoine.

"What interest could an heir to the Carter Chandlery and the chief of police have in a warehouse full of cotton?"

Neither of us had an answer to that, but Bishop Lynch did. When we confided in him a short while later, he thought immediately of an economic cause for a greed-driven secret plan.

"With war talk endemic in the nation, and with the anticipated need for uniforms and bandages and tents suddenly very obvious, cotton prices are expected to boom. The South's overly abundant crop yields of 1859 and 1860 are about to run out, although prices are still low everywhere. I would think that cotton purchased now will appreciate substantially in the coming months."

"But if Annie Carter and Becknell are planning to make a great profit in the cotton market, Excellency, why do they need to be so secretive?" I asked. "One would think that haste would be more important than subterfuge. Rising cotton prices must be a common expectation among the mercantile set."

176   **PAUL A. BARRA**

"True, no doubt. Since the South produces almost all of the cotton available in America, however, the real money is to be made north of the thirty-sixth-and-a-half parallel, I'm afraid."

I rose to my feet in a most undignified manner.

"What? You mean they intend to sell two ships full of our cotton to the Yankees? Why, that's, that's treasonous."

"Not quite, Tom. War has not been declared officially, so their sale would be legal, at least in a technical sense. I wouldn't want to vouch for either of their reputations if the local populace found out about their plot, though. Nor for the safety of their persons."

"What can we do about this, bishop?"

"Well, I believe the first thing is to remember that we have no actual proof of such a scheme. We should notify President Davis of our suspicions. He would want to put a stop to any source of supplies to the enemy."

Antoine, who seemed perfectly collected and calm in the face of these sensational speculations by the bishop, inexorably found his voice. "And might I suggest, Excellency, that speed is of the essence for us? Once the second ship is unloaded tomorrow night or soon after, the contraband cotton bales will be aboard in another day or so. If they get to sea, we've lost, since none of our warships could expect to slip past the federalist blockade of Charleston harbor to give chase to the Carter merchantmen."

Bishop Lynch and I stared at Antoine for a short second. It was the first time he'd spoken up since greeting the bishop thirty minutes ago. Of course, he was perfectly correct. Merchant ships heading north were one thing. Armed Confederate men of war chasing them would be taken under fire by Union warships almost certainly, even though the blockade was more threat than substance since the shelling of Ft. Sumter.

"You are absolutely right, Father. We must move quickly. I will put this all down in a letter to my friend Davis, while you two find

FULL OF EYES: A REBEL BISHOP MYSTERY 177

me a runner and a strong mount for the trip to Savannah. I believe that Jefferson Davis is addressing the Southern Baptist Convention there on the weekend."

I went out on the mare to find Bones—wondering all the while of the ironies wrought by war, not only the greed of two prominent people but of an Episcopalian from Mississippi addressing a Baptist convention in Georgia—while a stable hand made Jasper ready for the run south. It seemed further ironic that Bones, who had caught up Jasper when he broke free from downtown and then tried to extort money for his care, would now be trusting his health to the care taken of that same animal. But Jasper was in fine fettle and ready to travel. Bones had nothing better to do, not surprisingly, and was easily tempted by the prospect of an adventure and a little spending money when he returned. At his age, riding fast across the country held no fear. His aunt Flora made him a packet of foodstuffs for the trip.

He was soon thundering off for Savannah, just more than 100 miles distant, with Bishop Lynch's letter to Davis in his saddlebag. I felt that things were moving awfully fast.

Antoine had a class to teach and some pastoral duties that would take up the rest of the day and evening, and I was similarly committed. As I made hospital rounds and spoke with parish groups, my mind constantly swerved around to Savannah with a query about Bones and his mission. But, of course, I had no answers. We didn't expect to hear anything from him until he returned in person.

Bishop Lynch was scheduled to travel to Columbia for a church dedication, but he was anxious also to hear from Jefferson Davis. He was probably as tempted as was I to ride over to The New Town for a peek, but we were both able to restrain our curiosity. Certainly, we didn't want Becknell or the Carter girl to get wind of our interest.

When I came back from a supper meeting of the Ladies Guild, a trying affair, as usual, with the women seemingly torn between acts

178   PAUL A. BARRA

of genuine charity and social justice on the one hand and scheming politics on the other. These women were sharp and influential. The layers of southern civility that each could peel away and recover in an instant, as the immediate occasion demanded, rendered a rudimentary analysis of events impossible. It was all I could do to follow their machinations, if only to steer clear of the fireworks when they erupted. Not that the women wanted me involved in their skirmishes. I was at the meeting to offer a prayer at beginning and end and to advise them on needy charities and what other parish organizations were doing. I like to think that the presence of a Roman collar in their midst served to temper their vitriol a bit. All of the women were older than me and much surer of their authority, so I never even thought of censuring any outbreaks.

They kept their own books and, certainly, their own battle plans. Even so, they were able before the evening ended to manage their affairs, settle disputes and learn all the news in town. Their witticisms and knowledge of events amazed me and kept me on my toes all during the meeting, so it was draining, and I was happy to hear the last Amen. I did learn one tidbit, however, that interested me. One of the women heard on the grapevine that the Charleston Police Department considered the murder in the cathedral a robbery, probably by an unknown assailant, and that the case was unofficially closed. This was gossip, not fact, but it made me think when I overheard it that it may, after all, be up to three Catholic priests to solve the crime. I walked home slowly thinking about what we knew and trying to fit the pieces together in my mind. I did not have enough information yet.

In the big house, I met Flora in the dining room. She was putting silverware up in felt-lined drawers. Once, nearly two years ago now, when I came upon her in the market district, she was speaking with a group of Negro women in Gullah. It was lovely to hear, but utterly incomprehensible to anyone who had not grown up with it. It was the language of slaves here in the Lowcountry. When I expressed an interest in learning more about it, Flora diplomatically agreed to pass on the slave gossip instead. Surely they did not want a white priest able to interpret their conversations. So Flora had gotten into the habit of telling me what the slave community was going on about when I asked, a trade of gossip for continued confidentiality.

"Any news from the marketplace these days, Miss Flora?"

She had given me a biscuit and honey for a late snack to go with the buttermilk I'd gotten from the window ledge where we kept it in the cool six months of the year. She hadn't asked.

When I plunked down with a sigh at the dining room table, she just went back to the kitchen and made up the biscuit. She knew that Ladies Guild suppers were not filling enough for a young man.

"The preacher man's acting the fool again, I hear tell."

"What's the Reverend Quillery on about now?"

"Bad stuff about our church."

"He cannot stomach Catholics, can he?"

"He told my friend Caroline that the Catholic Church be the whore of Babylon. Got it straight from the Bible, he says."

"Yeah, Revelation. It's pretty obvious to anyone with the sense to check out the history of the book that the writer was talking about the Roman empire, but some anti-Catholics insist on interpreting the allusions to Rome as if John meant the Roman Church. At the time, there was only one Christian church. Be awful silly to curse your own church now, wouldn't it?"

"Oh, I do agree, Father Tom. I suspect that some folk listen to the preacher man and don't know no better, though."

"Um, yes, I'm sure you're right about that."

"He was right wild yesterday, though. More than usual. Yelling about statues, idols he call them, and how they can poison a house and stuff. He sounded crazy enough to scare some of my friends near to death. He looks odd to me."

"Odd?"

"Yeah. Maybe like he going crazy, 'stead of just sounding like it. He's got this big long coat all buttoned up, even in the sun. When he was hollering about Mary one time he pulled at his hair. Maybe his brain been hurt or something."

"What was he saying about Mary?"

"He was going on about her craven image, whatever he mean by that."

I told her that Quillery was either mispronouncing graven, which meant carved, or that he thought the statues in Catholic churches and in some Anglican ones were cowardly ideas because we were afraid to confront Jesus or God directly and had to resort to intermediaries, hence craven. But while I was explaining that to Flora, part of my mind was harking back to the morning we discovered the murder. Chief Becknell had used the same language, calling the statue that had been used to kill Jamieson Carter a craven image.

Quillery was having a problem coping with reality, it seemed. He must have been driven by some obsession to dare break into a Broad Street residence, especially one belonging to a Catholic primate. He had acted in a bizarre manner when Antoine and I visited him at his house. And now he was raving badly enough to frighten slaves. I visited with Flora for a while longer, letting her calm gentleness ease the strain that I had accumulated trying to keep up with the women at their meeting. I told her the news and the gossip, as best I remembered it, from the meeting as she stood polishing silverware with a cloth so old and soft that I could see her dark fingers through it as she worked. It occurred to me that she never sat when I talked with her. She always found work to do, as if she was keeping the separation between our positions clear even as we socialized. Even so, I valued her advice, and so I asked her what she thought of the character of Gretchen Becknell, who could not be entirely eliminated as a suspect in the murder of her illicit lover Jamieson Carter.

Flora took a breath and looked down at me when she spoke. "That woman treat me like some white folk do, like I ain't there. It prolly don't mean much, but I think that way of thinking mean the person don't be good in her heart, know what I mean? I hope I ain't insulting your friend, Father Tom, but that's what I think."

"Please don't fret about insulting my friends, Flora. When I ask your opinion, I do so because you tell the truth."

"Well, I don't know the Becknell woman too much, you heah? I know about her, and I drive her home that night. That's what I think."

Flora's opinion bothered me more than I let on to her. She was perceptive about human nature and naturally charitable. She spoke highly of Mrs. Ryan, for instance, who could not have been an easy person to work with. But then I never witnessed Mrs. Ryan treating Flora as if she didn't exist. The two women seemed to work the episcopal residence as equals. My soul was in turmoil when I finally left Flora in the dining room, but I managed to sleep soundly nevertheless.

Late the next morning, after Sunday services, I went looking for Andrew Quillery. I wanted to hear his rantings for myself. I found him easily enough. One of his obligations to his God was to proselytize in the public square, unabashedly trying to convert people, any or all people, to his brand of fundamentalism. The tactic irked other ministers, who were concerned more with converting the many unchurched Charlestonians than with members of other congregations. The other ministers were generally quite a bit subtler in their approach to evangelization, as well. None of that bothered Reverend Quillery. He harangued and bellowed out accusations and railed against heretics of all stripes. He did it nearly every Sunday. I admit that my dislike of his tactics and his theology was tempered by

182   PAUL A. BARRA

an admiration for his courage. It couldn't be easy trying to evangelize on a street corner.

This day he had chosen the sidewalk in front of the Southern Clothing Emporium on King Street. Since he had set his crate in front of a store owned by two brothers named Levy, I thought his tirade would be directed against Jews. He was brazen that way. Jews had been a part of Charleston since the late seventeenth century, and for a while following the American Revolution, there were more Jews in Charleston than in any other city in the nation. What's more, they were granted citizenship and voting rights, both, before Catholics. The local nativists have sort of avoided antagonizing them in their efforts to politically castrate Catholics from the old country.

One thing I had absolutely to avoid in observing Quillery was to become embroiled in public argument with him. Not only would that be unseemly and uncharitable in my brand of Christianity, but it would surely result in more embarrassment for the Catholic Church. The fundamentalist was a master debater, and I was hoping to witness some of his skills without becoming victim to them as I spied on his tactics. I stayed in the shade of another storefront, so that I was slightly behind the speaker, facing the crowd obliquely from a distance of twenty feet or so. The Reverend Quillery stepped up on his overturned box without so much as a glance in my direction and raised his hands and eyes to heaven. The Negroes in the crowd, mostly middle-aged women, looked fretful and stood close to one another. The children, of both races, had their eyes opened wide, as if the preacher was about to start telling ghost tales. White men lounged about nudging each other or smiling around their cigars.

Quillery drilled them all with his eyes, and even the men got still there in the street outside a clothing store in the full sun of a coolish April day.

"Ladies and gentlemen," he said quietly. Bodies leaned toward him a tad. "Brothers and sisters," he bellowed. Everyone jumped or

FULL OF EYES: A REBEL BISHOP MYSTERY   183

started, you couldn't help it. His voice hammered out at you, and its pitch caused a sharp pain in the cavity behind the eyes for a split second.

"I have come to tell you a tale today that is so sordid, so sinful, so egregious in ere implications, that you will scarce believe it. But it's all true, brothers and sisters, all too, too true. It's the story about a man who were struck down by God in the flower of his manhood for the hideous—hideous!—sacrilege he performed. He were not a man of the cloth, but he were a churchman nonetheless, and he paid for his dastardly sins with his very life. "

My throat felt dry and I swallowed hard. I had a horrible feeling that this sermon was going to be more than I wanted to hear.

CHAPTER 20

As Quillery spoke, it became immediately and abundantly clear that the preacher had not garnered his reputation and popularity by brimstone alone. He may have gotten their attention that morning in front of Levy's store by scaring the tar out of his audience, but he soon began to weave a mesmerizing tale of love and betrayal and murder.

It was forbidden love, of course, so we knew the betrayal was bound to come. I certainly knew it, for the man was telling the story of Jamieson Carter. He used no names, called Gretchen the blond woman and Carter the church elder, but he told their story so clearly that I was stupefied. How could Quillery know all that he was telling? When he got to the ultimate sacrilege and the final betrayal, the crowd was staring at him, not a whisper nor a cough to be heard, not a jiggle of impatience nor a shift of weight. His burred accent carried clearly through the morning air.

"Then, my friends, the two who could not control their passions, who had fallen so far in their illicit union, plummeted to the very depths of depravity. They met in a church one night. Yes, in the very sanctuary of God. Even there, in that holy place, their souls were consumed with lust. It were not in one of our own churches where the two met, uh uh. Twas in a foreign, a European church.

FULL OF EYES: A REBEL BISHOP MYSTERY 185

And if the church leader were a wrongheaded man, an anti-Christ even, the people of this story was not to be blamed for that. They considered their church a holy place, so that when the couple of this tale consummated the lust that truly consumed them—right there, folks, right there in the verra sanctuary of God—they realized that they had done a deed so evil that Christ himself could not forgive them."

Quillery was fairly bellowing by this time. Spittle flew from his lips, and an unholy rage was etched into the craggy features of his face. The nostrils of his hatchet-sharp nose flared like a horse in full gallop.

"And they reacted to their final depravation according to their characters, friends. The church elder, which were basically a good man except for his uncontrollable desire for the blonde woman, fell to his knees in futile supplication. He become overwhelmed with his sense of guilt and pleaded with his God for mercy. He knelt sobbing at the altar, shamed to his very marrow and begging the forgiveness of the Lord."

The preacher man stopped suddenly. When he spoke again it was in a quiet voice that had me straining to hear.

"We will never know if his voice were heard. We will never know because the woman acted out her reaction to their heinous, egregious sin. She offered a sacrifice to the God of that there foreign church. She swept up a craven image from the altar and crushed her lover's skull with it while he knelt in prayer. Right there in front of God, in God's house.

"And that is how they exist today, my friends, one in hell and one on the way. Even though she still walks among us, a personified evil, looking to do more of the devil's work, she is damned for eternity."

After a short stone silence, the people watching Andrew Quillery began to fidget. They wanted desperately, I knew, to ask the identity of the protagonists in his story, for there was never any doubt in our minds but that he was telling a true story.

The preacher man did not produce fabrications for the entertainment of the populace. To his listeners on Sunday afternoons, his stories were real and told to strike the fear of God into his listeners.

A man raised his hand and spoke above the murmuring that had begun to spread through the crowd like the stirring of dead leaves at dark.

"Was that there murder done in a synagogue, Reverend?"

Quillery fixed the hapless soul with his piercing eye, his rising color and sharp inhalation testimony to the wrath that was about to be spewed upon the questioner.

"Jews? Do ye think these evil people was Jews, for God's sake, man? Do ye think the religion that give us the likes of Mordecai Cohen, our senator and servant of the people of Charleston for all his adult life—do ye think that faith could also produce scum the likes of which I just told thee about? Were ye drinking already before noon, man?"

The people hardly spent any sympathy on the poor excoriated man who had the audacity to speak out. His foolhardy question—or was it brave, do you think?—had answered all their questions in one fell swoop. If the foreign church where the abominations had taken place was not a temple of Judaism, then it perforce had to be Roman Catholic. The people in the street now knew with certainty that Quillery was referring to the murder in the cathedral when he told his story. After all, Carter's braining was second in gossip value in April of 1861 only to the bombardment of our fort. The preacher man's sharp attack on the questioner had dispelled all doubts. Some people needed absolute assurance.

A few other men patted the embarrassed man's shoulder as he reddened furiously, but most were driven to great animation. The only religion considered foreign to Charleston other than Judaism was Catholicism. Many Charlestonians regularly referred to us as the Roman church. More ignorant ones called us papists, as if the appellation was a slur of some kind. It was a time-honored exclusion that was only now beginning to yield to education and familiarity. The British parliament had never allowed Catholics to vote in the New World when they were in charge of the colonies. "Protestants, Jews and Quakers" were naturalized by an act of parliament in 1740, but Catholics were specifically excluded. You can put off that discriminatory action by the English to a lingering apology for Henry VIII and his anti-Catholic sentiments, if you want, but things did not change appreciably in the immediate aftermath of the revolution that drove the heirs to Henry's concupiscence from our shores. The British may not have beheaded Catholics as Henry did Thomas More, but the discrimination they practiced was live and official. It rubbed off on the colonists. Even after the American victory in the revolution over British rule, Catholics could not hold office.

Things were markedly better by 1861, thankfully, but not so much that the people listening to Quillery's story of perfidy had any difficulty interpreting what judicatory he referred to as a foreign church, once the Jews were ruled out.

Quillery had alluded to the influence of the Holy Father in his talk, calling him an anti-Christ. Now the crowd's suspicions were confirmed. Quillery had not said so directly, the dirty Pilate, but everyone would be able to figure out that he had just told the true story of Jamieson Carter's murder. I realized in a sudden, intuitive flash that had to come to me through the grace of the Holy Ghost, what would happen as soon as the gossip coalesced and people started to demand action. Someone who had heard other malicious gossip would make the connection very soon indeed. There were not all that many adult blonde women in the Holy City. Word had undoubtedly leaked from the meeting at the Becknell cottage that fateful evening a few nights ago that the chief's wife was staying out late. Once they eliminated a few possibilities and identified Becknell's wife as the blonde of Quillery's tale, lynch fever might heat up rather quickly. Nothing would appeal to the salacious side of mob violence greater than the vision of a voluptuous woman accused of murder and adultery. Quillery had stirred them with zeal now and they would want a way to vent that feeling.

I slipped around the corner from Levy's store and headed home in great haste. Gretchen had to be warned.

Without spending a moment to notify anyone, I went directly to the stable and saddled the mare, Jasper being on the road somewhere between Savannah and Charleston carrying Bones Fletcher and, we hoped, leading back some of the Confederate Army. My blood was surging and I was ready to bolt away from the rectory at top speed. The mare hadn't heard Quillery preach, however, so she was still yawning and stretching as I flung the tack on her. Our ride was the first exercise she'd been called on to do for the day. She was a little stiff early on, so I forced my sense of urgency into a harness of its own and walked the beast until she warmed up. It was that slow start that may have saved my life.

As we came up on the Lockwood path that led along the Ashley River and up the west side of the peninsula, I was thinking of urging the animal into a canter when I heard the unmistakable sounds of a killing field—a gunshot, followed by a sharp cry, more gunshots and cheers. There were no trees on this low terrain, but a watch post that was not usually manned in fair weather stood near the point looking over the harbor entrance to the river. I stood in the saddle, looked around and couldn't see where the action was taking place. It had to be behind the guardhouse. The structure was on a little rise and I was below it and probably hidden from view to whoever had made a man cry out, but I knew I had to go forward to render assistance. It was my ministry in life.

Still, I dismounted and moved cautiously. I always remembered everything about the timing of that morning. No more than a minute later more yells and cheers ripped the air, followed by the pounding of hoof beats. A half dozen horses by my quick reckoning, maybe more. I remounted in a hurry, not sure where the horses were heading yet. When I realized they were moving away, uptown, I spurred the mare into a startled run and headed for the guardhouse. As we came around the side of the tall, narrow building, I could see the dust of riders moving up Lockwood, but I was not alone. Uncle Williams was waiting for me.

His tongue was sticking out of the front of his mouth, and his teeth were clamped down on it. His eyes were bulging and the crotch of his pants was stained. I noticed his pants first because they were at eye level to me as I rode up. Uncle Williams was drifting in a circle from a rope looped around his neck and tied off on a beam that jutted out from the top of the guardhouse. The beam normally served as a hoist for the rescue boat stored inside. The old man had been hanged from the block and tackle used to lower the boat.

I knew instantly that his neck was broken. The angle of his head was not possible to duplicate in life. I leaped from the saddle anyway, hoping against hope and too afraid for my friend not to act, and ran for the ladder. I dug out my small pocketknife as I climbed past the swaying body and began sawing at the rope. It was thick and coarse, and I was grunting and praying aloud in a kind of chant of agony as I worked. I was high, above the hanged man, and stretched out to reach the rope.

I could see that he could not have stretched his body enough to reach the ladder with his feet, for he was much shorter than I, but the possibility must have taunted him as he struggled for his life. I thought, and prayed, that the jolt of the hanging had killed him quickly. His lynchers must have thrown him from the lookout platform at the top of the guardhouse. He was hanging too high to have been astride a horse for the lynching.

Finally, the rope parted, and the body of Uncle Williams dropped to the grass below. I climbed down and knelt beside him on one knee, panting and dripping sweat on him. He was warm, but when I tried to move him, his head lolled about and I could see that his neck had indeed been snapped. Blood seeped from two bullet holes in his chest. He was dead.

I gave him the last rites and then sat with my back against the side of the building, trying to recover from the trauma of finding my second murdered acquaintance in two weeks. Uncle Williams had been a kindly person. All he wanted out of life was to survive and do a good turn now and then. I thought of the children of Beulah Mae back in the Devil's Hole, listening to the old man tell ghost stories around a fire at night. Now his eyes stared at nothing. The children might not even recognize this shabby, dirty shell of a man as their friendly relative, but their lives had been diminished by his death. I hoped then, as I whispered a quick prayer to Our Lord, that they never came to realize his final horror, how frightened he must have been when his murderers tied him up and carried him to the parapet like a sack of rotted apples. Had he known beforehand that they were going to pitch him off once they tied the rope around his neck? Dear God, grant him the serenity of ignorance this once.

If only Jasper were available and not off to Savannah with Bones, I might have gotten to the murder scene in time to prevent it. More likely, I suddenly realized with a twinge low in my belly, I would have gotten there in time to join Uncle Williams in the hereafter. The gunshots that followed the hanging could as easily been pumped into me as they were into the victim as a coup de grace. I got to my feet at that thought. Was this lynching associated with the murder in the cathedral? And if so, how? Before I could determine any association, though, I had to deal with the immediate threat. Violence was in the air and Gretchen must be warned.

Minutes later, I clattered to a stop in front the Becknell cottage on Partridge Lane. Still in a turmoil from the lynching, sweating yet and in a state of dishabille, I lurched to the door and pounded on it. Gretchen flung it open, wide-eyed and pale. Her hair had come partly out of the comb that pushed it into a shore wave above her forehead and ran down her neck in golden rivulets. I could not help but see her breasts pushing against the thin cotton of her dress as they rose and fell. One hand held the door, the other touched her mouth. She was barefoot, but I didn't notice that until I was driven closer to her feet a moment later.

"Wha—what are you doing here?"

"I—I've come to warn you, Gretchen."

"Warn me?"

At that, she turned her head to the noise behind her. I looked over her shoulder and saw Gordon Becknell coming to the front door, carrying a pewter cup of ale and snarling. He banged the cup down on a small table in the hallway, slopping the brew over but paying it no mind. His blazing eyes were on me, small but bright under his round bald head. He shoved his wife forward. As I raised my hands to catch her, he struck me in the face. The blow caught me on the cheekbone. It jarred me badly and knocked me to the ground. I felt my face and tried to focus my eyes. I realized at the same time that nothing was broken and that Gretchen's feet were bare. I scrabbled to my feet but had to sit back down. I was dizzy.

Becknell stood with his hands on his hips and legs spread. A snarl disfigured his lips and leaked into his speech. "What in the hell do you want with my wife, papist?"

"Gordon—"

"Hush, woman. I'm talking to him, not you. What you doing, thumping on a married woman's door like that?"

"You hit a priest, Gordon."

Becknell's reddened face underwent a subtle change, enough to notice, though, as the color left it gradually and his brows lifted, widening his pig eyes. I'd been having an enervating day, but God granted me the strength to get to my feet then and the acuity to realize I had to take the opening his expression offered.

If I was not yet mentally capable of exploiting his hesitancy, at least I could stall for time. He was worried suddenly that he might have acted precipitously, or at least he was thinking he might have to worry. Police chief or not, he was in the wrong punching a cleric outside his front door and for no apparent reason.

"I came to warn your wife of imminent danger, Becknell. I can't imagine why you felt you had to attack me."

"Why, I thought you were a danger, crashing in here like you did. What you talking about, anyhow?"

I felt clearheaded enough finally to press my advantage.

"I didn't crash in anywhere. I was standing outside your house when you assaulted me, but we'll deal with that later. Right now I'm talking about a danger your wife faces, and one you should know about if you're doing a proper job as police chief. Reverend Andrew Quillery has accused Gretchen of complicity in the murder of Jamieson Carter."

If Becknell was surprised at my charge, his wife must have been shocked. His eyebrows shot up again, and his mouth opened. Behind him, Gretchen gasped, flung her hands to her face, and doubled over. Her action threw Becknell into further consternation.

"What the hell?"

I found that I could not answer. Gretchen's reaction was so profound that it could mean but one thing. I didn't want to put a name to it. It was clear enough to put paid to my denial, however.

She had trouble breathing, and her husband went to her, patting her back and whispering over and over. "It's okay, girl. It's okay."

It was not okay. This kind and open woman, an admitted partner in an illicit love affair with a married man, now murdered, was also involved in that murder. That was the only analysis possible of her reaction in front of her husband. The tension must have broken something inside her. To hear that she was publicly accused of murder must have been the final tug. Gretchen started coming apart just when she needed most to be strong.

For my part, I didn't know what to think. I did realize that she needed more than anything else just then to be spirited away, hidden until the zeal of some townsfolk cooled, hidden until we could unravel this mystery.

"Take your wife off, Becknell. You can sort out things later, but she needs to be taken somewhere safe. Now."

He mumbled that he knew of a hunting camp along the banks of the Edisto River that was secluded and easy to defend. He turned from me back to her.

"Pack some clothes in a hurry, Gretchen. We probly ain't got much time."

She nodded dumbly and staggered into the house. Becknell stood looking at the door opening, his thick fingers opening and closing along his pant legs. He turned back when I called his name. He stared at me as if he were seeing something dark in his own soul. I knew this couple was in for much more than a hidden weekend in the deep woods. They had some serious explaining to do to each other.

First, though, Chief Gordon Becknell had some explaining to do to me.

CHAPTER 21

ho's responsible for Uncle Williams?"

"Who?"

"Uncle Williams, the old gentleman you and your cohorts chased off to the Devil's Hole."

"Oh, that ol' nigger. Shoot. Nobody chased him off. He just figured life would be a right bit easier out yonder with his own people. He'll be able...er...wanting to come back here anytime. I got enough troubles on my plate without worrying about him just now."

He looked back at the house. Maybe he was expecting to see Gretchen ready to go. All he did see was the empty front hallway.

"Uncle Williams has been hanged, down by the guardhouse at the Lockwood Point."

Becknell turned back to me slowly. His eyes seemed to focus a little at what I'd said, but he showed no outward sign of shock or guilt. None that I could interpret, at any rate.

"That boy's been lynched? Damnation."

He rubbed the stubble on his chin with the palm of his hand. He sighed, and his shoulders drooped some more. He swung his big head back and forth, his chin rolling across his chest.

FULL OF EYES: A REBEL BISHOP MYSTERY 195

"I purely ain't got time to mess with that now, Reverend. How 'bout you get ahold of James Moseley when you get back to town? He can handle it till I get back."

"You don't seem overly perturbed that a man's been killed, by a mob, right in the city."

"I'm...uh...I'm concerned, right enough. I just got other things to take care of right this here minute."

As if on cue, his wife walked out of their home then, a soft-sided cotton bag in one hand and a kerchief wrapped around her head. She moved slowly, as if she had taken laudanum or some other opiate. Her eyes were glassy, unfocused, her mouth slack and the tips of her lower teeth showing. She walked to the corral, and her husband trailed after her. She sat in a small buggy while he rigged it up with some alacrity. Neither looked at me or said a word, not to me or to each other. He climbed in, the rig tilting to one side, and tapped the horse with the reins. They creaked off. Neither looked back, neither said so much as goodbye.

I didn't know exactly what to do. By the time the Becknells were around a bend in the road and out of sight, I realized that I was infected with the same sort of lassitude that had gripped the couple. I forced myself back into the saddle and made for town. I went the long way, skirting around the path that led along the Ashley and past the guardhouse, where the flies were already buzzing and the odd scavenger beast no doubt sniffing around an old man's stiffening corpse.

By the time I located James Moseley, the police officer, and explained to him what had happened to poor Uncle Williams, animation had returned to my body. Moseley stood awkwardly in the station house where I'd found him. He was a trim man dressed in a vest and coarse cotton trousers. His gold badge was pinned to the vest, and he rubbed along the engraved star on it while we talked.

Moseley shifted from foot to foot and looked down at the battered wood floor of the station every so often.

"Tarnation. Another man murdered, you say? I best be over to inform Chief Becknell about this. Thank you kindly for telling me."

"I'm afraid Chief Becknell has left town. His wife has been threatened, and he decided to spirit her away. He told me to tell you that you are in charge now. I think you'd better act as if you've taken over as interim chief, James."

"Whatever for, Father Tom? Ol' Gordon'll have my hide if I try to do his job."

He smiled when he said that, but it was a tentative smile, as if he was hoping that I was joshing somehow.

I lowered my voice when I answered him. "Chief Becknell is implicated somehow in the distressing incident at the cathedral, James. He and his wife have left town, and I expect that he will not be functioning in any official capacity for the foreseeable future."

Moseley gaped at me until he could make some sense of what I'd just said. I don't think he did, not then at any rate. He pursed his lips, thinking, and maybe getting ready to probe for some more information. I hoped he wouldn't ask, because I was not at all sure what more to tell him. He was basically a man of action, so I think he decided the best thing to do was to act, and worry about the meaning of it all later.

He nodded at me and touched his finger to his forehead. "I reckon I'll go off and see to that po' ol' nigger man."

The policeman walked away, and I hurried over to Bishop Lynch and told him what I had discovered. He blessed himself and closed his eyes for a moment. Then he left in a hurry aboard the same mare I had been riding and had left tied outside the chancellery.

"I'm sure you administered the Last Rites, Father Dockery, but I want to see that Uncle Williams's body is properly cared for. We'll make funeral arrangements when I get back."

FULL OF EYES: A REBEL BISHOP MYSTERY 197

Then he was off.

Word of the lynching spread quickly throughout the Negro and Catholic communities. Workday or not, the large cathedral was a good bit more than half full for the Requiem Mass the next morning, Monday. Every service had its own personality. Sometimes the masses said at different times in the same church on a Sunday morning can be entirely distinct from one another, depending on the demographics of the congregation each attracts, the length and solemnity of the liturgy, the time of it and other factors. A good preacher needs to gauge the tenor of his audience and be prepared to alter, maybe subtly, the deliverance of his prepared sermon.

Special occasions, such as funerals, weddings, feast day celebrations and the like can also take on a flavor of their own. Imagine the funeral of a young person killed in tragic circumstances contrasted to a service for an old woman who had been suffering at the end of her life. They would be different to the extreme. Well, the Mass of the Dead for Uncle Williams was different from any funeral I had ever attended.

The personality of the liturgy was not that of a grieving loss. Worshippers spoke in loud whispers to each other in church. No one greeted old relatives or friends they hadn't seen in a while. No one much cried, just a few of the ladies who cry on command and didn't realize that this funeral was different. Bishop Lynch knew immediately that it was different. He felt the same sort of unfocused anger, resentment even, that I could detect rippling through the church. People were not hopping mad, not ready to foment riots or pursue justice. There was not an intolerable grief at the death of Uncle Williams either. He was a good man, I guess, but not a hero to folks here nor a special person. He had been a freedman who never really took advantage of his freedom, the age at which he gained it notwithstanding. He was just a man who survived, hung around the church, not a man possessed of a vibrant personality or an endearing

198   PAUL A. BARRA

way about him. Just a man. That's why, I guess, the anger I felt at my back was diffused. I did not expect trouble over the lynching, but I knew people needed healing. They felt wronged. A human life, however lacking in real value it may have been, had been taken with an almost disrespectful casualness.

When the bishop stood before the coffin, the coffin that had been cobbled together the night before as Uncle Williams's body lay waiting in the tack room of the cathedral stables for it to be finished and lay now on a catafalque covered with a glossy black pall that had been embroidered by the Ladies Guild, he placed one hand on the fabric and surveyed the crowd. His presence and demeanor had quieted them. The quality of his preaching was a form of entertainment to the faithful. Although I would never deign to mention that to His Excellency himself, his parishioners were prepared as always to rate it according to its appropriateness. Sometimes, of course, when the bishop was in high fettle he could, and often did, change the mood of a congregation by the power of his speech making. He could wake up and charge a lazy audience. He could make people think about their very lives when the Spirit took him. He could bring listeners other than the crying ladies to tears with the emotion he could induce.

On the morning of Uncle Williams' funeral, though, with the dull thunder of practice cannonades at the battery in the background reminding us of the imminence of war with our northern kin, Patrick Lynch looked at his people, and he spoke to them. The bishop told them that Uncle Williams had been deprived of life with an apathetic disregard that frightened him.

"He was a Negro, true, and one not worth a large enough price to warrant an auction either in the bad old days. But in God's eyes, this poor man was a human being, the only species of creatures on earth God loves so much that He gave them immortal souls and wills that can act freely. God grieves today, my friends. He grieves over Uncle

FULL OF EYES: A REBEL BISHOP MYSTERY 199

Williams as He grieved over His own son. This man"—he thumped on the box—"was made in the very image of his creator.

"Old Uncle Williams was thrown from the parapet of the Lockwood guardhouse like a worthless sack of old grain. His withered neck snapped like a chicken's. He deserved better. God deserved better. Freedman or slave, Uncle Williams will now get what he deserves, eternal rest in the bosom of his Lord."

The bishop paused, his head high, eyes closed to heaven. Then he startled everyone in the church by beginning to hum. Softly first, then more and more loudly. Like most churchmen, he had a well-trained voice, a tenor that could carry a tune. After I got over the shock of the Bishop of Charleston humming at a funeral mass in the diocesan cathedral, I began to recognize the song. It was a Negro spiritual, The Water is Wide. Other people, the coloreds at first, picked up the hum. When it grew to fill the church the bishop suddenly began to sing in a clear, high voice. People responded with the chorus lines at first. When Bishop Lynch raised his arms, they took over the singing. Negroes had their eyes closed. They swayed and began to clap their hands softly. I could see the strains of emotion even on the pale faces of the few regular churchgoers in the front of the church.

The hymn ended high, leaving the people almost deflated. Their anger had gone, and they grieved for their brother finally.

When the service had ended, people filed past the bishop and me, nodding and occasionally putting out their right hand to him. He shook hands solemnly and quickly, never smiling and never slowing the procession into the clear, cool morning. One man shook his hand firmly enough to cause the bishop to reconsider the face in front of him. He was a tall, lean figure, strong features etched into a craggy face, dressed in an elegant brown frock opened at the front, cream vest showing through. Gray eyes, one dull and the other bright, a thin nose and skin tight across his skull. The bishop smiled and pulled the visitor to him, clapping him on the shoulder. I saw Bones Fletcher standing just behind the stranger, watching the exchange with his mouth slightly open, and I realized that Jefferson Davis, president of the Confederate States of America, was speaking to my bishop.

"That was powerful preaching indeed, Patrick, as good as any I ever heard, even from the Dominicans at school. It moved this flinty heart of mine."

"I'm glad you got here in time for it, Jeff. It does my own heart good to see you again. I'm sorry the circumstances are so dismal. I don't want you thinking ill of this holy city."

"Dismal circumstances are becoming a way of life for me, I'm afraid. Please don't worry. I know that lynch mobs represent a small percentage of southerners and that they pop up, like poisonous weeds, in the best walled gardens."

Bishop Lynch smiled again at his friend. He introduced me as his assistant pastor.

"Tom is also an accomplished detective, Jeff. He it was who uncovered the scheme I called you to attend to. I believe it concerns the very security of the Confederacy."

"I'm happy to make your acquaintance, Father Dockery. Bones here spent much of the journey from Savannah bragging on your capacities. You have made a friend there."

I bowed to Bones, and we all smiled and laughed. Bishop Lynch swept off to the vesting room to get into his clerics. I sent Bones to attend to Jefferson Davis's big gray horse and Jasper. "I'll meet you at the stables in a little while, Bones, and we can settle accounts, as it were."

The young man grinned at that and made his way down the front steps to the hitching rails where the animals were tethered. By this time, people were looking into the cathedral from those steps and

FULL OF EYES: A REBEL BISHOP MYSTERY 201

the street. Someone had surely recognized our visitor, and the word would spread quickly through the city.

"You may have to make a public appearance, Mr. President."

He glanced outside with a quick smile and a nod to the crowd.

"I expect I will, Father. People need reassurances right now. I'm mighty sorry that I am not in a position to give them."

Davis looked pained when he spoke. He had the reputation of being a sensitive leader, one who cared for his people. I knew that as a United States Senator he had opposed secession until the very end, until he felt that there really was no alternative. He was a secessionist leader now, had accepted the mantle thrust upon him by circumstances he could not influence directly, but he was worried about the future of a country divided within. He had studied at West Point and fought in battle with many of the generals who would be commanding the Union forces. He knew that some of them would be killed by his own men, and that all of them would be responsible for the deaths of thousands of loyal American boys and men. Jefferson Davis, Mississippi planter and veteran of the bloody war in Mexico, was afraid for the lives of the people he was expected to lead.

He was also pained physically, I had heard, plagued by a type of nerve disorder that was starting to show up in his one eye, but none of that in any way diminished his presence. The people gathered on the steps of the cathedral had that open-mouthed, awed expression of those in the company of greatness.

The president walked out a few steps to the top landing of the cathedral and raised his hands to the people gathered there. They clapped politely, still too moved by the funeral mass for cheering. He moved back into the interior shadows of the building. Jefferson Davis facing me with his head bowed slightly, as some of those people continued to look in at him. The bishop came back in through the vestry. With a nod to me, Davis left with him.

Twenty minutes later, after I had prayed over the earthly remains of George "Uncle" Williams and had consigned those remains to the light sandy soil of the Negro graveyard behind the cathedral campus, I looked out at the city to marshal my thoughts. Was I implicated in the murder of this poor old man? Was it my investigation that had brought him to ruin? It was probably common knowledge by now that I had visited the Devil's Hole and had been asking for Uncle Williams. Any one of the patrons in that first roadhouse where I had stopped would have answered questions about my visit for the price of a drink of cheap rum.

Had he happened on some information? Was the information he overheard so important that men would kill to keep it secret?

As I gazed overland, pondering these questions, I saw the bishop and the president walking side by side into town, toward the Cooper River and the chandlery business run by Annie Carter. Based on Jefferson Davis's reputation for decisiveness, I thought I might know some of the answers soon enough.

Indeed, before the dinner bell rang that very noon, Charleston was in an uproar. CSA troops, dressed in matching gray and red uniforms, had raided two merchant ships tied to piers outside Carter's Chandlery. Both were nearly full of baled cotton. It was a precision raid, carried out in the predawn darkness before the funeral and done so swiftly that Annie Carter, who was overseeing the loading operation, had not the time to run back to her office to destroy or hide the bills of lading that lay prepared on her father's big desk. It was clear from the paperwork that the cotton had been destined for the North.

Charlestonians of every stripe were in the streets late in the morning, red-faced and wide-eyed over the news of the raid. I heard the word "treason" uttered in hoarse angry whispers, but there was no violence. The only casualty of the whole affair was one sailor who had fallen hard while trying to run away in the dark. Fourteen

FULL OF EYES: A REBEL BISHOP MYSTERY   203

Negroes, six mariners, and Miss Carter were apprehended. The injured sailor, who had fractured his jaw and knocked out three rotted teeth when he crashed into a bollard on the way down, was taken to the army infirmary on State Street. The rest waited in the brig on Sullivan's Island.

Jefferson Davis and Bishop Lynch sailed out to the military jail on a periagua, a sort of enlarged dugout boat that was often rowed or poled in the rivers and along the coasts of Latin America and had been adopted by southern Americans. I went along to record their interrogations of the prisoners, especially that of the oldest daughter of Jamieson Carter. Since the police chief was a suspect and had anyway made no progress in his investigation of the murder of Jamieson Carter, a church official, it had fallen on the bishop, Antoine, and myself to solve the crime. That was why I was chosen to be secretary for this visit, presumably at the behest of the bishop. I didn't ask how he had arranged it. I was just happy enough to be included. It occurred to me that some of the revelations I would record might have a bearing on the murder.

It should have been a pleasant trip over to the island, for the water was calm and the boat quiet. An occasional fish slapped the surface and seabirds drifted by on a mild breeze in sunny skies. Everything smelled clean in the sea air. The men on the boat were quiet, however, since the task that lay before us promised to be anything but pleasant.

The oarsmen tied us up to the military pier, and we walked past palmetto palm battlements to a log building deep in the confines of the fort itself. Anne Carter sat on a scruffy mattress with horsehair drooping from one of its corners. The mattress was on a plank bed raised slightly off the stone floor. I imagined armies of hungry bedbugs moving around the mattress, but in the gloom of the low prison cell, her eyes were all we could see at first. She still wore a sailor's cap over auburn hair that stuck to her face and in her mouth.

She made no attempt to improve her appearance as Davis and Lynch entered the cell. They were backlit. She stared at them blankly. When the jailer placed a candle on the packing crate in front of her, she recognized the bishop and jumped to her feet.

"Your grace."

"Hullo, Annie. How are you feeling, dear? Are you in any pain at all?"

"No. Nossir. It's just a little damp in here, is all."

Lynch removed his cloak and put it around her shoulders gently. She pulled hair out of her mouth.

"Sit down, girl. We mean you no harm."

The jailer left us, and President Davis stayed in the shadows with me and an army officer, but the young woman had no eyes for anyone other than the Bishop of Charleston at any rate. The two of them sat on the old mattress.

"Did Gordon Becknell persuade you into joining him in the scheme to sell that cotton up north, Annie?"

"Oh, good God almighty."

"Yes, dear, I'm afraid we know all about it, so there is no point in discussing that. I do wish to know, however, the background of it all. How did a girl like you, the daughter I baptized some years ago, come to align yourself in business with the likes of our defamed chief of police? It's a perplexing conundrum. Can you enlighten us?"

At first, I thought she wasn't going to answer. Then she sobbed once and began to chew on a knuckle. She talked that way. We had to lean closer to catch all she said.

"He told me it wasn't illegal yet. We weren't actually at war and could still trade with the North. Technically."

The woman looked up with wet eyes and a stricken appearance to her face. I thought she was so distressed at having to acknowledge this iniquity to her bishop that she would burst into tears. She maintained her composure, though and resumed speaking.

FULL OF EYES: A REBEL BISHOP MYSTERY   205

"I surely knew that it was immoral, Excellency. I surely knew that we shouldn't ought to sell our Southern cotton to the enemy. I knew that. I surely did know it."

Annie Carter paused in her confession—for that is what it was, despite the other men standing in the shadows of that brig room. For the young woman, it was her and a priest alone. Some of what she said was not clear to anyone farther away from her than the bishop, yet it was clear that she was confessing her sins and was suffering the pain of remorse. Bishop Lynch, for his part, knew when a confessor needed to probe or cajole. He knew when a confessor could ease the process with sympathy, or with silence. He said nothing, sat perfectly still.

"Daddy hadn't tended to the business as well as he should have the last few months. He wasn't prepared to profit from the war, and he wasn't ready to help the Confederate cause with the kinds of supplies we are going to need. He was preoccupied or something. Maybe he was getting tired. When he was, uh, killed—" She blessed herself when she said that, kissing her thumbnail at the end. "—I had to take over. Momma is ill equipped for business, and the boys are too young yet. I'd been doing Daddy's books for a while now, anyway. I knew we needed some capital quick-like, needed to make some big purchases before war was declared. At the speed the other states was starting to follow South Carolina in cutting loose from the federation, even a fool could tell we had but weeks to get ready. I made a quick decision to go for a pot of gold and, as God himself is my witness, I'm sorry I ever did. I'm so sorry, Father."

I was startled to see Bishop Lynch sketch out a blessing. He was giving her absolution right there in jail! He was not wearing his stole, Annie had not started the confession with the formula required, they were not in private, were not in a confessional box, but the Bishop of Charleston granted absolution to a sinner anyway. When he told Antoine and me about it later, I argued against the form's validity. It was a mockery of the sacrament, I said. It was truly intended, he said, and Annie needed the grace of the sacrament right then.

What about the seal of confession? I asked. Other people had heard at least some of the confession. They could speak of it to other people, in court, for instance, although by the time the case came to court, the fury of full-scale war would probably be upon us and interest in Anne Carter and her indiscretions would be minimal. She tacitly granted a waiver of that right, the bishop said, by making a public confession. Besides, the proof of her thwarted crime was plentiful without her sacramental confession. She never did deny her part in the plan.

"As to the form of confession," he said, "Annie did mumble the introduction and make an Act of Contrition. You may not have realized that."

I did not know that. Even so, Bishop Lynch's cavalier way with the structures imposed by the Church of Rome in this instance was disconcerting to me, especially since he was normally so careful that way. I knew him to be a compassionate and caring priest, obedient to the Holy Father and normally meticulous in attending to the many rubrics of the Church, so I assumed that he knew better than I how to digress under extenuating circumstances and I ended up agreeing with his handling of the Carter girl confession, as we later came to refer to it. Antoine Gagnon, for his part, had no compunction at all in applauding the bishop's actions, even from the beginning. One might expect that sort of daring willingness to depart from official policy from a Jesuit, a Jesuit from a French province, no less.

After granting her forgiveness from her sins, Bishop Lynch asked Annie Carter how she ever came to know Gordon Becknell well enough to pair up in a disreputable scheme that had to be at least unethical, probably immoral and possibly illegal. They hardly traveled in the same social circles, and Becknell was virulently anti-Catholic.

FULL OF EYES: A REBEL BISHOP MYSTERY   207

"I knew his views, Your Excellency, the same way I know he didn't murder my father. I spent many nights in his company."

CHAPTER 22

Although the Most Reverend Patrick N. Lynch was but a middle-aged man, he had been ordained to the priesthood early in life and had, therefore, heard thousands of confessions over the years. He had nearly a decade of the clergyman's experience on me, so I knew that he could no longer be surprised or dismayed to learn the evil things perpetrated in the name of concupiscence, the ways even good people sometimes choose to separate themselves from their creator by sin. He knew, as did I, of young and well-bred women who fell to the temptations of lust. He knew of many who ruined their lives and the reputations of their families with serious transgressions. Still, the two of us had to admit that the thought of sweet Annie Carter fornicating with the likes of Gordon Becknell was a shock to our sensibilities.

Assuming he had mistakenly construed her admission that she had spent the night with him, Bishop Lynch questioned Annie as delicately as he could, always conscious of the other ears listening in the cell. Now that she had blurted out that she could alibi Gordon, he felt that he had to clear up exactly what she meant to say before the gales of gossip destroyed what was left of her good name in Charleston.

FULL OF EYES: A REBEL BISHOP MYSTERY   209

"You were in the company of Chief Becknell the night your dear father was murdered?"

"Yes, Excellency."

"Was this in some official capacity, dear?"

"Not exactly official, but I'd hoped for it to become thus."

"Ah."

"I'm not making sense yet, am I?"

"I'm sure you should be, but I'm being dense, Annie. Treat this conversation as if you were telling your tale to a young child. Make me understand it."

"I'm sorry, sir. Let me tell you just what I did."

"Please."

"I joined the Know Nothing Party about a year ago."

Lynch opened his mouth to express his shock, but when Anne held up a palm with a thin grin, he snapped it closed and nodded for her to continue.

"I realize the Know Nothings are famous for being anti-Catholic, and not particularly amenable to ladies among them even. I wanted the inside information about that. I wanted to know why some people are opposed to whole groups of people, most they don't even know, haven't even met. I wanted to find out why the Know Nothings dislike immigrants so much, especially the Irish.

"Carter sounds English enough, so most people who don't know my family assume that I am not Catholic but Anglican or Presbyterian. You'd think there were no Catholics left in Britain, for heaven's sake. Anyway, at school—I went to William and Mary. Did you know that, Bishop Lynch?"

"Yes, I think I did. Please continue."

"A classmate of mine at school sort of recruited me into a kind of feminine auxiliary of the Know Nothings. She is not a Charlestonian, rather a Savannah girl, not an intellectual giant either. As I said, I was interested in exploring the motivations behind

210   PAUL A. BARRA

nativism, so I let myself become one of them. We met in Washington a few times and once or twice in some Virginia towns. The men ran the meetings and we served refreshments and then sat on the edges. Frankly, the meetings were boring. Especially at first. When the war talk started, things got a little more exciting, but none of the groups seemed to be up to much besides talk. Over Easter last year, I invited my friend, Celia, to visit on her way home. We went to a Know Nothing meeting here. I thought the jig would be up once I was recognized. They were pathetically eager, however, to further their cause and welcomed me, like I was a convert or something. This group was more, er, animated, if you will. They drank some whiskey, although not when the women were in attendance of course. They are Southerners, even if they may not qualify as gentlemen exactly. So, it was exciting. Sort of like a sorority prank or something. Nothing much came of it, although I did meet Gordon Becknell at the meeting. I was polite to him because he is the chief of police.

"I sort of still belong to the party now, a year later, although I am not active. Gordon looked me up shortly before my pater's funeral last week. The week before that he had made a proposal, in outline, and had the idea that I could try to talk daddy into trying it. My father was uninterested in trying anything with enthusiasm by then, at least as far as the business went. I think I told you that. So I didn't act on Gordon's idea at the time, but we did meet once to flesh out the details. That meeting was on the night my father was killed. We had met at a Know Nothing meeting, like I said, so he felt he could approach me as a sort of friend, I guess. Anyway, he said he had some business that might help the store and now that I was going to be in charge of making it go again. His scheme sounded good at the time. I realize, of course, that his...er...enthusiastic membership in a nativist group should have disqualified him as a partner in any kind of business arrangement. To say nothing of social. I knew pretty well his feeling about my own faith, and I recognized the petty nature of

FULL OF EYES: A REBEL BISHOP MYSTERY 211

his mind, but he is the chief of police, and I thought that his position might assist us in pulling off this plan. We stood to make a small fortune, you know. Then father died, and I didn't go back to college. The plan suddenly sounded better, and I pressed Gordon for further details. I decided to go along with it."

Lynch nodded at that.

"So the two of you were at a meeting of the Know Nothings when your father was killed? Is that what you're telling me?"

"Actually, we were at the store, the chandlery, going over the basics of the plan. We had to pre-sell the cotton, get an invoice and bill of lading together in order to get past the Union ships outside the harbor. He was taking care of all that. I was not actually committed to the plan. After I truly realized quite suddenly one night that Daddy was no longer around to make decisions and that the job of keeping Carter Chandlery alive was suddenly all on my shoulders, my resistance kind of weakened. Up until then, my mind had accepted his death and my new responsibilities, but my heart must not have done so. Deep inside I must have been refusing to believe the truth that was staring me in the face. True acceptance came all at once. And it was, er, breathtaking. So, I was sort of numb when Gordon and I finalized the deal."

She paused for a moment and passed her hand over her eyes. I thought she might be fighting tears, but the bishop sat silently. Annie Carter continued. "But the night of my daddy's death, we were setting up the paperwork we needed if I decided to go along with it. I was worried even then about my father's preoccupation and the business, so I may not have been as sharp as I could have been, but I'm afraid I do remember quite clearly that Gordon was either in my company or in my sight until well after midnight. We often worked at night on the...er...project, to keep from prying eyes. The night my daddy was killed, we were talking about how we could make the final purchases of the cotton from merchants and the sales contracts. I can

212 PAUL A. BARRA

prove all that with dated papers and the like, because we drew some up, the ones that would look like legitimate purchases."

The young woman paused, her face drawing closed again.

"Now those same trails of paper will be enough to exonerate Gordon Becknell of murder, and enough to convict me of treasonous activities."

Annie Carter's last words were spoken so softly that we had to again lean toward her to hear her. Her eyes reddened, and two fat tears bubbled over her lids and rolled down the freckles on her cheeks like wax beads across a map of sea islands. One minute she was an exuberant college girl telling of a slightly naughty adventure, the next she was burdened with the cares of maturity and facing the ramifications of her human weakness.

She made no move to wipe the tears away, neither sobbed nor snuffled, just sat and wept silently. Lynch patted her on the shoulder and got to his feet. Jefferson Davis followed him out into the open air, leaving Annie Carter sitting with her back bowed in a cell of the military prison. She looked alone and fragile in a dark and forbidding place, I thought. She was still wearing the bishop's frock about her shoulders.

The two men stood for a minute breathing in the salt air, glad to be out of the dark, dank cell. Lynch knew full well the cause of Jamieson Carter's "preoccupation," of course, but he could say nothing to his friend. Davis was president of the Confederacy and could presumably have helped Annie Carter had he known of her father's liaison with Gretchen Becknell, but the bishop could no more break a confidence to tell him than he could to tell the murdered man's daughter.

"I must admit that I sympathize with the child, Mr. President."

"Aye. Be hard not to, wouldn't it? She's in for a rough time, regardless of whether or not she's prosecuted for their scheme. But I anticipate a long war, Patrick, much as it grieves me to say it, and

FULL OF EYES: A REBEL BISHOP MYSTERY   213

she'll have ample opportunity to make amends. Perhaps she'll turn out to be a great patriot, after all."

Bishop Lynch smiled his thanks and the two men strolled out to the ramparts and gazed across the shipping channel to Morris Island. I followed at a distance, giving them ample room to talk as old friends. Looking out to sea, Jefferson Davis said, "Key now is to catch up Gordon Becknell. See if he will corroborate Annie's story. I know this whole episode does nothing but complicate your search for the murderer of Jamieson Carter, but it has been a coup for the Confederate Army."

"True enough," replied the bishop of Charleston. "The cotton must be worth a lot of money and the publicity will no doubt raise the enthusiasm for the Confederacy to even greater heights. As far as the murder in the cathedral goes, Becknell could still have planned the death of Jamieson and had somebody carry it out in his name. And it is probably just possible that he could have done the deed after leaving the company of young Annie. I'll be anxious to talk to him once you get him."

Getting the fugitive chief of police was no easy matter, however. Davis sent a contingent of soldiers out to the Edisto. They located the river camp without too much trouble, but neither Becknell was to be found. The men did find signs of recent habitation in the crude cabin, but the fire remains in the chimney were cold. Clumps of horse manure in the barked sapling corral were still moist, if cool also. They turned the dogs loose but were prepared for a long search in the wilds of Colleton County.

The governor of South Carolina, meanwhile, had traveled to Charleston from Columbia to visit with the CSA President. Many other state leaders assembled with Governor F. W. Pickens in the council chambers at city hall. Jefferson Davis was a soldier first and foremost, so he had military strategies to develop in the border states as soon as they too left the Union. According to what the president told the bishop, Lincoln's demand for conscripts from each state—the infamous proclamation demanding 75,000 militiamen—was anathema to the South. Virginia, North Carolina, Arkansas, Kentucky, Missouri, and Tennessee had refused to honor Lincoln's proclamation. Virginia had already seceded, and Davis was going to begin his military campaign there, in the same northern locale made famous by John Brown, Harper's Ferry. He was known as Osawatomie Brown for an uprising he had staged in the Kansas Territory the year before, trying to keep that western state from legalizing slavery. John Brown had then fomented a slave revolt at the federal arsenal in Harper's Ferry in the fall of 1859. It was put down by Robert E. Lee, ironically, as it turned out, then a colonel in the federalist forces, and John Brown was hanged for his crimes against peace in December.

The federalists had not yet been reduced to singing about his exploits as if he were a hero rather than a rabble rouser, but Jefferson Davis had a war to plan, and John Brown's body was incidental to that planning. He scarcely gave a thought to him, but he did have to journey up to the place he made famous. And he had to do it soon, for thunderheads of war were drifting ever closer. So Davis agreed to address a joint meeting of state and local politicians before leaving South Carolina. He felt he owed it to them, he told Bishop Lynch, to be truthful about the immediate future.

That night, the city council chambers were full to bursting. The sergeant-at-arms had thrown open the windows in the second story room and Antoine and I were crammed into a nook that caught at least some of the breeze. I wasn't complaining about the tight quarters, though. I felt fortunate to have gained entrance at all. Father Gagnon acted as if it was no more, no less, than his just due to be present at the historic occasion. He managed somehow to appear patrician even with scores of people jammed under and around his slightly raised nose.

President Davis, wearing the same clothes he wore at Uncle Williams's funeral, stood as Governor Pickens introduced him. Everyone else in the council room got to his feet at the same time, clapping and cheering so loudly that I could feel the floor tremble beneath my soles. The wildness lasted. The president bowed. The people raised the level of tumult. He raised his arms. The frenzy escalated yet again. Finally, Jefferson Davis assumed the classic orator's stance, and the crowd grudgingly permitted him to speak.

He spoke in formal tones, a flowery kind of language that seemed odd to me but was perfectly acceptable to the politicians gathered to hear him. Maybe that was how they all spoke on official occasions. Three reporters, one of whom I recognized as the senior man for Robert Barnwell Rhett's *Charleston Mercury*, were scribbling furiously as the president spoke.

Flowery or not, Davis wasted no time appealing to the patriotism of the assemblage or inflating their sense of adventure. He said at the beginning that the war between the states was going to be long and bloody.

The people that night were somewhat disappointed, although some I heard afterward were chastened and sobered by Davis's dire warnings. His concerns were destined to be warranted in the years to come. Not only were we outnumbered better than two to one, but a third of our nine million inhabitants were slaves. Davis said that we could not count on them to fight with their masters.

Industry gave the north another great advantage. Pennsylvania alone made twice as many goods as all of the Confederate states. The South did have a unity of purpose, what the president referred to as "one purpose of high resolve."

He spoke about the newly signed Confederate Constitution, recently written in Montgomery, Alabama, as the document that the

Southerners who wrote the original constitution had intended back in 1776.

"In our preamble, we seek the favor and guidance of Almighty God," Davis said. "We will need the God of our fathers to guide and protect us in our efforts to perpetuate the principles which by his blessing they were able to vindicate, establish and transmit to their posterity. With the continuance of his favor, ever gratefully acknowledged, we may hopefully look forward to success, to peace, and to prosperity."

As we left City Hall, Davis confided in my bishop his great concerns over the impending war. He was an accomplished military man, and he knew full well the superiority the Unionists enjoyed.

"I see many troubles and thorns, Patrick. We have little machinery to wage war, little money to buy any and, I fear, other countries will not want to risk the disfavor of Washington by assisting our effort. The going will be difficult."

"Please let me know what I can do to help, Jeff. I am but a simple churchman, but perhaps there is something..."

Davis smiled at his friend. "You are a good bishop, and the Confederacy may have need of your talents one day. For now, I think, it will be well for you to tend to your flock, keep their spirits up. Your sisters have already begun sewing for the troops. We will probably need them for hospital work also. Can you see that they are trained?"

"Consider it done. Now, what will you do to keep your spirits up?"

"There's nothing like the tonic of work. I'm off to Virginia to set up a capitol and some battle lines. I won't have time to become despondent. My only prayer is that the federalists will leave us in peace, but I'm afraid the time may have passed for that."

Jefferson Davis rode off on his beautiful gray, a fine figure in the saddle, back straight and his slender body moving easily with the rhythm of the horse. We hated to see him go, especially since he

FULL OF EYES: A REBEL BISHOP MYSTERY   217

took the troop with him before they had located the whereabouts of Gordon and Gretchen Becknell. Finding the Becknells seemed more urgent than ever.

We walked back to the bishop's home and found the front door locked again. Mrs. Ryan answered my knock, and Bishop Lynch addressed her once we entered the foyer.

"You and Flora run this house the way you see fit, Mrs. Ryan, and you have been doing an admirable job of it. I have no complaints whatsoever. I do have a question, however."

The old housekeeper looked quizzically at her employer. The lines that ran down from her eyes and mouth seemed to me to be stretched, and she was paler than usual.

When the bishop posed his question, she flushed.

"Why ever have you suddenly taken to locking the front door of the house? We never did it before."

Even though Bishop Lynch spoke gently, Mrs. Ryan stammered and pulled her apron up to wipe her face.

"I'm afraid to tell you, Excellency," the woman said in her thick brogue. "It don't seem proper, this being a part of the Church and all."

The bishop and I exchanged a quick glance. I had no idea what Mrs. Ryan was referring to, and neither did the bishop, apparently. He said to her, "Fear not, dear. Tell me what's bothering you."

"It's that nun."

"A nun? From the convent across the street? Which one, and what has she done?"

"I don't know her name, your Excellency. It's not one of the wee ones we usually see at mass, but a big creature. Her face looks like thunder. She been prowling around the house here, scaring the Devil out of me with her looks. I'm afraid she might come inside. I don't know how I'd handle her."

218 PAUL A. BARRA

"Well, don't worry yourself anymore about her, Mrs. Ryan. Father Dockery here will visit the convent and find out who the woman is and what she's doing in the vicinity of this house."

It was Monday, April 23, 1861, nearly two weeks since the barrage on Fort Sumter.

I knew I'd have to settle this question of the lurking nun quickly, for I had a murderer to find before the War Between the States took over our lives.

That thought stopped me for a minute. I was in a hurry to get back to the murder in the cathedral, yet the business of the nun skulking around the chancery could be important in its own right.

"Bishop Lynch."

"Tom?"

"Do you think I'm becoming obsessed with the murder of Jamieson? I seem to be thinking about it all the time, and I always ask myself if any bit of information I learn could somehow be connected to it."

"I hardly think of it as an obsession. The murder is on my mind also. We are fairly certain, are we not, that the police have decided not to investigate further? If they did at all? It seems as if the investigating may be up to us alone. You are the one among us most equipped to carry out such an investigation."

"That's what worries me, the sin of pride."

"Pride? Is this a confession, Tom?"

The bishop smiled when he said the last. It was a tentative smile, though, as if he wasn't sure if his question could actually be serious. I smiled back at him, reassuringly, I hoped.

"No, not a confession, Excellency. I just feel confused in my mind."

"In that case, let me reassure you. The murder in the cathedral will go unsolved if you and I, and Antoine, don't dig deeply and try to find out what happened. Even more, Tom, if we don't do it

FULL OF EYES: A REBEL BISHOP MYSTERY 219

quickly, the coming war may overtake us, and we may never find out who killed Jamieson Carter. We owe it to his memory, for all the time and energy he poured into our church community."

That was true enough. I knew from my experiences in uniform in New York that police departments were rarely interested in major investigations. Their main role was to protect the citizenry, so that once a crime was committed, the policeman's work was over. If anyone was going to find the murderer, it would have to be us. I had to keep my mind focused on the crime.

The bishop's words reassured me, and I left him with a short bow of appreciation. I hurried across to the convent, hoping to settle the issue of the nun who had decided to sneak around the chancery—and hoping to do it quickly.

CHAPTER 23

She was dressed in black and was too busy with the slaughter to notice me at first. Sister Bernadette Miller had a small white chicken in each hand. She lifted them gently by the heads and then suddenly twisted her wrists and the birds' necks. The birds spun in a circle and then drooped from the nun's hands, dead. They didn't squawk, but I fancied I'd heard neck bones crack. There was no blood. It looked quick, efficient and painless. She flipped the chickens into a sack that lay near her feet bulging with maybe a half dozen other carcasses. She rose up to look for more. That's when she saw me watching her from the outside of the pen. Her ruddy face cracked into a huge grin beneath the white veil of her order, the Sisters of Charity of Our Lady of Mercy.

The OLMs, as we all called them, were the original congregation of women religious of the diocese, founded by no less a personage than Bishop John England himself. They taught and tended sick people and performed what we referred to as corporal works of mercy, things such as feeding the poor and delivering clean clothes they had begged from businesses to the worst of the Negro shanties on the peninsula. They were teachers and nurses and social workers. The nuns had migrated to work other parts of the state as well as Charleston. Their unstinting efforts were appreciated wherever they

FULL OF EYES: A REBEL BISHOP MYSTERY 221

went. Their reputation was so sterling, in fact, that the general public had lionized the order. Even the press had written in grudging praise of their charity and humility, and the papers other than our own United States Catholic Miscellany were not particular friends of the Church.

The OLMs were human beings, though, and no more exempt from the jealousies and politics that afflict most of us than any group of basically good people. They engaged in turf battles with other orders now and then, but, generally, the sisters were so busy and so involved with God's work that they had scarce time for pettiness in their lives.

So I felt confident going to them for assistance. Sister Bernadette's smile encouraged me further.

"Good day to you, Father. Welcome."

The OLM convent was across the street from the cathedral on Friend Street, so close that many of the nuns came to daily mass in the lower church. Occasionally, a priest would enter the convent to give the last rites or to bring communion to an ailing member, but since the order was young, we didn't often need to visit.

I raised my biretta to her and bowed.

"Hello, sister. Please don't let me interrupt your work."

"Nothing to it, Father. I've killed enough birds for dinner already. Who is it you wanted to see? I'll take you on my way to the refectory."

"Actually, I came to see you."

I walked with Sister Bernadette across the yard and into the thick stone main building of the motherhouse. We chatted until she began dunking the birds in scalding water on the big black stove in the convent kitchen and plucking them. Then I talked business. Bernadette was the superior general of the congregation, but she drew kitchen duty along with everyone else and seemed not to mind the work. She did mind the news I broke to her as I brought her up to date on goings-on since the Carter murder. She prayed aloud for Annie Carter and for the state of South Carolina. Her complexion reddened even more than usual as I told her about Jamieson's affair with Gretchen Becknell as delicately as I could. The nun busied herself bleeding the chickens into a pot—saving the blood for the pigs, she said—and eviscerating them. She cleaned the gizzards and removed the livers. The smell of blood and offal seemed to make the telling of the war news easier somehow. She recognized my discomfort too, the way people who spend their lives helping others were wont to do, and encouraged me with little exclamations and a question whenever I faltered.

Finally, Sister Bernadette was up to date. I was relieved.

"These are terrible burdens you've had to bear, Father Dockery. I'm glad you told me, so we can share them some. Now then, how much must I bear in silence, do you think?"

"None but the most obvious, Sister. I'm sure that your own sisters will be full of the story of Annie Carter and her cotton when they return for dinner at noon. And war news, of course, will be everywhere after last night's meeting at city hall."

"So, we can discuss all you've told me then, excepting, of course, poor Jamieson's...er...liaison with the Becknell woman. What about Reverend Quillery's involvement?"

"Common knowledge, or soon will be. Not only has he gone public himself, but I was hoping to enlist your support in my investigation. Your sisters are all over town every day. Someone may have heard or may yet hear something that could help me. I find a lot of holes in all my theories. Plus, we desperately need to find the Becknells."

"We will be happy to help. I'll quiz them all this very day and assign them the secondary duties of listening and asking, where appropriate, of course."

"Of course."

FULL OF EYES: A REBEL BISHOP MYSTERY   223

"Now, may I ask you a question?"

"Please."

"Will you stay for the noon meal and help us eat these tender chickens, since you didn't help clean them?"

She laughed out loud at that, and at my obvious embarrassment. It never occurred to me to offer to help in the kitchen. Had the tables been turned, had I been at labor while she talked to me, the nun would have been up to her elbows in the task without hesitation. She wiped her hands after patting the birds into a baking pan and said she was only fooling.

But she had let me know in a friendly way that we were all equal in the sight of God, not only white and brown but male and female too.

I felt heat on my ears and the kind of shrinkage of the lungs that afflicts us when we know we've made an obvious and stupid blunder.

I swore to myself that I had learned the lesson well that day, that I would at least offer to help someone else at his or her work if I was visiting when the work was being performed. The basic function of priests is to serve the faithful, even if that entails getting down into a dirty job with them.

Would I have offered to help if the work had been a man's job instead of kitchen labor? No ordinary man of my generation would consider for an instant doing the work of a woman, but then, I was not an ordinary man, was I?

I was a priest, consecrated to service. Sister Bernadette was probably not more than a few years older than I but seemed much the wiser in the ways of human relationships.

"I should have helped. It's unforgivable that I stood around watching when I could have been helping. I'm sorry, sister."

"Think nothing of it, Father Dockery. Had you helped, it would have been the first time a man touched food in this convent except to

224 PAUL A. BARRA

consume it, and that not very often either. Please, I was only having a bit of fun at your expense. But you will stay to dinner, won't you?"

"No, I'm afraid the bishop is expecting me. In fact, sister, he is expecting me to tell him whether you will assist the Confederacy in the war effort."

That stopped her. She was chopping parsley without lifting the French knife from the block and paused with it poised on its tip.

"The Sisters of Charity of Our Lady of Mercy are committed to peace, Father. I don't know what sort of assistance the bishop hopes for, but we can hardly engage in the coming war, can we?"

"Of course not. I'm being obtuse again, I'm afraid. President Jefferson Davis asked Bishop Lynch to recruit the OLMs as a nursing corps and to set up field hospitals. I fear he thinks the need will be great."

"Yes. How awful. We would have done that without asking, but I reckon you are thinking of advance planning. One of the things we do is nurse the sick or wounded. I'm sure President Davis knows that some of us are nurses already. We should be able to set up a training program of some sort. It needs be done immediately, I presume?"

"Yes, Sister, I'm afraid so."

"Well," she said, resuming her rocking chopping, "you've certainly given me enough to talk about at dinner today. The girls will be energized."

"Another good reason for me to leave before they return from their labors. As usual, the diocese is indebted to your order, Sister Bernadette."

"As usual, you have only to ask, Father Dockery."

I smiled and nodded to her. She grinned back and patted me on the back as I took my leave. It was the same motion she had used plumping the chickens in the baking dishes.

As she walked me to the door, I pondered how to question Sister Bernadette about the sister who had been worrying Mrs. Ryan

FULL OF EYES: A REBEL BISHOP MYSTERY 225

with her odd behavior. It was a delicate question to pose to the head of a good-hearted order, wondering about the behavior of one of her sisters. Before I formed a question, however, we heard loud footsteps stomping down the hardwood floor of the entrance hall. Sister Bernadette stiffened. I turned to see who would provoke such a response in the kindly nun and saw another figure in black heading for us like a man-of-war under full sail. She was a large woman, her face set in a frown and her red, beefy hands clenching and unclenching as she strode toward us.

"Who might this be, Sister Bernadette?" Her voice was loud and aggressive

"Why allow me to introduce Father Dockery, Bishop Lynch's aide. Father, this is Sister Mary Lucille."

I smiled at the big nun, but before I could say a greeting she fairly growled at me. "The bishop's right hand man? Are you another one who favors the Ursulines in Columbia over your own diocesan order?"

"I—I beg your pardon?"

"The Ursuline Order, Father. Surely you know who the Ursulines are?"

"Yes, of course, but—"

"The congregation where Bishop Lynch's sister is the mother superior, and where he sends all his money instead of giving any to us?"

She clamped her mouth shut and stood glaring at me with her brows arched and hands on her hips. Her head jutted forward, looking for all the world like a 300-pound alligator snapping turtle, the most fearsome predator of our fresh-water creeks and ponds.

"I know the Ursulines, certainly, Sister. And I know the bishop's sisters, Sister Bautista and Sister Laura—"

"Then you presumably know that he extends his largess to them at our expense."

"No, I don't know that at all. He is generous with his kin as he is to all—"

"Not to us. We have to scrimp and make do while those women live well."

Sister Bernadette, whose face had lost its color and who stood with her hands over her face, suddenly thrust herself forward. Spots of red bloomed in her cheeks. "Really, Sister! That will be quite enough."

Sister Mary Lucille puffed up her formidable chest at the interruption, her eyes large and wild.

"I know about it, Mother. I know things you don't know."

The big nun took on a look of triumphalism, as if she were a child who had found out something she was not supposed to know. I realized as I looked at her glowing face that she was not right somehow. She didn't appear to be much older than fifty, but she had the look of senility about her. Maybe worse. Maybe she was quite mad, I thought.

"Well, suppose you just tell us what it is you supposedly know, Sister Mary Lucille," Bernadette said in an icy tone.

The mother superior was angered. Perhaps if she hadn't been, things would have turned out differently, and I would never have had cause to think the unthinkable—that a woman religious had the capacity for violence. But Sister Bernadette's waspish tone released the passions building in the brain of the older nun. Her face took on a high color, and the blood vessels in her neck threatened to burst. Her voice was a screech.

"I will indeed tell you what I know. I know that Bishop Lynch is sending money to the Ursulines in Columbia and that he was using that unholy creature Jamieson Carter to hide his crime."

"Crime?"

"Oh, indeed, Father Dockery. For the money that is making the convent in Columbia a veritable house of luxury is church money.

FULL OF EYES: A REBEL BISHOP MYSTERY   227

Money that the good people of Charleston donate to the cathedral parish is being spent on His Excellency's relatives. To sustain them in the manner to which they had become accustomed in his father's house."

Sister Mary Lucille was ranting. Her eyes bulged dramatically, and her clenched fists were pumping up and down in her agitation.

"That vile businessman Jamieson Carter was using his businesses to get the money to them without anyone knowing. I know because I confronted him with his shenanigans, after I discovered him with an evil yellow-haired temptress he had no grace to resist."

Sister Bernadette and I stared haplessly at the frenzied nun. She was not yet finished with her ravings.

"Why do ye think his head was crushed, then? He had to pay for his sins. He had to pay for thieving from God's church. And, God rest his soul, he had to pay for his disgusting sins of the flesh!"

Sister Mary Lucille fairly bellowed the last sentences. Then, giving us one more look of total triumph, she stormed down the hall, a monstrous black ship leaving nothing but debris in her wake. She threw open a door and was gone.

Her mother superior looked as if she might cry in the sudden silence that followed her departure. It was as if the air had been sucked out of the hall behind the marauding nun.

"God knows, I'm sorry, Sister."

"No, no." Sister Bernadette swallowed hard. "You've nothing to be sorry for, Father. It's my fault. We've known for months now that the poor dear had become...er...unbalanced, as it were. She's not been right for a while, and we haven't done anything about it. We've assigned her to duties in the house, of course, but she disappears at odd times, and we have lost control. Sometimes she is not in her cell when we waken for morning prayer."

"Can you not hospitalize her?"

"How can we? Her mind is sick, but her constitution is as strong as a horse. The hospital can do nothing for her."

"Perhaps you had better keep someone watching her."

"Yes. We've talked about a rotating schedule, with someone always assigned to keep an eye on her. To see that she doesn't cause mischief and to explain when she does embarrass herself. And us."

"Well, then. That's probably the best you can do. Watch her and pray for her."

"Aye, Father, it probably is. I just hope we've not left it too late."

"I haven't heard any of her exploits in town, and I surely would. Her habit marks her as a member of the Roman church and, I can assure you, there are many here who do not hesitate to inform us immediately when there is a complaint about us. She has frightened the bishop's housekeeper by wandering about at odd hours, as you say, but we've heard nothing from Charleston proper."

"I was not thinking about her rantings, actually. I pray to Jesus, Mary, and Joseph that her imbalance has not caused her to harm anything or anyone that we may not know of yet."

I left the convent on that foreboding note, wondering if the big nun with the big hands could be capable of violence, after all. Was her insanity advanced enough so that she actually believed that Jamieson was an agent of the Devil? How had she known about Jamieson and Gretchen Becknell, and what damage might she have done on one of her nightly forays? It was not a clear suspicion in my mind, but judging by the spiteful manner in which she spoke of Bishop Lynch, I felt it my obligation to advise him of the episode which had so disturbed Sister Bernadette. He needed to be warned.

CHAPTER 24

Antoine was waiting for me in the rear yard of the chancery. The lower floor of the episcopal residence to the back doubled as the chancery of the Diocese of Charleston.

Our administrative tasks were so slight—we had less than a dozen priests in the entire state—that we had no need for a separate building for diocesan work. One room served as an office and storage space. The Jesuit was pacing the shade of the hardwoods there.

"Thomas, where have you been?"

"I'm sorry I didn't know you were waiting for me, Tony. I had some few duties to perform."

"Well, never mind. Come along then, we have an important matter to discuss."

"First, I must see Bishop Lynch about a pressing matter."

"I'm afraid the good prelate took himself off to a communion breakfast at the Hibernian Hall and has not returned. What is it you're so frantic to see him about?"

I told Antoine about the episode with Sister Mary Lucille. It seemed even more bizarre and threatening in the telling. He looked quizzically down his nose at me when I finished the tale.

"You think her capable of braining poor Jamieson, then?"

230   PAUL A. BARRA

"Well, Tony. I hadn't put it into words like that before. I can scarcely believe that a woman of God could have the capacity to do such a thing."

"Ah, but righteous anger, man. Many an evil deed has been perpetrated under the thrall of righteous anger."

"Perhaps you're right."

"If I am, God forbid, then we must speak to the bishop immediately when we next see him. But I agree it's long odds that she had anything to do with our little murder. Meanwhile, I have something else to occupy your mind."

He took me by the elbow, and we were soon strolling down Queen Street in deep conversation. The sky had clouded up, concentrating the smell of jasmine and dogwood, and it was pleasant walking. Not so pleasant was the news my brother priest had for me.

"Reverend Quillery is at it again, I'm afraid. Yesterday he as much as accused the Catholic church of causing the murder of Jamieson Carter."

"What on earth did he say?"

"He ranted and raved during one of his public preaching episodes. He's gone 'round the bend, you know, Thomas, really wild-eyed and crazed and rambling. I declare that people would boycott the talks except that he always manages to pique our interest with some tidbit of news or some accusation or..."

"Our interest? Do you mean that you attend these sermons?"

"Of course. How else would I keep abreast? Know thine enemy, you know. My contacts offer only second hand information and, as useful as that has proven to be on occasion, nothing can substitute for a primary source. Vigilant observance can yield much more than mere facts. Yesterday, for instance, when he was on the verge of losing his crowd because he had fumed and fussed to the point of irrationality— I mean, even the Negroes were starting to fidget and look bored. How much of that Bible thumping can one take? How

FULL OF EYES: A REBEL BISHOP MYSTERY 231

many thous and sayeths can one assimilate before it all starts to sound like a foreign tongue? Quillery seemed to take stock of the situation suddenly. It happened precisely when he caught the eye of Peter Fletcher. The lawyer, you know him?"

I nodded, remembering Fletcher as a good source of information, civil enough, if I didn't exactly trust him. He was not the kind of man I would offer confidences to, but he had been helpful in a peripheral way after we discovered Carter's body in the cathedral.

"Well, Fletcher motioned to Quillery, and the preacher suddenly broke out in a clear voice. He said that the murder of a prominent Charlestonian would never have occurred had he stayed away from a foreign church. The man's attachment to papist temptations, Quillery intoned, were his downfall."

Antoine had assumed the tenor of the preacher's voice as well as his manner of speaking. The mimicry was so accurate I couldn't help but smile at it. But such an accusation was nothing to smile at, so my humor was short-lived.

"Whatever could he have been talking about?"

"'Tis a mystery, Thomas. He smiled, no smirked, directly at me when he said it, so I believe he was tossing us a bit of cornbread, giving us a clue that he is sure we won't be able to decipher. His cockiness is vexing, but it may be his ultimate downfall."

"Yes, indeed. If only we had some idea what the clue meant. Jamieson was killed because he was a Catholic?"

"I must admit to having no earthly idea either. We'll have time to hash it around, though."

"How's that, Tony?"

"Antoine, please. Try to get in the habit of referring to me by my formal given name in public. Someone might overhear us as we walk."

"I certainly hope not."

"Anyway, one of my friends caught an exchange between Fletcher and Quillery as the sermon crowd was breaking up. She heard the lawyer—"

"She? You mean you employ females as spies too?"

"Whyever not, m'boy? Come, come now, it makes perfect sense. Many a man will speak freely in front of women, just as they might before slaves. Assuming they won't be understood even if heard, I imagine. It's pure stupidity, I agree, but it happens, and I see no reason not to take advantage of it. Here is what the woman caught. Fletcher and Quillery agreed to meet at five o'clock. It was all very side of the mouth and surreptitious, if you know what I mean. I'm intrigued enough to want to find out more, aren't you?"

"Indeed. How could we do that?"

"We lie in wait and follow them."

After getting over my shock at the mere suggestion of such unseemly conduct from two men of the cloth, I argued and lost. Antoine Gagnon could convince a bay netter to buy shrimp, I swear.

So that was how we came to be waiting in the shadows down the block from Quillery's townhouse later that day. We were dressed as common working men, in cotton blouses none too clean looking—although they didn't smell bad—and denim pants. We both wore caps and had darkened our faces with soot. He had provided the clothes, from one of his inexhaustible sources, while I had thought of the head paraphernalia and facial camouflage. I knew from my years on stakeouts with the police department that people didn't suspect dirty, tired workers to be threats and that the uniforms of cops had become so identified with their function that street clothes were the perfect disguises. The same should be true of clergymen, I supposed.

Of course, I had no way of explaining to anyone else why we were disguised as common laborers. Our best, nay only, defense was that

FULL OF EYES: A REBEL BISHOP MYSTERY 233

no one would ever recognize us from any distance. Especially not Quillery or Fletcher.

We waited in nervous silence, keeping our heads bowed as if in weariness and humility, slouching against the smooth bole of a leafing out crepe myrtle tree. Time passed. Insects droned. I think Father Gagnon may have nodded off by the time I finally espied the two suspects dart out the side door of the Quillery home. I elbowed my colleague and started off after them. They were moving fast and managed a block lead by the time Gagnon caught up to me, puffing slightly.

"My, are they ever in a hurry."

"This works well for us, though, Tony. They will never imagine that we are following them, even if they happened to see us from this far back."

"As long as we don't lose them."

"Amen."

We didn't, as it turned out, although we had a breathtaking chase that alternated between playing at our weary roles and racing to catch sight of our quarry. Finally, we paused under a spreading mimosa, hearts tripping, and watched Quillery and the lawyer enter the train station at Morrison, part of the South Carolina Canal and Railroad Company. By 1861, rail service was available all the way to the Georgia border at North Augusta on the main line, and to Camden on a secondary line. I hoped the two we were following weren't planning on a long trip by rail.

We'd scarcely had time to catch our breath, when minutes later the two, escorted by a large, well-dressed Negro, walked out on the main platform and down a set of steps at the end of it. They crossed two rows of tracks and boarded a tender car on a small spur line off by itself. Antoine and I looked at each other in dismay. How in the world could we ever hope to follow them now?

"Maybe we could rent horses," I suggested.

234 PAUL A. BARRA

"Dressed like this? Doubtful. Very doubtful."

We watched Quillery and Fletcher disappear down the tracks, the Negro pumping the drive handle with long, powerful strokes. Neither white man looked back to see us standing under the tree watching them, and the colored man was too busy working the rail car. They were either very secure in their knowledge that no one could hope to follow them or they were so intent upon their destination that they overlooked any possibility of pursuit. We washed our faces in a rain barrel next to the depot and stuffed the soft hats we'd been wearing into our hip pockets. We combed our hair with the water and made ourselves look as presentable as possible. Then we walked into the train station.

There were a few Negroes here and there, one sweeping the dry wooden floor lethargically with a clutch of straw, another asleep against the back wall. Three women sat together on a bench. From their ages and facial similarities, I deduced that they represented three generations of a family, daughter, mother, and grandmother. They all had the same look of strained anticipation on their faces, as if they were waiting for something or someone who was late enough so that they suspected it or he wasn't coming after all. They cut their eyes to us when we walked in, but the two younger women looked away almost immediately. The older Negress, a motherly type, allowed her gaze to linger on us—actually on Antoine Gagnon—a little longer before she too went back to an unfocused stare. Antoine walked right up to her.

He bent over, and the two talked. I was too far away, and their voices were too low, for me to understand the words, but the woman's gestures and expressions made it abundantly clear that she suddenly recognized him and was surprised at his dress. The other two women then took an active interest in their conversation, although the men in the little house might as well have been on the moon. The women smiled at first, and I was encouraged, and then

FULL OF EYES: A REBEL BISHOP MYSTERY   235

looked aggrieved, and I was discouraged again. We might never find out what Quillery was up to. Darkness would hide him for good in another hour or so.

After the soulful period of their talk, Antoine became animated, and the women perked up too. Abruptly, the priest reached into his pocket and pulled out some coins. He gave them to the youngest, who got up and left hurriedly. Antoine sauntered back to me.

"It seems that Mrs. Manigault's grandson had been sold in Maryland some years ago. She's a parishioner at St. Mary's, by the way. I always make a point on Sundays of greeting the slaves at the stairs to the balcony, so I recognized her. She was...er...interested in the manner of my dress once she realized who I was, but I told her we were trying to remain inconspicuous in order to uncover some unjust chicanery. I left it vague, and she was so distressed over her own plight that she didn't press for details. Fortunately. It's all a happy coincidence, Thomas, at least for us."

"What, exactly, is the coincidence?"

"Ah, yes. Poor Mrs. Manigault. Her grandson was separated from the family in 1859 and has been working on a farm of some sort outside Baltimore. The owner sold out. At least that's the rumor. So the boy, a man really, was purchased by a slave trader in the city of Baltimore two weeks ago and was being transported to Charleston to be re-sold. I believe we knew or had heard about profit to be made by buying slaves where they are cheaper?"

I didn't know what he was talking about, but when he paused for confirmation, I nodded because I wanted to find out where the younger woman had gone and how this chance encounter was going to benefit us in our surveillance. He continued.

"This woman's grandson is supposed to be among the slaves being brought this very evening to Charleston. Of course, it's all done surreptitiously, since slave trading is technically outlawed except for the private auction houses in the city. This sale is illegal,

I guess because it's unlicensed. Sam is the brawny buck we saw pumping Quillery and Fletcher away on the tender. She thought that he was going to drive them to the site of the exchange in a wagon. Sam had agreed to let the three women accompany them, for a fee. When the white men decided to go by rail instead, their hopes were dashed. I revived said hopes by agreeing to rent the wagon instead. They will, for their part, direct us to the point where the exchange will take place."

"The young woman has gone to get the wagon?"

"Yes. It's supposed to be waiting at a stable nearby."

Ten minutes later, we were underway in a beat-up slatted wagon drawn by two large gray horses, one of which looked as if he should have been donating his hooves for glue instead of pulling people around. But he moved along at a decent clip, kept up with his younger partner at a hard walk. We were out of sight of the railroad station in minutes and thumping through open country. The youngest woman drove. Her name was Rebecca, and she was the sister of the slave they hoped to greet tonight. Her mother was the thirtyish woman, named Sarah. The grandmother was barely middle-aged from the look of her. All three were Manigaults. They shared the front seat and didn't talk much. Rebecca kept the horses moving. The three women sat stiffly, hoping for their plans to work out.

"All they hope to do is to verify that their boy is here," Antoine said. "Then they'll try to find out where he's being taken and eventually reestablish contact."

"Sounds to me like big odds for disappointment."

"They do have a pretty good system of communications. It follows what some people have taken to calling the Underground Railroad. It's a type of conduit for escaping slaves as well as for communication, I gather. As the whole issue of slavery becomes more and more an execration to the northern states, the value of the slaves themselves has dropped. A matter of demand and supply, I'm told by men who fancy themselves economists. The demand for slave labor continues at a regular pace here in the South, but Lincoln and his followers have created a surplus of the commodity up north. Astute businessmen have been buying slaves cheap up along the Mason-Dixon and selling them more dearly down here. It's reputed to be quick and substantial profits. And slaves or freedmen like that big boy Sam travel the pipeline in both directions bringing slaves to market, so the lines of communication are pretty good. Slow, maybe, but good. Sam and others of his ilk make extra money for themselves by reuniting families and the odd friends."

"Everybody wins but the slaves themselves."

Antoine did not reply to that. We fell into a numbing silence as the horses pounded along and the sky darkened. It was a deep black night by the time the blowing horses slowed. My back hurt from the pounding in the buckboard. We were all silent. Rebecca walked the animals without clucking or any other noise. When we rounded a bend in the road and saw a lightening sky before us, she steered into a lay-by and stopped the wagon under some trees. We got down and started walking up the road toward the light. Antoine and I outdistanced the women and could soon make out a bonfire and movement around it. When we were close enough to see clearly, we stopped to slow our breathing and to let the women catch up. A clump of slaves stood in front of the huge fire. We could smell the burning pine resin and see dozens of white men, some accompanied by a colored or two, talking to each other and occasionally walking over to the clump of Negroes. A passenger train sat idling on the tracks adjacent to the fire. There were no structures in sight except for an open, roofed affair that I assumed to be available in case of rain. It stood on the outskirts of the firelight, empty this clear night.

I was about to turn to Antoine and precipitate a planning discussion when a small light flared up ahead of us on the road.

238   PAUL A. BARRA

I could see a man's face suddenly and briefly as he lit a cigar. The five of us immediately ducked into the woods and hid behind trees. We hadn't spoken since leaving the wagon, luckily. The guard's cigar glowed occasionally, and I calculated that he was about 100 yards or so ahead of us. He had the big fire and the noise from the gathering behind him, though, so it was unlikely that he would espy us, and he apparently had not heard our approach. I didn't see how we could get past him, without resorting to violence, that is. Then Antoine whispered in my ear.

"I'll distract him, then y'all get closer to the action."

Before I could ask what he had planned or why, he spoke briefly to the women and then stepped out on the road. He began walking toward the fire as if he were on a Sunday stroll. In a few minutes, we could hear him start to whistle. The tune was "Amazing Grace."

I touched the arm of the woman nearest to me. I couldn't see which one it was, but it didn't matter. I began to follow Antoine. I assumed the ladies were coming after me but didn't stop to make sure. When I could make out voices, I slowed. Pretty soon, I could see my brother priest talking to a man on the road. They laughed and then began walking together toward the fire. More men were coming in from what I reckoned to be the west, so I just followed along and soon blended in with the crowd gathered around the fire. A good many of the men were smoking, and a few smelled of liquor. The only women I saw were colored folk, not counting the slaves who stayed in the same group we'd seen earlier. I saw Antoine and a man I assumed to be the road guard walk over to the clump of slaves. They talked together and pointed into the group once in a while. Then Antoine patted the man on the shoulder and walked off. I met up with him.

"They're going to auction off these slaves in a few minutes, Thomas. We probably ought to keep to ourselves on the fringes, so that we're not recognized. Silas, the gentleman who was watching the

FULL OF EYES: A REBEL BISHOP MYSTERY   239

road, said there's a good many Charlestonians here. He was looking out for police, by the way, and to escort any prospective buyers to the sale."

We drifted off to the perimeter and watched the goings-on for no more than a few minutes before the crowd started to coalesce near the grouped slaves. The sale was about to begin. If Quillery had come to buy a slave or two, then we had gone through a lot of trouble for nothing. I was grateful for the opportunity to experience my first ever slave auction anyway, and we were bound to learn something this night.

A man stepped up on a crate in front of the rest and the crowd noise simmered down. The man began to speak. It was Peter Fletcher. We moved closer.

"Gentlemen. I represent the owner of these fine slaves."

Antoine and I looked at each other. I imagine my mouth was open as far as his. Was the Reverend Andrew Quillery, righteous preacher of fire and brimstone, a slave dealer? I turned back to look for him as Fletcher addressed the terms of sale—cash and immediate responsibility for the product purchased. I finally caught sight of the thin, hatchet-faced Quillery standing near the slaves. He was in front of and facing the crowd of buyers, like Fletcher, not on a box but not among the buying public either. As the sale started, the big Negro Sam took the money for each purchase and put it in a pouch hung round his neck. He took a piece of paper from the slave who was sold, marked it, and gave it to the buyer. The bills of sale must have been preprinted.

Fletcher introduced each slave, spoke his or her particulars—age, weight, children, in the case of females, and skills. The lawyer waxed enthusiastically about a slave's physical characteristics. "Look at this buck's shoulders and the width of his chest, now. He can work all day, built like that."

240 PAUL A. BARRA

Some of his descriptions provoked comments and bawdy jokes from the crowd of buyers, especially when the auctioned merchandise was a young woman. The sales went off quickly, though, and the slaves brought what I thought was big money.

After six transactions of that sort, Sam walked quickly over to Quillery, and another Negro took his place at the side of Fletcher. I saw Sam give the pouch to the preacher man. Quillery was the slave dealer! No wonder the sale was being held under cover of darkness and with watchmen about. Quillery didn't want it common knowledge that a preacher was selling slaves bought in the north.

By the time Sam went back to Fletcher's side with a presumably empty pouch, a dozen slaves had been auctioned off, and thousands of dollars had changed hands in less than an hour. The unsold slaves were chained together. They were released a few at a time, given their sales slip and brought forward by a rough-looking character, a ramrod, with a pistol strapped to his waist and a short whip in one hand. He pushed the slaves in front of him. They seemed cowed. Fletcher described the particulars of the slave in a rapid voice. Some of the auctioned slaves smiled when the bidding started, some kept their heads bowed. As I was watching the ramrod, I saw out of the side of my eye some movement within the cluster of chained slaves. The two younger Manigault women were standing with a man, talking animatedly with him. I assumed that was the long lost brother. Antoine was still next to me, and the grandmother was with him.

After the next batch of sales, the ramrod went back into the knot of slaves to bring out a few more. He fooled with the chains a bit, unlocking the next group to be sold. One of them was the Manigault brother, who stood with his paper in his hand, ready to be sold. Suddenly, a flurry of action burst out.

The rough-looking ramrod jerked his head up while he was standing in front of the Manigaults. He raised his whip hand and

FULL OF EYES: A REBEL BISHOP MYSTERY   241

brought the leather down across the shoulder of Sarah Manigault. It was a soundless assault from where I was standing, but the woman bent over in obvious pain, clutching her shoulder, her face twisted in agony. Then, in a blur, her son swung his fist. The ramrod himself was down on his back, and the Manigault slave man was standing over him. The Negro's chains were off, and he still clutched his sale paper in his now closed fist. *Good Jesus Lord*, I thought, *did a slave just knock down a white man in authority?*

The eldest Manigault woman left us and ran toward her daughter and granddaughter. People realized something was happening about then and a general frenetic movement started all at once. Slaves pushed forward. White men started running, some toward the slaves, others away from the action. Fists were raised, hats flew off. I could hear a roaring sound of voices. Some single curses burst out of the maelstrom of noise and activity. I heard a scream and another cry of anguish. The moving feet raised a dust cloud, and the center of the fight became difficult to see. I snapped a look to the outer edge, where the sales boxes were, and I saw Fletcher and Quillery in a small group of other men, including Sam and another black man. The two principals, and their money, were being protected. Behind them, the youngest Manigault woman, who had been in at the start of the melee when her mother had been attacked, raced from the dust cloud, keeping her head down and followed closely by the slave son, her brother. They made the woods before anyone seemed to notice them. Antoine and I turned and ran back down the road in the direction from which we had approached the auction. Silas loomed out of the dark suddenly.

"What's going on over there?"

"Looks like some of the slaves have begun to riot, Silas," Antoine said as we ran past him. "I can't afford to get caught in that mess."

Then we were gone, and Silas was pounding down the road to the fire. We found the wagon and eased the horses out onto the road,

242 PAUL A. BARRA

turning them to face Charleston. I stood in the bed of the wagon as Antoine assumed the reins. Two pitch torches were jammed into brackets on either side and just behind the driver's seat. I lit one and held it up. We waited. Presently a horseman rode by at a gallop, not slowing to talk. Then it was quiet again. More minutes passed, and the noise from the riot tailed off. I was at the point of assuming that the Manigaults had not effected their escape after all when a small voice pierced the blackness around my flickering torch.

"Father, that you?"

"Yes, dear," Gagnon answered unhesitatingly. "Come get in the wagon before we are all discovered."

The young woman, Rebecca, and her brother climbed over the tailgate and sat quietly in the bed, breathing hard from their trip through the woods. I could see scratches on their arms, and the young man had a cut on his forehead.

"Where's your mamma?" I asked.

"She went back for grandma. She say they'll make it back on their own directly."

At that Antoine started the horses off with a lurch that almost pitched me from the wagon. I stamped out the torch on the floor and left it there to smolder itself dead.

"How is Sarah's shoulder?" I asked Rebecca.

"It still hurts some, she say, but it ain't broke."

I climbed up to the seat with the other priest.

"No sense worrying about the other women, I don't suppose?"

"No, Thomas, I don't think so. They will get back to town the same way the rest of the slaves make it back, once the brouhaha calms down. Besides, we've got plenty enough on our plate just now. We need to put the pieces of this puzzle together and try to figure out what it all means. And, we've got an escaped slave in our buggy. Lord, what an eventful night."

"Amen."

CHAPTER 25

We dropped off the escaped slave without even learning his name or what plans the family had for survival. Antoine had spent all his money on the wagon rental, but I had a few dollars in my pocket, which I gave to Rebecca. It was a good deal of money for me, but I thought I could envision a need in the immediate future for her and her escaped brother. She whispered a frightened thank you and slipped a piece of paper into my hand before she kissed it, like I was the pope or something. Then she stepped over to render the same gesture of gratitude and obeisance to my friend.

Antoine's face screwed up when Rebecca clutched his hand. He didn't pull away, but he looked like he might have wanted to. I had noticed that same behavior in the presence of Bones one time and wondered then whether or not poor Antoine had an innate aversion to contact with colored folk. It couldn't be innate, naturally, but it could be a result of his upbringing or some kind of hygiene phobia. I wasn't the only one who noticed it. Rebecca's brother stood back watching the exchange with a neutral expression on his face.

The siblings disappeared into the night near the Devil's Hole, and we continued on to the train depot to return the buggy.

Walking home finally, tired from the excitement and the hour, but easy of mind now that we were alone again and no longer pretending to be workingmen, I asked Antoine what he thought it meant that Andrew Quillery was a slave trader.

"Well, for one thing, it accounts for the fine furnishings in his home. And probably for his association with the ruffians you overheard coming from Gordon Becknell's house. Dealing in slaves is a very lucrative enterprise. However, that does not speak to other problems the man represents for you—er—us. Is his wealth a factor in the murder of Jamieson Carter, for instance? Or does his hypocrisy make a difference as far as his anti-Catholicism is concerned? I don't know."

"Imagine that rascal playing the high and mighty with those poor colored folk, and him all the while buying and selling them! I wish now that I had gotten some better blows in when I found him in the bishop's house."

Antoine began to laugh at my vexation. Suddenly he stopped, stopped laughing, stopped walking. I stopped myself and turned about to look at him. His nose was high in the air and his mouth slightly open. His long lashes played against his cheek for a minute. Then he stared at me, as if he had discovered a hidden gold coin in his trousers pocket.

"That's it, Thomas. Of course."

"What in the world are you going on about?"

"His wealth. Quillery said that he was in the bishop's house because he was looking for something, and you surprised him there. I've spent hours trying to think of what he may have been looking for, and then the coincidence of the Becknell woman arriving outside the house just as you fell off the porch. It must all connect to his money somehow."

"Could he have wanted to buy something from Gretchen, do you mean?"

"Or possibly he was going to pay her for something. Blackmail. Or a criminal enterprise of some sort."

FULL OF EYES: A REBEL BISHOP MYSTERY   245

"What could the bishop's house have to do with anything like that? I don't see any connection. Neither Gretchen Becknell nor Andrew Quillery could have any conceivable reason to be interested in the home of a Roman Catholic bishop. At least, I can't see any reason."

"Humm. That is a conundrum to be sure. Let's sleep on it, shall we?"

As it turned out, there was a while to go that night before either of us found time to sleep. What we found instead was the mother superior of the Sisters of Charity of Our Lady of Mercy waiting with Bishop Lynch in his study.

The bishop, a gracious and mannerly man in all circumstances, introduced Antoine to Sister Bernadette Miller. Neither of them made any comment about our dress, acknowledging no anomaly in two diocesan priests looking as if they had just completed some rough adventure and smelling, I'm sure, of soot and horse sweat, if not our own. As if to accentuate their non-judgmental acceptance, bishop and superior invited us to join them at the coffee table, which was set with bone china and Hayden & Whilden silverware. I noticed that four cups had been set out and that the plate of biscuits in the middle was untouched. Antoine was relating the story of the slave auction in a droll and witty style, hoping no doubt to seem unaffected by the barbarity of the process and the danger of our experience, when Flora came in with a silver teapot. He finished his tale just as she began to pour.

"Did you know that the preacher man was buying and selling slaves, Flora?" I asked.

"I heard tell, yessuh."

"Common knowledge, would you say? Among the coloreds, I mean."

"I believe so."

"Well then, I don't understand. Why on earth would slaves listen to the man scold and berate them and fuss like he does if they know he's profiting from their hardships? Slave trading is an evil exercise and the persons suffering from its excesses should not—should not authenticate it by allowing themselves to be an audience for his preaching."

"I don't think I understand, Father."

I sighed inwardly and said, "Why do the slaves go listen to that man when they know full well that he is a bad man?"

"Well, they go 'cause he calls them."

She stood holding the silver teapot and bent slightly toward me. She looked as if I had asked her why man uses fire to cook. Flora was always too mannered to frown, as Mrs. Ryan sometimes did, when she thought you were missing a point, but she did manage on this occasion to show her surprise at the depth of my ignorance.

"He a preacher man, Father Tom."

All of a sudden I felt foolish. I said thank you to Flora a few times, and she scooted out of the room as if glad to be away from my questions.

"I'm afraid you were asking her to explain the obvious, Tom," Bishop Lynch said. "The Negro hasn't been trained to ask questions. They have been subjugated for so long in this country that they are fundamentally and profoundly incapable of thinking freely. They go listen to Andrew Quillery because he expects them to do just that, and he has the power of God behind him. At least in their minds. Slaves have a long way to go before they will be able to discriminate among options. That's why this war talk is so worrisome to me. We have been pushed to fight a fight we almost certainly must lose in the long run. Then the northerners will force us to release all the slaves at once, and they will be ill-prepared for the sudden freedom."

"But every man has been granted free will by the Creator. Surely that gift is always present to us?"

FULL OF EYES: A REBEL BISHOP MYSTERY   247

When the bishop didn't reply, I went on, sorry to have asked but too far into the argument to just end it. "You do agree that they must be freed, Your Excellency?"

"In God's good time."

I let it go then because I knew we had other issues to discuss. Otherwise, no nun would be sitting in the bishop's parlor at the approach of midnight. Sister Bernadette looked as pleasant as she had in the forenoon, and as well rested. I wondered if the nuns of Charleston took naps. At any rate, there was no time for the wanderings of minds now, since the bishop was prepared to get serious. We leaned forward slightly when he cleared his throat.

"Sister Bernadette is gracing this room because she is the bearer of some intriguing news, gentlemen. She heard it from some of her sisters at supper and carried it to me afterward. She has been waiting since then for your arrival. It's something we need to discuss as a force, so to speak."

We all looked at the nun.

"Sister Alice James and Sister Bertha were feeding the hungry at our mission on America Street earlier this evening when they heard a commotion in the line. They went outside to look, because we have had drunken fights there on occasion, and that is one thing we like to nip in the bud. They saw a carriage driving off rapidly and a man laying in the gutter. He had apparently been run down. The man, one of our...er...clients, was not badly hurt as it turns out. Before she realized that, however, dear Sister Bertha, whose heart and compassion are as big as creation itself, sent a postulate after the carriage. Mary Turner is a young woman, not yet wearing the habit, so Sister Bertha thought she might pass with less notice. She told young Mary to follow the carriage.

She was thinking, you see, to determine ownership in case the injured man required costly medical treatment or some form of compensation for his injury. Well, the Negroes in the soup line said

248   **PAUL A. BARRA**

that the driver was a white woman with yellow hair. When Mary returned, she reported that the carriage had turned in at a house on State Street and parked in the walled back yard. The woman had exited the carriage before Mary caught up, but she waited—partly to catch her breath, for she had run the whole way. Fifteen minutes or so later, a woman came out of the house carrying what looked for all the world to be a statue, a wooden statue of the Virgin Mary."

We all gaped at Sister Bernadette. What did this all mean? Was the woman in the carriage Gretchen Becknell, and had she gone to Reverend Quillery's house on State? Could the statue be the murder weapon? The mother superior finished her report.

"Mary was astonished and so decided to follow the carriage farther. Once on to Meeting, however, the woman put the beast into a trot and poor Mary was unable to keep up for long. She made her way back to the poorhouse and reported her findings to Sister Alice and Sister Bertha. They told me about it at supper and I, in turn, questioned the nuns and reported to His Excellency."

I was still letting this news sink in when Antoine started firing questions.

"Was the buggy still on Meeting when Mary saw it last, Sister?"

"Yes, Father."

"How far up, would you know?"

"The dear girl was courting a swoon by the time she gave up the chase, so she wasn't perfectly clear about where she was, but she said that it had crossed Calhoun and was heading north."

"Was the blonde woman alone in the carriage?"

"As far as we know she was."

"What kind of carriage was it?"

"A small covered affair, like a physician or a priest might use for house calls."

"How big was the statue?"

FULL OF EYES: A REBEL BISHOP MYSTERY 249

"Perhaps we'd better ask Mary Turner herself, do you think, Father Gagnon?"

"She's here, then?"

"Yes, waiting in the kitchen."

At that, Bishop Lynch tugged on a satin cord hanging near his chair. A scarce minute later Flora opened the study door and let in a wisp of a girl, who could not have been more than sixteen or so. Her eyes took up her whole face. Her lips were bloodless, her skin pale. She stood half in the doorway, looking as if she was trying to decide if it was safe to enter. The bishop got to his feet with a smile.

"Come in, child. Please."

Mary sidled up to the table and sat in a straight chair the bishop held out for her. She looked directly at Sister Bernadette.

"You have met His Excellency?"

The girl nodded. "This is Father Dockery, the bishop's associate pastor, and this is Father Gagnon of St. Mary's."

She darted her eyes at both of us in turn and said "Good evening, Father" twice in a voice we could barely hear.

Sister Bernadette spoke to her softly. "We were wondering, Mary. Could you describe the statue you saw the blonde woman carrying out of the State Street house?"

"It was dark, mother. Not black but dark."

"How did you know it was made of wood, then?"

The question from Antoine seemed to shock the girl into silence. She looked blank with her mouth working slightly and no sound emerging. Sister Bernadette smiled in a motherly way and reached over to pat the girl's knee.

"It's all right, Mary. We just want to know what you know. Can you answer Father Gagnon's question?"

Never taking her eyes from the nun, Mary Turner answered, "Yes, Mother. It didn't shine like gold or silver, and it wasn't painted like a plaster statue. It wasn't heavy like a marble statue is. The woman moved it about like it was not too heavy. I thought it was wood. Maybe it wasn't."

"Was it large?"

"No, Father. The woman didn't have any trouble carrying it. Fact, she held it with one hand when she climbed into the buggy. It was about this tall."

The girl opened her hands and stretched them about three feet apart.

"Was the woman young or old?" Father Gagnon asked.

"Uh, maybe in the middle. No, old. That is, uh, not like a schoolgirl but not as old as Your Excellency. About like you, Father."

That drew a few smiles and seemed to calm the girl's nerves a bit. The rest of the questioning went more easily.

Mary told us that the buggy was pulled by a brown horse, which matched the description of the Becknell's bay that I had seen when I went to warn Gretchen of Quillery's wild accusations.

When last seen by me, the animal was hauling both Becknells to the Edisto River.

The postulate also described the driver so well that there could be no doubt that it was Gretchen, and that she had stopped at Quillery's house to pick up the statue that had been the murder weapon.

"All that seems to remain is to determine where Mr. and Mrs. Becknell are hiding and then to determine who of three possibilities is the murderer," Bishop Lynch said. "I fear that it must be either Gordon Becknell, his wife, or the Reverend Quillery."

I disagreed. "Has Sister Bernadette told you about Sister Mary Lucille, Your Excellency?"

The bishop looked at the nun. "No, she has not."

"I'm sorry, Excellency. I thought that Father Dockery would have told you that earlier today."

He looked at me.

FULL OF EYES: A REBEL BISHOP MYSTERY 251

"You hadn't yet returned when we left to follow Reverend Quillery, Excellency. And we just now got back from the auction."

The bishop nodded at that and turned to Sister Bernadette.

"One of our sisters is becoming a bit senile, I'm afraid," she said. "She went into a sort of tirade this morning, claiming that she knew about—"

She paused suddenly and looked directly at Mary Turner. The youngster blushed and stood. She curtsied to the Bishop of Charleston and fairly scurried out the door. After the door closed behind her, the mother superior continued.

"Sister Mary Lucille claimed that she knew about Jamieson Carter and Mrs. Becknell. She went on in a rage about how poor Mr. Carter had to pay for his sins, not the least of which was a scurrilous accusation that he was channeling money, church money, to the Ursuline order in the state's capital. She had made these accusations before, although always in the privacy of the convent. I'm mortified that poor Father Dockery had to witness such an outburst today."

"The poor thing," Bishop Lynch said. "I assure you that the diocesan accountant can confirm that any funds I send to my two sisters come from my own personal account."

"We had never doubted that for a moment, Bishop Lynch. In fact, one of us knows an Ursuline well, and we know through her that the order is as impecunious as we are, maybe more so. That's the very reason why we never mentioned poor Sister Lucille's ramblings before. She's not right. So we prayed for her and trusted that her accusations would never reach outside our doors. I'm sorry to have to bring it up now."

"I think the bishop would also be interested to know how Sister Mary Lucille came upon the information about Jamieson and Gretchen Becknell," I said.

"I have no answer to that, Father. I questioned the other sisters about it, but no one knew anything."

252   PAUL A. BARRA

"We do know that she is occasionally absent from the convent, sometimes at night. Maybe she eavesdropped and overheard something incriminating. How else could she have known?"

Before the nun could answer, Bishop Lynch spoke up.

"The question that intrigues me is what she may have meant by her claim that Jamieson had to pay for his sins. Is she robust?"

"Indeed, Excellency," I answered. "She's a big woman and strong looking. When she made her accusations this morning, she acted in a rage. It was a frightening display."

"Was she inflamed enough to commit murder, do you think? That's the question in my mind. She may have been in the cathedral, for all we know, and mad rage is motivation enough to crown someone in passion. We need to look into this further, Tom."

No one had anything to add to that analysis, so the meeting broke up slowly. I escorted the women to the convent across the street and returned to find both Antoine and the bishop suppressing yawns. I also found the paper Rebecca had given me in the pocket of the blouse I was still wearing. It was a receipt describing the sale of Wade Manigault to Andrew Quillery, datelined Baltimore and signed. I thought it might be handy to have as evidence against Quillery's slave trading if we ever needed it, so I showed it to Antoine, who passed it on to Bishop Lynch. The pontiff laid it on his desk.

The Jesuit said that he would accept Lynch's kind invitation to spend the night. He wanted to be at the bishop's house when we notified the police the next morning.

CHAPTER 26

As it turned out, we didn't have to bother notifying them. When I finished the seven o'clock mass in the lower church, I found James Moseley, acting police chief in the absence of Gordon Becknell, waiting for me in the vestibule.

"An interesting sorta service there, Father. You folks go to church everyday?"

"Yes. At least some do, James. Daily mass is not mandatory as it is on Sunday. You could see by this morning's attendance that most Catholics go once a week as do most Protestants, I would imagine."

"Probly so. My wife's family are powerful strong Baptists. They go Wednesday evening and most of the day on Sunday. But it's almost all talking. I notice you never preached at all this morning."

"That's right. We don't usually give a sermon during the week. People are in a hurry to get to their day's work, so we concentrate on the Eucharist, which is the center of our worship. We read from the Bible every day, though."

"I noticed that, all right."

"You interested in learning more about the Catholic faith, James?"

"Maybe. Sometime. Right now I come to give you some news."

254 PAUL A. BARRA

When I raised my eyebrows at that, he grinned widely, showing a missing tooth on the bottom. The acting police chief was hatless, as usual, his sandy hair rustled like Moses's burning bush after he ran his hand through it. He was dressed in the brown long-sleeved shirt that was the pro forma uniform of the Charleston police and had his gold badge pinned to its pocket. He had a revolver holstered at his waist. Moseley said, "This could be a big break in two cases, Father Tom. We picked up a man on drunk and disorderly charges last night. One of the boys recognized him as a friend of Gordon Becknell. Becknell's been removed as police chief by the city council pending the investigation of charges against him, did you know that? Well, ol' Gordon went visiting with this here fella, name of Jack Madden, by the way. When we started asking Jack about Gordon's whereabouts, he went to babbling. He's said some strange things, some concerning a hanged man. I thought you might want to be on hand when we take his formal statement this morning."

I did indeed want to be on hand and made arrangements with James to meet him at the downtown station house at nine. I skipped breakfast to get some early paperwork done and was waiting inside the police station when Sergeant Moseley came in from his own meal at a local cafe.

He led me to the holding cells in back.

"I'd like you to get a look at this fella before he gets his drama face on for the interrogation. As soon as we open this here door, he'll be the one in the cell facing us directly. I'll pull the door, and you step in quick-like and have a look, okay?"

I nodded, not at all sure what this was all about, but more than willing to cooperate. Moseley pulled the door toward him, and I stepped through in a fast stride. A man sat on a stained board bed held off the floor by ropes. He had just looked up when the door squeaked open and still had his chin in his hand. He was unshaven and rumpled. His eyeballs were shot through with lines of burst blood vessels, a whitish crust lined his lips. Most of his teeth were missing.

The prisoner and I both started as we took stock of each other. His mouth opened and a sort of plaintive groan sneaked out. He closed his eyes. I recognized him immediately as the man who had been holding what I had taken to be Uncle Williams's head outside my window three nights ago. The sight of him caused an involuntary tremor in my chest, but the shock of atavistic fear was momentary. The smell in the windowless room and Moseley's voice brought me immediately back to reality.

"On yer feet then, Jack. Quick now."

Moseley was barking out the orders like a volley of gunshots as he unlocked and swung open the barred door to the cell. I was a bit surprised at the authoritative nature of my friend, although I realized that I could not have expected him to display deference in front of criminals. Madden reacted to the bullying by standing. He got up so fast that he swayed slightly, the effect no doubt of the alcohol dissolving still in his brain. He was medium-sized and slightly bow-legged. It was the same shape as the figure that chased my buggy on the way home from Ritter earlier in the week.

"You frightened my horse badly on the road between here and Ritter, Mr. Madden, and you upset my sleep."

I didn't want to admit how badly he had frightened me that terrible night of the vapors. I kept my voice low and casual to the ear. He groaned again and put his hands to the sides of his head. He started to shake his head but stopped with a grimace. Beads of sweat popped up at his hairline. When he started to speak his voice grated as painfully as the movement of a rusted gate hinge.

"I didn't mean nothing. T'were a joke."

"Yes. I imagine a funny enough one after a few years have passed. But it wasn't your joke, was it Mr. Madden?"

256   **PAUL A. BARRA**

He looked at me with a jerk that made his brow furrow. He clutched his forehead as if to keep it from splitting in two. His moan had a question mark after it this time.

"Who told you to play the jokes, now?"

"Why, nobody. Them was my own idea, Reverend. I swanny. I'd had a beer or two and felt like some fun, that's all. I painted up a face and had a little firecracker that puffed out colored smoke, like."

James Moseley came into play then. He stepped right up to the prisoner and growled in his face, looking for all the world like a rabid bulldog. Madden backed away until he came to the far limits of the room. There he tried to duck away from the cop, but to no avail. Moseley was after answers, and no sodden disgrace of a human being was going to deny him. He cuffed Madden sharply on the arm, almost toppling him, and pushed his head against the wall by griping his jaw in one hand and poking a finger of the other one between his eyes. The drunk squirmed in pain.

"Now answer the gentleman's question like a gentleman yourself, Jack, or I'll make yer life even more goddam miserable than it already is. Who put you up to the joke?"

"Twere Gordon hisself, James."

The man's breath on his face must have been all Moseley could stand but he never gave an inch. "Do you work for Gordon, then? Why would you do what he says?"

"We're in the same...er...club. Twere a favor, is all."

"What did he give you for this favor?"

"Just a coupla pennies, is all."

"Where is the scalawag now, Jack?"

"I don't know."

"Don't play with me, man. I'm not in a mood for playing."

"I—"

FULL OF EYES: A REBEL BISHOP MYSTERY   257

"Tell me the truth, Jack, or you'll rot in this cell with nothing but piss-warm water to drink for the rest of the spring. You're trying my patience now."

He threw Madden back up against the cell wall and stood with his fists clenched, staring hard at the cringing prisoner.I wanted to intervene, to invoke some Christian charity, but I sensed that Madden was about to tell everything that he knew. It was Moseley's brand of justice, surely gentler than Becknell himself would dispense. I assuaged my conscience by noting, as I kept my hands to myself, that Madden was not really suffering from the grilling he was receiving at Moseley's hands. If he had not spent the night before imbibing alcoholic beverages he probably wouldn't be suffering at all. At any rate, the treatment and his suffering were enough for him.

"I think he's still out to the Devil's Hole somewheres. That's where he told us he was going to hide out till the war done started. Said he was gonna get a commission. Artillery."

Madden cackled at the very idea, but his throat phlegmed up, and he stopped to spit in the corner. His incipient smile disappeared completely when he faced Moseley's fierce face again. I could sense any resolve he had mustered to resist dissipate, like ice cream melting on a summer's day. He wiped his brow and started talking rapid-fire, his face twisted in discomfort. He told us that a half dozen Know Nothings had lynched Uncle Williams after Becknell told them that the old Negro had overheard his scheme to sell cotton to the Yankees.

"We was gonna use the money from that deal to make us a lively party again. Preserve Charleston for the Charlestonians."

And three of them were already under arrest and incarcerated in the Confederate prison on Sullivan's Island. They were caught loading the contraband cotton. Madden stood there in the damp cell, panting, aware that he had said too much.

There was something else that I had to know. "Did the ones who lynched Uncle Williams find him in the Devil's Hole?"

Both men turned to look at me. Their heads were close together, and both faces registered surprise. It was almost as if they'd forgotten I was there.

"Why, er, no, Reverend. We caught him on the peninsula—that is, I was there but never partook of the action, heah? That poor old nigger said he was on his way back home, called his church his home. He wasn't making much sense, I don't guess."

We left the man after that. Moseley told the jailer to get Jack Madden some flapjacks and coffee. We sat in his office until the jailer came back.

"Do you think he's telling the truth, James?"

"Aye. I think so, Reverend. I'm sorry if I got a bit rough in there, but I know from experience how to handle those kinds of men. Madden's a weak fella, needs pushing. He'll make a good witness, I believe."

"Yes. All you have to do is find Becknell and arrest him."

Moseley nodded at that, his persona back to the diffident man I thought I knew. Of course, his treatment of Jack Madden was not cruel by the standards of the day. I thought he was slightly embarrassed because he had shown any meanness in front of a man of the cloth, even if it was calculated to achieve an end in the quickest way he knew how. He smiled over at me.

"Aye again, and that's where you could help me out."

"Me? How in heaven's name could a priest help?"

"You're a bit more than a priest, Father Tom. Besides being a former policeman yourself, you have been to the Devil's Hole recently and would know where to start at least. It's an unknown country to most of us."

More than a priest, the man said? Was James Moseley beginning to realize that Catholic clerics can be normal southerners too? At any

FULL OF EYES: A REBEL BISHOP MYSTERY   259

rate, I could hardly say no after all the help he had been to my own investigation. Plus, I thought then that Gordon Becknell might be the key to unlocking the puzzle of Jamieson Carter's murder.

"If my bishop is agreeable, I'll be happy to accompany you out there."

"You have to get permission? We could go on your own time if that would make it easier."

"Catholic priests promise obedience to our bishop, James. I'll have to ask his permission."

"I understand," he said, looking as if he didn't understand at all. "We'll come by after we make a few arrangements. Maybe an hour or so?"

"That will be fine."

I left then and hurried back to the bishop's house, where Bishop Lynch and Antoine were waiting in the study. I told them what James Moseley had found out at the jailhouse.

"With any luck, this could unravel some of the knots of this mystery, Tom. Take Antoine here with you and Godspeed."

CHAPTER 27

We rode out to the Devil's Hole at a rapid clip. We were ten strong, including Antoine on the cathedral mare and me on Jasper. I took the party straight to the house where Uncle Williams had holed up, figuring that Beulah Mae might be more amenable to helping the authorities than the habitués of the roadhouse would be, assuming any of them were still sober enough to help this close to the noon dinner hour. That was an uncharitable observation, I thought, and glib—even if I did make it only to myself. Sober or not, however, they would not be pleased to see a posse ride up to their hideout.

We found Beulah Mae under a shade tree to one side of her house. She and the oldest child were looking collards.

Looking collards is what the Negro in South Carolina referred to when she was cleaning the broad collard leaves and picking off bugs and beetles. I never knew why they bothered—except that it was a good occasion for socializing—since the collards are cooked for hours with fatback, so that nothing on them could possibly survive in recognizable form. Besides, wouldn't a quick wash in the nearby river serve as well?

The two females stopped conversing and watched us approach, each with a collard leaf in hand, until we were close enough for the mother to recognize me. We stopped under a gnarled old oak a few

FULL OF EYES: A REBEL BISHOP MYSTERY 261

yards from the house. I dismounted and walked across the sandy yard to them, while the rest of the men stayed on their horses and looked about. I swore I could smell the rankness of the pigsty from here, but no one else commented on it.

"Morning, Beulah Mae."

"Reverend."

"How're you feeling?"

"'Bout the same. It ain't come and go none today. Stays 'bout the same all the time."

"Then you must refrain from exerting yourself. Let your children do the running around."

"Sounds good to me. You wanna tell 'em?"

We both laughed at that. She was wheezing by the time she stopped, and this was just polite laughter. I waited a minute until her breathing was normal again and then asked her had she heard about Uncle Williams. She nodded. She angled her head at the police.

"They the ones that did it?"

"No, no. No, ma'am. These are the police. We're looking for the man who ordered the lynching, in fact."

"That got to be the white man who be hiding out here. Knew something was wrong when he first come, on a big black horse. He a big man hisself, not so tall as you but big 'round. Bald head, pig eyes. He ride out everyday when everyone else taking a sleep after dinner. My kids seen him."

It was still morning. I looked up at the sun and then pulled my watch from its pocket. Almost noon. We had to find Becknell's camp and then arrange to raid it so he couldn't get away.

"You got plenty of time, Rev."

"I'm sorry?"

"I mean that white boy ain't going nowhere anytime soon. His horse got stole last night. He went down to Mazie's for a beer or something, and someone rode off on that nice horse while he in

262   PAUL A. BARRA

there. He walked back home, and he was mad as fire. We could hear him cussing from inside the house."

"He's living close to here?"

"Uh-huh. Ain't too close, now, but he got to pass close by on the trail."

Beulah Mae described the location of Becknell's camp, less than a mile up the river. I asked if there was a woman with him, knowing that she would have mentioned a blonde long before this if there had been. She said that Becknell was alone, although he had visitors twice, two or three men riding on horseback. I figured those were his Know Nothing cronies bringing news and supplies and that he was visiting Gretchen when he left everyday. I thanked Beulah Mae and gave a silver dollar to her daughter. I didn't want to put her mother in the position of having to accept charity in front of her, but I was fearful that the family would soon suffer from the debilitating effects of Buelah Mae's lung problems. It was all the money I had left, although I normally had little need of money. And a whole silver dollar would go a long way toward supporting the little family in the Devil's Hole. The child whispered her thanks with a shy smile, the only words she spoke while I was in her presence.

James Moseley instructed his men after I relayed to him Becknell's whereabouts. The police were to spread out to surround the campsite as we approached. Moseley himself would give the signal to rush the place, a sort of breathy whistle he had apparently perfected.

"It'll sound sort of like a wheedling wind when you hear it," he said.

Antoine and I looked at each other, remembering the words of the prayer for slaves that described their cries and moans as a wheedling wind. I had never heard that expression before.

Antoine and I were to ride with James, making the official entrance from the path to the Becknell hideout. The posse moved off, leaving the three of us behind. While we waited for the other men to get enough ahead to take up positions through the woods, I asked the acting chief where he got the word wheedling.

He grinned self-consciously. "Made it up, probly. It's the way I think the whistle sounds, like a pig I heard on our farm one time after my daddy cut its throat. He was hurt, but he sounded like he was trying to sweet talk daddy at the same time, save his life like. I don't know if wheedling's even a word or where exactly I got it from."

"Perhaps you're a poet, Chief Moseley," Antoine said.

"Not too likely, I'm afraid. It's all I can manage to fill out reports. I could never write poetry."

"Lots of poets don't write down their poetry."

We didn't talk anymore after that. We set off holding our mounts to a slow walk on a trail following the riverbed, single file, for fifteen minutes. We stopped when we saw a clearing ahead with an old Army tent erected on it. No smoke came from the campfire spot and we could see no movement in or near the site. Pines didn't like it this close to water, so the forest was mostly oak and cypress, heavily wooded. We knew that Moseley's deputies were hiding around the place but could see no one. My back felt itchy in the heavy silence, the trees close. Anyone could be hiding. We'd never see them. Where was Becknell? Had he heard us coming and waited in ambush? Or was he hiding inside his tent? We assumed that as a police officer, regardless of his legal standing, he had access to weaponry. Moseley urged his horse forward a couple of paces, leaving himself exposed. He brought his hands to his mouth.

"Gordon! It's James Moseley. Come out where I can see—"

A sharp pain in my shoulder kicked me from Jasper just as I heard the explosion of a gun go off behind me. I landed on one side, facing the horse's hooves, dazed from the loud blast and from hitting the ground hard. Antoine and James spurred for cover when they heard the gunshot. Becknell, looking like a wild Indian, jumped from a tree holding a long pistol in one hand. He snatched up Jasper's reins and flung himself onto his back. He wheeled the frightened beast and took off back down the trail the way we had come in. Jasper's feet dug deep and threw clods of dirt over me.

After that, it seemed silent for a short second. Then men and horses were coming out of the woods thundering in pursuit, and Antoine was on one knee beside me.

"Can you move your arm, Thomas?"

I could, although the attempt was painful enough to wrench a stifled cry from me. The other priest seemed pleased at that.

"Means, I do believe, that nothing is broken. The ball hit in the thick back muscle behind your chest and looks to have bounced off your ribs. At least, there's another hole under your arm where I think it came out again. The bad news is that it's bleeding copiously and didn't miss your heart by much." He stopped talking and probed gently with his fingers at my clothing. "Can you ride, do you think, Thomas?"

I grunted in the affirmative and got to my feet with Father Gagnon's help. It was a painful trip up. The journey home seemed a frightful ordeal to anticipate, but I knew I needed treatment. I climbed into the saddle of the old mare, and the other priest got behind me. We walked out of the woods slowly. Even so, every jounce of the horse brought fire to my upper torso and water to my eyes.

We heard shouts and gunfire as we made our way slowly to Beulah Mae's house. When we rode off the trail into her clearing, the first thing we saw was Jasper standing alone. Through squinted eyes I made out two Negroes, a man and a woman, standing in the shadows near the horse. They stepped forward when we drew near. Rebecca Manigault was the woman, with her brother, the escaped slave named Wade.

FULL OF EYES: A REBEL BISHOP MYSTERY   265

They helped me down and led me over to the same table Beulah Mae and her girl had been using for cleaning vegetables. Rebecca ran to the house and came out immediately with Beulah Mae.

While the older woman bound my wound with leaves and herbs and ground paste of some sort, using strips from my own ruined shirt to tie the dressing off, Wade told us what had transpired in the past few minutes.

Beulah Mae had rushed her children into the house as soon as she heard the first shot, the one that felled me. Rebecca and Wade peered from their hiding place near where I had seen Uncle Williams on my first visit and saw Becknell hurtle out of the woods with the posse in hot pursuit. The police opened fire when they left the woods, and the noise apparently unnerved Jasper. He bucked the fugitive police chief off while the house was between him and his pursuers, and ran into the woods. Becknell, who may have been hit by one or more of the police bullets, was thrown almost into the trees. He rolled under cover and stayed still until the posse went by in a cloud of dust, chasing a riderless horse up the trail.

Becknell got to his feet and staggered into the pigsty. The police didn't see where he had gone.

"They think he still on that horse, so they off in the woods and down the road, looking," Wade finished up. "The horse done come back by hisself a few minutes ago."

Antoine swore. "Why in heaven's name didn't you tell them where the man went?"

"They never stop long enough to ask. Besides, master, I's a slave that's loose, so I don't show myself to no po-lice."

Antoine nodded at Wade in an understanding manner. "Of course," he said. "Stupid of me to ask."

He knew the runaway could never afford to draw the attention of officials. I could see him looking around as the women ministered to me. He walked over to a patch of sandy yard that looked darker

266   PAUL A. BARRA

than the rest. He squatted down and touched his finger to the spot, then looked back at us.

"Blood," he said as he got to his feet. "Look like a fair-sized spill."

We were quiet, and we could hear a strange sound from the direction of the pigsty. I guess it was shock setting in, for I almost giggled at the noise. It sounded like a wheedling wind to me.

Antoine and Wade paid me no mind, but stood watching the sty intently. The priest walked over to the slave. "We can't let that man bleed to death in there."

Wade looked away. After a long minute, he sighed deeply and nodded. Antoine patted him quickly on the shoulder. The two of them made their way slowly to the filthy, stinking pen across the yard. They avoided the doorway once they reached the hut itself, moving one to one side and the other to the other side. The rest of us were an unmoving tableau under the shade tree, me sitting on the table with my legs dangling off it and the two colored women staring at the scene in front of them with their hands folded at their bellies. We heard Father Gagnon speak into the darkness of the pigsty, telling Becknell who he was.

"We want to come in and bind your wounds. Please don't shoot."

We heard no reply from within. The Jesuit genuflected and blessed himself. He ducked into the lair of the wounded beast. Wade stepped in behind him.

There was no gunshot, no noise at all. Within seconds the two men came weaving back out, carrying a body between them. I slid off the table. Beulah Mae began tearing strips out of what was left of my shirt. Antoine and Wade put Becknell on the table. They nodded to each other. A wave of recognition of the shared danger passed across the priest's face. I knew he'd crossed some personal Rubicon in his own mind, some vague distaste for interacting with actual Negroes he had managed to overcome when he asked Wade for his help. Antoine had always maintained his Christian love for the colored

FULL OF EYES: A REBEL BISHOP MYSTERY   267

man in his mind and, I suppose, in his soul. Now he seemed willing to accept him as a physical partner as well.

My attention could not linger on my friend, however. I had to find out what Becknell, the enemy, knew. His face was white and a pink froth bubbled out of one corner of his mouth when he breathed. But he seemed to be breathing easily and quietly. Beulah Mae went immediately to work, wiping away the gore from a pulpy mess on the man's belly. Antoine pried a pistol from the former police chief's clenched right hand. I leaned over to Becknell. "Gordon. You are badly hurt. May I give you a blessing?"

His eyelids popped open, surprising me, and he moved his lips. No sound came out. I wiped the froth from his lips with my fingers as he tried again to speak.

"Don't—don't want—no papist blessing."

Then he grinned. It was a lopsided affair and was attended by another gurgle of bloody foam.

"Where's Gretchen, Gordon?"

"Saved the...last...the last...for her."

He raised his right arm slowly until he could see it. He seemed surprised to find his hand empty. He let the arm fall and closed his eyes. He said nothing else.

I moved away slowly, letting the black women continue to bind Becknell's wounds. Antoine helped me sit in the sand beneath a tall gangly pine.

"Did you learn anything, Thomas?"

"Not much." I breathed in short, shallow puffs. When the pain from my ribs subsided some, I went on. "He did seem to be bearing a grudge against his wife. I suspect she may be the key to the murder of Jamieson Carter."

"Where in the world could she be?"

"At Andrew Quillery's house."

The other priest stared at me as if my loss of blood had addled my brain. "What?" he uttered.

"Yes. I believe the two of them are adulterers, together."

He stared at me some more, disbelief fairly written on his face, for the image of the blonde woman with the haggard, toothless Quillery was a bit much to accept. Especially as we had last seen him at his house, with teeth out and hair as wild and out of control as his eyes. But the police started arriving back at Beulah Mae's place just then, and Antoine's observations had to wait.

They fashioned a gurney for Becknell after he was bandaged up and hung it between two riders. I rode the old mare by myself, left arm in a sling. Wade and Rebecca had faded into the woods when they heard the posse coming back, long before we started out on the journey to Charleston. No one mentioned either of them when we told the story of finding Becknell in the pigsty.

I was in pain when I thanked Beulah Mae for her help, and it got worse once we moved out. I felt hungry, tired and weak. I was anxious to make it to Broad Street, however, to sound out Bishop Lynch about my theory.

CHAPTER 28

We had the conference in my room, for I could no longer remain upright. It would have seemed strange indeed under normal circumstances to see the Bishop of Charleston there in the humble quarters of a junior priest, but I'm afraid that I was too weakened from blood loss and the constant agony of that long ride home from the Devil's Hole to appreciate the uniqueness of the occasion. I knew that I was grasping, ever so tenuously, the end of my rope by then, and I wanted to convey my suspicions to Bishop Lynch before I left the conscious world for a time.

James Moseley waited down in the kitchen, eating Flora's biscuits and drinking her dark coffee, while I told Antoine and the bishop that I thought Becknell had not killed Carter in the cathedral.

"He would never have used a Catholic icon to do such a deed. He had guns and other weapons at his disposal, or he could as easily have dispatched poor Jamieson with his bare hands, I dare say. He could even have had his men string him up like they did Uncle Williams."

"Well, who then, Tom?" Bishop Lynch asked. "Surely not the woman who has admitted to being Jamieson's...er...partner in an adulterous liaison? Or do you think the mad nun did it?"

"My suspicion is that Andrew Quillery was smitten by Gretchen and killed Carter out of jealousy."

PAUL A. BARRA

Then I closed my eyes for a minute and forced myself to recall the night when I'd fallen off the porch while fighting with Quillery. Gretchen had been so tender afterward, nursing me and, if the truth be told, seducing me. We may not have succumbed to sins of the flesh, but she had seduced me into caring for her. Why, I had to ask, would she not have tried the same ploy on Andrew Quillery? I dared not confess this in such conspicuous clarity to my bishop, not even to my brother priest, but I could make them understand that Gretchen Becknell was an essentially unscrupulous person.

"The devil is doing his work through Gretchen, Excellency. I'm afraid that she is the instrument of his evil."

I didn't know, as I slipped off into a deep slumber, the extent of her evil nature.

James Moseley organized a search for the woman I had accused. Three days later, one of his men espied her buggy in an outbuilding on Quillery's property. They knew what to look for because I had described the lightweight single-seater I had seen the Becknells drive off in after the terribly conflicted Quillery had denounced Gretchen in public. The acting police chief didn't share with us how the man came to see inside the shed, but he did invite Antoine and me to accompany him when he went to search Quillery's house. By that time I was finally awake. I was propped in a chair in the dining room being spoiled by Flora and, will wonders never cease, Mrs. Ryan, when Antoine came in and shook his head in mock dismay at the treatment I was receiving.

"Tea and strawberry scones. Really, Mrs. Ryan. This man is supposed to be serving humanity, not being served."

"I take it that means you'd like some for yourself, Father Gagnon?"

As Flora chuckled and went back to the kitchen for more scones, Antoine made some noises to Mrs. Ryan about her being perspicacious as well as talented and settled himself across from me. He told me about Moseley's discovery.

"The bishop and I are going to accompany James to question the preacher man, Tom. I thought you might want to tag along, as it were."

"I do, indeed. I'm still bandaged rather heavily, so I may not be much good for chasing down malefactors, but—"

"Fear not, my friend. I have already harnessed the mare to the larger chancery buggy, so we should make it down to Quillery's place in relative comfort. I'm anxious to see what other of Quillery's secrets we may expose."

We must have presented a sight to the residents of State Street as we stepped down from the curtained carriage and walked to the Reverend Andrew Quillery's house—three men in black and two armed police officers. When no one answered our knock, Moseley instructed his man to guard the front door, and we walked around back. We found the reverend pottering in the garden behind his fine home. At least, we thought he was gardening in the dark, rich loam. In reality, Quillery was digging with some purpose other than horticulture, so much so that he did not hear the four of us walk up behind him. He started when Moseley addressed him and, without so much as a glance over his shoulder at his visitors, tried to complete the covering of the object he was burying. Moseley bent over, hooked his hand in Quillery's elbow and drew him out of the soil. The thin man kept shoveling, even when his motions caught nothing but air. He dropped his small digging tool and meekly allowed James to lead him to the house. Bishop Lynch said to Antoine, "Please uncover the statue and bring it into the house. And be prepared for action. I fear that Pastor Quillery may have been expecting a visit."

The bishop was sitting with the minister at the glossy pine table in the kitchen, the rear room of the house, Moseley standing behind them, when Antoine and I entered the room and placed an ebony heartwood statue of the Madonna on the table. Fine particles of damp dirt clung to it. The lustrous face of the mother of God was exquisitely carved, but no one was looking that high up. Our gazes were concentrated on the thick base of the statue, at the section of the rim that had been pitted and splintered slightly, as if it had been brought to bear with some force against a hard object. Despite all the handling it had received since being removed from the cathedral two weeks ago, the statue was perfectly smooth everywhere except in that one place. We were all visualizing in our minds what had caused the damage. Bishop Lynch touched the carving with his index finger, noting as I had how it still carried in its wood the cold from Quillery's early garden soil. He moved his finger up from the blemished base and, as the dirt sprinkles came off before it, we could all see the thin crack that led from the splintering almost up to the knee fold in Mary's cloak. It was a beautiful carving, much too beautiful to burn or otherwise destroy, apparently.

"Why did you not dispose of this evidence, Reverend Quillery?" Bishop Lynch asked.

"It is a lovely thing, and I wanted to keep her."

"So, how did it get damaged?"

"I were angry, see, and I hit him."

"Why were you so angry?" James Moseley asked.

The preacher man moved his head ponderously, as if it was almost too much burden for his neck to handle, and looked up at Moseley.

"Why, she were seeing that there papist, man. Why else do ye think?"

"So what? She ain't your wife, is she?"

"Aye. Don't I know that too well."

Then he stopped talking and would say no more. Moseley tried cajoling, then threatening and pleading. All to no avail. The preacher man had ceased to speak. Bishop Lynch got to his feet and went to the window that overlooked the walled yard and small stable. He turned to Quillery. "I see Mrs. Becknell's buggy out back. Does that mean she is here?"

Quillery's eyes jumped open, but still he said nothing. From the doorway that led upstairs came another voice, a soft, feminine one.

"Yes, I am here."

Everyone in the kitchen turned to look at Gretchen Becknell. She was dressed again in white, as she was the first time I had seen her, kneeling in her garden on the day we discovered the body of her lover. Bishop Lynch was wearing his biretta, the one with the amaranth red plume on top. He tipped it to Gretchen, bowed slightly and spoke in a quiet voice.

"Do you agree with the Reverend Quillery's rendering of the facts as they occurred in the wee hours of April eleventh, madam?"

"I don't wish to make testimony against a friend of mine, Father. Or are you more than a father, sir?"

"This is Bishop Patrick Lynch, Mrs. Becknell," Antoine said.

"Well, Bishop Lynch, I trust that you do not expect me to incriminate someone on second-hand information."

"Second hand, my dear lady? Do you deny that you were in the Cathedral of Sts. John and Finbar on the night when the murder of Jamieson Carter took place?"

Gretchen hesitated and Quillery, who had been staring at her countenance with what can only be described as devotion, spoke out loudly.

"Tell him ye agree with my avowal, fer God's sakes, woman."

"Well, Mrs. Becknell," said Lynch, with his left hand in his fascia and standing tall, "do you agree that Andrew Quillery battered Jamieson Carter to death in the cathedral?"

She put her face in her hands and whispered through them, "Yes. Yes, I do."

"And how did you come to know this, madam?"

"I—I was there as well."

She spoke so softly that we had to hold our breath to hear. The room was otherwise silent. Indeed, the entire house and property seemed devoid of noise as this drama played itself out.

"You were there, and you saw Andrew Quillery strike Carter on the back of the head with this statue?"

"Oh, my—"

"Please, madam. You must answer truthfully. This commissioned officer of the peace is taking down all that is said. Your reply could result in this man earning a noose around his neck. We must know the truth."

Gretchen looked at Quillery. Her face was blanched and stricken, as if she were on the verge of falling away faint. The preacher met her eyes. His were full of resolve. He inclined his head at her so slightly that I could never after swear that Patrick Lynch had actually seen him nod at the woman. She seemed to gain strength from the intercourse, however, and spoke again.

"Yes, sir. I saw Andrew hit Jamieson over the head."

Then she looked straight at the bishop and said in a firmer voice, "But it was not murder, sir. It was a fit of rage. Jealous rage. He could scarcely control himself."

"Why would this man be jealous of Jamieson Carter?"

She began to cry then. She shook her head and would not answer. Quillery reached out to her and seemed about to rise, but Moseley put his hand firmly on the man's thin shoulder.

"I were jealous, man, because I love this here woman as God himself loves all of us. I couldna bear to see her with him."

That assertion by Quillery stopped all conversation again. In the quiet, Gretchen's sobs and Quillery's hard breathing were all anyone else could hear. Until Bishop Lynch spoke again, sharply and with authority.

FULL OF EYES: A REBEL BISHOP MYSTERY   275

"So you decided to bear her guilt for her, Reverend Quillery. Have you thought about the guilt she'll feel before God when she watches you swing from a rope? I don't think you are doing any of us a favor here, especially not this woman."

"What—what do ye mean?"

"I mean, Reverend Quillery, that you were in Baltimore buying slaves on the night Carter was killed. Or more likely, on the train home that very night. Wade Manigault held a bill of sale showing your signature and dated April 11, 1861 in Baltimore. That was the day you purchased the slaves you sold two nights ago. He escaped during the melee at the sale site, still holding the sale document he was given for his auction. He gave it to Father Dockery. I have it here."

He pulled a paper from the pocket of his cassock and flourished it at Quillery.

"Gretchen Becknell has woven her spell over you, Reverend, and you are trying to protect her. When you learned that she had killed Carter, you decided to cover up the deed. When that didn't work, you decided to take the blame. An admirable effort, my friend, but of no consequence. I doubt any jury of your peers will convict you of conspiracy to conceal a crime once they see the evil ways of this woman. She has deluded you, to say nothing of poor Jamieson and even her husband."

The preacher shook his head. Moseley spoke up. "Mrs. Becknell has admitted to being there in the church, Reverend Quillery. Since you couldn't have done the dirty deed, that points the finger of guilt directly at her."

"No!"

Quillery's cry was a bellow of agony and despair. It galvanized Gretchen Becknell. She whirled and bolted from the room.

"Quick, James. Her horse is hitched up," cried the bishop.

PAUL A. BARRA

James Moseley was a step slow in recovering from Lynch's remarkable analysis of events, but recover he did. As he took a long stride toward the fleeing woman, Quillery leaped from his chair and crashed into him. Moseley was knocked sideways and into Antoine. Both tumbled to the floor. Without thinking of the damage to my side, I went after Gretchen.

She was almost to her little buggy when I caught up with her. I tackled her, and we both fell under the horse. The animal shied and began to move around nervously. I tried to keep Gretchen from its unshod feet by placing my body over hers.

"Tom," she whispered. "Let me be. I'll meet you at the Hell Hole Inn later tonight."

I must have hesitated, pulled up to look at her face. She shoved me hard in my ribs, and the intense pain caused me to gasp and shift my position. Gretchen pushed her way out from under me, and I did not have the strength suddenly to hold her. I heard the wagon creak as she boarded and whipped the horse. Her bay gelding was now in a wildly confused state. He didn't like the pressure of the people beneath him. His instinct was to run, but I was still under him and against his back legs when Gretchen laid the buggy whip to his back. He whinnied loudly and reared, twisting to one side and dancing to be free of this torment and turmoil. I curled myself up, afraid of the stomping animal's hooves. I heard the whip crack again. The horse lunged, pulling the offside wheel over my back. With a great cry, I raised up with my good side and felt the buggy tip. As it went over on its side, the stays came loose as they are supposed to in an accident, and the horse bolted free. He ran down the street, traces trailing, the bit between his teeth.

James Moseley was there, shackling Gretchen Becknell before she could recover her feet. Antoine helped me up. I could barely stand. The bandage that wrapped my ribs was soaked with blood where I'd taken Becknell's bullet. I could feel it, warm and sticky, easing between my fingers as I sought to clamp down on the pain. My friend and my bishop assisted me to the diocesan carriage while the acting police chief whistled up the constable at the front of the house.

Later, in a courtroom before a magistrate, Bishop Lynch, Father Gagnon, and James Moseley heard Gretchen Becknell deny her guilt and try to lay the blame on first Andrew Quillery and then on Father Tom Dockery.

I was again sitting in bed, listening to Antoine. When he said my name, my eyes opened even wider.

"Me? How in heaven's name could she think to blame me?"

"She said you were infatuated with her, Thomas. She even gave a treatise in opposition to celibacy and said that years of it had driven you to unslakable lust, so much so that you tried to, er, have your way with her one night in this very house. Because you were unsuccessful, you followed her to the cathedral in frustration. When you saw her meeting with Carter, you killed him. She said that you cried out that if you couldn't have her, no one would. It was very melodramatic, but we all knew by then that she was grasping at straws. When Quillery heard her accusing you, his Christian decency reasserted itself, finally, and he told us under oath what had happened."

"Maybe it was less Christian decency that motivated him than it was the scales falling from his eyes."

"Perhaps. I'm trying to be less cynical and more charitable in the telling, Thomas. Either way, she cooked her own goose with her wild accusations."

I gulped silently at that and listened while Antoine related what had transpired during the murder in the cathedral, at least the story as pieced together by James Moseley after he had heard all the testimony, including a deathbed statement from Gordon Becknell—although he was not yet dead and was, in fact, beginning

278   PAUL A. BARRA

to show some murmur of recovery from his wounds under the ministrations of the Sisters of Charity of Our Lady of Mercy. I wondered as an aside how that nursing assistance from papist nuns would eventuate in his biased mind if he did recover.

"Jamieson Carter had gone to the church to pray for forgiveness. He had ended his romance with Gretchen and sought the solace of his faith after a period of fateful lechery. She followed him, reluctant to give up so easily. Her motivation was hardly love, or even lust. She wanted his cooperation in the cotton scheme her husband had hatched, not knowing at the time that Gordon Becknell was meanwhile persuading Carter's daughter Annie into agreeing to the smuggling through their chandlery business. This was a new plan in case Gretchen's efforts to suborn Jamieson Carter's morals failed to achieve their end. Gretchen was still following the old plan she and Gordon had devised. She was to entice Jamieson with her flesh and then get him to go along with the scheme. Carter was guilty of illicit love, no doubt, but the idea of forsaking the Confederacy for greed was probably more than his conscience could bear.

"He refused her again in the nave of our cathedral and turned to pray. She was furious, she said, overcome with despair in fact, and fearful that her remorseful lover might reveal the whole scheme to authorities. She picked up the statue in a rage and bashed the poor man while he prayed at the communion rail."

Father Gagnon bowed his head for a moment at the sacrilegious nature of the murder before he continued. "Then she ran from the church, although she had maintained the presence of mind, somehow, to lock the door behind her. When she got near the rectory, she realized she was still clutching the statue.

Perhaps she was temporarily deranged. More likely so used to getting her way by using her feminine wiles on men that she could not accept failure. Anyway, she needed to dispose of the murder weapon. She had taken Jamieson's keys, to lock the church and

FULL OF EYES: A REBEL BISHOP MYSTERY 279

impede discovery of the body, so she went into the chancery office and hid the statue behind some of the files. She thought that one extra statue in the offices of a church known for statuary and other ornamentation would pass unnoticed. She never thought you would have noticed it missing from the cathedral so quickly.

"Later, when she had deceived Andy Quillery into doing her bidding, she thought she should dispose of it permanently. By then, she and everyone else knew that the constabulary had pegged the Blessed Mother as the murder weapon. The preacher man, by then totally under the spell of Mrs. Becknell, went to find it the night he accosted you in this house. He was apparently looking for the chancery on the bottom floor and gained entrance to the main floor instead. He went in the side door instead of the back. She was waiting outside for her new lover. When you fell off the porch in the struggle with Quillery, she told him where the statue was, and he went to retrieve it while she nursed you back to consciousness."

"So, that's when Bones saw him carrying the statue."

"No, no, Thomas. I must remember your precarious medical condition. You have lost a lot of blood and cannot be thinking clearly yet."

"How so?"

"He never gained possession of the statue until Gretchen was tending to you on the walk outside this house. Mr. Bones had seen Quillery two days prior to the attack on you here."

"So, what was Andrew carrying the night Bones saw him?"

"Onions."

I had to chuckle at that. We suspected the man because of nothing, attributed evil intent to someone who was doing nothing surreptitious at the time. The preacher man's reputation with the Negroes had colored Bones' interpretation of innocent movement in the dark. We were so eager for a suspect that we latched onto the fiction poor Bones had unknowingly perpetrated.

"So Andrew Quillery had never seen or touched the murder weapon until the night he attacked me?"

"Precisely. In fact, if the dear Blessed Mother would speak through the statue she could tell the story herself."

"Perhaps she would tell us that Sister Mary Lucille hid the statue after witnessing the murder in the cathedral," I interrupted.

That bold assertion gave Antoine momentary pause, but just that.

"I do suppose we have to consider that possibility. She acts as though she saw something that completed her derangement. But whoever put it there, Sister Mary Lucille or Gretchen Becknell, Quillery eventually located the statue hidden in the chancery. He took it to his house to hide it or burn it. The weather has been too warm for a fire in his grate, though, and he was afraid to draw attention to a fire outside, so Gretchen took it out to her meeting with her husband near the Devil's Hole. By then, Gordon understood that his wife was fornicating with the likes of Quillery and was apparently willing to prostitute herself with anybody for the appropriate gain. He came to understand also the true nature of his mate sometime during their lone sojourn together. She was not willing to live any longer in a rough camp with him, for instance, not for the sake of their marriage, not for the safety of her husband."

Antoine shook his head slowly at the perfidy of the woman Gretchen, his lips pursed in distaste. He had closed his eyes so that his lashes lay against his skin. Then he seemed to collect himself and spoke again. "I think also that Gordon was a patriot in his own way. He expected to fight the Yankees, for instance, although he was obviously not averse to profiteering from the war. He was not driven by greed, like Quillery, to abandon the Confederacy for the sake of making money. He must have shuddered at the thought of Gretchen meeting some Union officer during the war who was in a position

FULL OF EYES: A REBEL BISHOP MYSTERY   281

to help her out in some way. He refused to take the statue when she brought it to his camp, told her to bury it in Quillery's head instead."

Things began to unravel for the conspirators at that point. Gordon was being hunted by Moseley and his men for both the hanging of Uncle Williams and the failed plot to smuggle cotton north. The net of circumstances was closing. Afraid her husband would turn her in under duress, Gretchen coerced the preacher man into hiding the statue in his already tilled garden. The couple, Quillery and Gretchen, was planning to escape into the turmoil the war would surely bring. The bishop, the priests and the police turned up at his house before any escape was possible. So, she let Quillery offer to take the blame.

"What was the significance of Quillery's wealth, then?" I asked after digesting the solution to so many questions.

"I, ahem, hate to admit this, but its sole import to the case was as the attractant for Gretchen Becknell to Quillery. One would have thought that a man with his age and experience would have cottoned to something so obvious as her ploy. I mean, had he but looked in the mirror and then at her, he would certainly have known that she was using him for something other than his looks and vibrant personality. But lust blinds men, y'know."

"Was it mere lust, do you think?"

"Maybe not. He was smitten, no doubt. You were right about that. It was a remarkable bit of insight on your part."

If Antoine knew that I received the insight because I had almost fallen for the same sort of seduction by Gretchen, he was gracious enough to keep his suspicions to himself. In fact, he did not try to draw a confession of the sort out of me at any time, not then nor in the future. I remembered how I suspected him of political treachery when this whole mess had begun weeks ago.

The sea change in my thinking about Antoine was remarkable in the extreme. I felt the kinship of priestly brotherhood more strongly that day than ever before.

It was that same sense of kinship that drew me to the main service at St. Mary of the Annunciation a month later, on the feast of Pentecost. Father Antoine Gagnon was celebrating the solemn 11 a.m. liturgy with his pastor, Monsignor Reed, in attendance at the altar. The junior priest was scheduled to deliver the sermon.

He had been enjoined in no uncertain terms by the pastor that he was expected to deliver a talk denouncing abolitionism and defending the Southerner's right to own slaves, preferably using Holy Scripture to bolster his argument.

Antoine did not defend slavery in his sermon. He was my dear friend by then but we became even closer after he told the full house and the slave gallery that the possibility existed that God was allowing the South to be afflicted with the impending war because the people had embraced this uncharitable and greed-driven convention. He urged the South to disclaim slavery as a way of life.

"If that seems too much—and it may be too much at this juncture, brethren—then at least resolve in your hearts to treat your slaves as fellow human beings. Look for Jesus Christ in each one of them."

After mass, Antoine told me of the enormity of his decision to condemn slavery, and its consequences.

"Slavery is a great evil, Thomas. We southerners should never have allowed plantation owners to import the poor African to make the owner rich with inexpensive labor. The Church should never have gone along with this blight on our society. It is plain wrong to own other people, and it has always been wrong. I hoped, along with Bishop Lynch, that it would die out on its own. It probably would have, were it not for the war that will envelop us soon. Now it will not be allowed to die a natural death. Win or lose, the South

FULL OF EYES: A REBEL BISHOP MYSTERY 283

and slavery will have changed for the worse. If we win and gain freedom from northern oppression, then slavery will be imbued with new vigor. Many here and in the North think that this war will be fought over slavery. The Confederates will be loath to abandon it with victory, especially if many of our young men die fighting for it.

"If we lose the war, the North will terminate slavery in an instant, and we will also lose forever that marvelous bond of manners between the Negro and the white man of the South. Either way, either if he is further subjugated or if he is summarily freed without adequate preparation for freedom, the Negro loses. And we are culpable under God for having subdued him for so long."

That turned out to be the last extensive conversation Antoine Gagnon, and I had before the winds of war blew our world into confusion and chaos. Knowing that he could no longer continue to serve under Monsignor Reed after his defiant sermon on Pentecost, Father Gagnon petitioned Bishop Lynch to permit him to return to his religious congregation in New Orleans. The bishop could hardly refuse.

With Antoine Gagnon off to Louisiana, I was left alone with my thoughts about slavery and my slave-owning bishop. Less than 500,000 of the five million or so white Southerners owned slaves in 1861, so preserving the institution for the sake of profits was probably not the main reason 90 percent of white southerners fought to keep slavery. It was more a matter of preserving the culture of the South, in my mind, and Bishop Lynch was deep into the culture of his diocese. And, the bishop was at least as persuasive in defending his slave-holdings as Antoine was in calling slavery a great evil.

The indignity of the market in humanity that Antoine and I witnessed stayed in my mind as spring turned into bloody summer. I prayed then that the coming war would allow me enough quiet time to further consider my own final decision on the matter.

Epilogue

By that feast of Pentecost, 1861, Gretchen Becknell had been remanded to the county gaol, and Andrew Quillery was placed under house arrest. James Moseley was investigating his slavery dealings and the preacher man's participation in the concealment of the murder, as an accessory after the fact. The arrest may have saved Quillery's life, as well. Many Charlestonians became aware of his anti-secessionist leanings by then. Most thought they were fueled by his enormously profitable slave-trading enterprise. A united North and South would have kept the profit margin high for someone who was willing to skirt the law to buy slaves whose value had cheapened where abolitionist sentiments were strong and sell them in the pro-slavery South. A war between the states would not only make the trade impossible to conduct, but a northern victory would end it all together.

If the preacher man was in danger of being lynched by a partisan mob, it never seemed to matter to him. He did not recover from the loss of Gretchen and became a sort of eccentric hermit. He stopped preaching all together, although people occasionally caught him strolling along narrow city streets, oblivious to the bedlam of war and talking animatedly to himself with wild gestures and facial contortions that frightened children.

FULL OF EYES: A REBEL BISHOP MYSTERY 285

Gretchen escaped hanging because of her gender, but she did not ever surface in Charleston again. She went to prison, and we all lost track of her after that. The years immediately following her arrest were times of great turmoil in our city and in our diocese, so the murder of Jamieson Carter lost its impact in the whirl of thousands of other stories of life and death.

Jamieson's daughter Annie never did make up for the loss of reputation that her family's name suffered because of her father's affair and her own dabbling in treason. Her mother stayed on to live out a spare aristocratic old age in the Carter home on one of the narrow cobbled lanes south of Broad. The house seemed to crumple and disintegrate along with her. Carter Chandlery went belly up, partly because of the Union blockade that restricted shipping from the Port of Charleston. The Carter children stayed in Charleston to work, except for Annie. She migrated upland twenty miles to the former summer colony now called Somerville. She eventually married a veteran of Vicksburg and raised a family, but was never again a factor in the mercantile life of the Lowcountry. She and her children did become prominent participants in the Catholic parish of the area. Her husband was a casual Presbyterian who took to drink and atheism late in life. Annie forgave him his excesses, telling her pastor that he woke from a nightmare one black night and confessed what had been affecting his dreams for the past ten years.

He had killed and eaten his favorite hunting dog in Mississippi, the one who had followed him into combat and stayed by his side. He told his wife on that dark night of his feverish dreams that both of them would have starved if he hadn't done it, but the need for it took some of his faith away. That is what Annie thought.

Former police chief Gordon Becknell had developed a serious infection by the time Civil War battles began in earnest and was suddenly doing poorly. The sisters told Bishop Lynch that they feared it was systemic in nature, and Becknell did eventually die from his Devil's Hole wounds.

In Charleston, a great fire, thought by some to have been begun by Yankee saboteurs, swept from one side of the peninsula to the other just a few weeks after Pentecost 1861. Except for the attack on Fort Sumter, there had been no real war action by that time. But the fiery disaster gave us an inkling of what was to come. Among the many victims of the fire was the grand cathedral on Broad Street, Sts. John and Finbar.

If Bishop Patrick Lynch was distressed by the loss of his diocesan church, he was to become used to the feeling and had, in any case, many other things to occupy his mind. He became the leading secessionist cleric in the South, actively defending the cause and supporting the Confederate Army with speeches, fundraising, spiritual ministry to the soldiers and with the nursing hospitals run by the nuns of the diocese. He organized the defense of many of the diocesan schools and convents from Yankee marauders late in the war, although he was unable to save the Ursuline Convent in Columbia from Sherman's army, where his own sister was the abbess.

When I took out Antoine's poem/prayer about the wheedling wind, which I did so often that it finally became worn through, but by then I'd memorized it, I thought not only about my courageous friend but also of my own failings. I still had not decided what stance to take on slavery two years later. By then, the Union army had suffered many defeats, including a devastating one at Fredericksburg. People in the South were beginning to talk of Lincoln suing for peace. No matter if the Confederacy was successful or not, I had to decide morally on the issue of slavery. I knew that full well at the time. I can tell you now, however, that before I made up my mind, Father Antoine Gagnon entered my life again to help me decide. He came because we had more criminalist work to do for the Rebel Bishop.

Author's Note

Unpopular because of his arrogant ways in the final years of his reign as Bishop of Charleston, the Most Reverend Ernest L. Unterkoefler, known as the German Shepherd, was at least an ardent advocate of civil rights and a true friend of people of color. When he finally left this vale of tears for his eternal reward after a twenty-five year tenure (1965-1990), he refused, in his will, to be entombed in the crypt of the Cathedral of St. John the Baptist in the city of Charleston. The alleged reason was that he did not want his body to rest in the company of one of his predecessors, Bishop Patrick N. Lynch.

For Bishop Lynch was a slave owner and, although he was ultimately much more substantive and important a character than that, it was this one failing that possessed the prodigious mind of Unterkoefler. Whether or not the burial story is apocryphal, Unterkoefler certainly felt no affection for Lynch, and Bishop Unterkoefler's mortal remains are not with those of the rest of the deceased Catholic bishops of South Carolina.

A spin-off of that dislike is that the diocesan archives were closed through the 1970s and 1980s for all practical purposes to research about nineteenth century Catholics in the South. There are many other sources, of course, but letters and articles, an actual commission to Lynch from Jefferson Davis, early diocesan newspaper clips—all were unavailable for a long time.

When David B. Thompson's episcopacy replaced Unterkoefler's in 1990, however, it began with an infusion of light and air into the hidden life of Patrick Lynch. When I was able to read about him and episcopal life during the Civil War, I was captivated. This novel began as a profile I did for Catholic Heritage on Lynch, who, as I mentioned in the text, was called "The Rebel Bishop" by no less a character himself than Horace Greeley. So, I'm grateful to Bishop Thompson for opening up a whole new field of interest for me.

288 PAUL A. BARRA

This story is fictional, although some of the recognizable characters are drawn true-to-life namely Jefferson Davis, General Beauregard, Major Anderson, Mary Boykin Chesnut, Pierre Toussaint, Bishop John England, and, of course, Bishop Lynch. Most of the characters in this book are fictional and are not meant to represent anyone living or dead. That includes the narrator, Father Tom Dockery, his friend Jesuit Father Antoine Gagnon, and his pastor Monsignor Reed. St. Mary of the Annunciation is a real church, standing proudly to this day on Hasell Street, but she never was administered by anyone named Reed—or any other pro-slavery pastor, as far as I know. Bones and the police chiefs are all fictional, as are Gretchen, Moseley, Mrs. Ryan, and even Andrew Quillery himself. I made up all the secondary characters out of whole cloth as well.

Devil's Hole is not real, but the slave parish at Catholic Hill is. The attack of Ft. Sumter is fairly portrayed. The sermon given by Bishop Lynch in chapter five was made up, but the historical discussion that followed is based on fact.

The history, the places, and the cultures depicted are done so accurately. For instance, at the behest of his friend Jefferson Davis, the Rebel Bishop ran the Unionist blockade on the Minerva and sailed to Rome on the open deck of that boat in 1864. He was there, trying to persuade Pope Pius IX to recognize the Confederate States of America, when Lee finally surrendered at Appomattox. Bishop Patrick Lynch endured the ignominy of having to swear allegiance to the Union at the American Legation House before being allowed to return to his diocese.

He then spent another lifetime rebuilding that Diocese of Charleston and paying off most of the enormous debts the Catholic Church in South Carolina had incurred through the war years—some $360,000 worth. He died after serving as Bishop of Charleston for twenty-four years, until 1882.

FULL OF EYES: A REBEL BISHOP MYSTERY   289

His house slave, Flora, was also real. The rumor was rampant that Bishop Lynch had originally purchased her to save her from the mistreatment of her former master. Lynch had, after all, paid more than $800 for her when she was already middle-aged and partially crippled—but verification never came from her or the bishop, as far as we know.

Also, the episcopal residence on Broad Street is real and elegant even today, but the Diocese of Charleston probably did not purchase it until 1868.

Some additional tidbits that the amateur historian might enjoy include:

John Forsyth, the former governor of Georgia, was secretary of state in the administration of Martin Van Buren when he accused the pope of being an abolitionist. Forsyth was undoubtedly thinking of his upcoming election challenge from General William H. Harrison, a Whig who favored the continuation of slavery. Pope Gregory XVI's apostolic brief condemned the trade in slaves and was thought by some to infer a condemnation of the practice of slavery itself. Forsyth argued that the pope's brief made him, in effect, an abolitionist. Abolitionists were generally conceded to be anti-Catholic at the time (1820s). John England must have resented Forsyth's electioneering at the pope's expense.

Bedford Forrest rose from private to lieutenant general, the only man in the War to do so. He was wounded four different times and had twenty-nine horses shot out from under him in four years of successful campaigning. The cavalry officer also had thirty confirmed kills in hand-to-hand combat before he surrendered his troops in Alabama. He became famous for his statement that he was "a horse ahead at the close."

A new church at Catholic Hill was not actually built until 1898, the year after Father Daniel Berberich discovered the faith community at Catholic Crossroads, as Ritter was known then, after it had been priestless for nearly forty years.

Paul A. Barra

Reidville, 2018

About the Author

PAUL A. BARRA WAS A naval officer for five years, earning the Bronze Star with Combat "V" and the Combat Action ribbon for his work on the rivers of South Vietnam; a bartender for ten; and has been a chemistry teacher for longer yet. Barra was the senior staff writer for the Diocese of Charleston and wrote for newspapers and magazines, receiving numerous awards from the South Carolina Press Association and the Catholic Press Association. He graduated with a BS from Niagara University and an MS from Loyola University of New Orleans.

His four supplemental readers were published by Houghton Mifflin in 2008, two years before Tumblar House released his non-fiction book about the founding of a private high school, *St. Joe's Remarkable Journey*. Barra's middle-grade adventure novel, *The Secret of Maggie's Swamp*, came out from Brownridge Publishing in 2012.

A Death in the Hills was short-listed for the Tuscany Prize before he signed a publishing contract with Argus Books in 2014. Argus also published his second mystery *The Mekong Junkman* in 2015. *Astoria Nights* (Black Opal Books, 2017) is his third novel.

Barra and his wife Joan have eight children and live with their dog, burro, alpacas, and chickens in Reidville, SC. Barra is currently putting the finishing touches on an historical mystery set in Charleston and featuring a real-life slaveholding bishop.

About the Author

Paul A. Barra's last novel, "Westfarrow Island," published by The Permanent Press, was called "exciting" by Publishers Weekly.

PW said, in part: "The relentless action in the dual story lines keeps the reader engrossed. Barra offers it all: murder, smuggling, chase scenes, romance, and international intrigue." It was shortlisted for the Silver Falchion award. His short story, *Assignment: Sheepshead Bay,* was selected for the MWA anthology "When a Stranger Comes to Town," released by Hanover Square Press in April 2021.

Barra has had five novels published, plus a non-fiction book about the founding of a Catholic high school without diocesan approval. He is a decorated former naval officer, was a reporter for local papers and the senior staff writer for the diocese of Charleston.

Read more at www.paulbarra.com.

Milton Keynes UK
Ingram Content Group UK Ltd.
UKHW012150090624
443713UK00001B/79